"Just what do doing, terrifyin **Elizabeth dema in the buggy to tower over him.**

"We need to talk."

He ripped the reins from her hands and tossed them to Gemma. In one quick motion he scooped Elizabeth onto his saddle, in front of him. Her eyes widened and she looked to be gathering another wail of a breath.

He looked hard at her. "Stop!"

She clamped her mouth shut.

"I'll bring her back as soon as I've had my say."

With that, he reined the Major away and, with Elizabeth cushioned in front of him, galloped off.

Author Note

I love stories about second chances—about people who fight for their happily-ever-after despite the curves life has thrown them. In *Familiar Stranger in Clear Springs*, Elizabeth must break through her fears in order to grasp *her* happy-ever-after.

As much as I love writing about La Playa, on San Diego's harbour, I enjoyed taking a trip with this story to Clear Springs—a fictional town that I modelled after Julian in the backcountry of San Diego.

I hope you enjoy Tom and Elizabeth's story.

FAMILIAR STRANGER IN CLEAR SPRINGS

Kathryn Albright

MILLS & BOON

First published in Great Britain 2016
By Mills & Boon, an imprint of HarperCollins*Publishers*
1 London Bridge Street, London, SE1 9GF

© 2016 Kathryn Leigh Albright

ISBN: 978-0-263-91676-8

Our policy is to use papers that are natural, renewable and
recyclable products and made from wood grown in sustainable
forests. The logging and manufacturing processes conform to the
legal environmental regulations of the country of origin.

Printed and bound in Spain
by CPI, Barcelona

Kathryn Albright writes American-set historical romance for Harlequin Mills & Boon. From her first breath she has had a passion for stories that celebrate the goodness in people. She combines her love of history and her love of story to write novels of inspiration, endurance, and hope.

Visit her at kathrynalbright.com and on Facebook.

Books by Kathryn Albright

Mills & Boon Historical Romance

Heroes of San Diego

The Angel and the Outlaw
The Gunslinger and the Heiress
Familiar Stranger in Clear Springs

Stand-Alone Novels

Texas Wedding for Their Baby's Sake
The Rebel and the Lady
Wild West Christmas
'Dance with a Cowboy'

Visit the Author Profile page at millsandboon.co.uk.

This story is dedicated to my beautiful sister, Phyllis, who has been with me from the start in this dream to write stories. You have offered unconditional love, support, encouragement, and fun.
It means everything to me. Love you!

Acknowledgements

I would also like to acknowledge and thank
Charlotte Mursell and Julia Williams,
my amazing editors at Mills & Boon,
who took the raw form of this story and
helped me see the nuggets of gold. You are the best!

Chapter One

Southern California, 1876

Elizabeth looked up from marking the last sale in her ledger and frowned at the youngster standing by the large wooden crate of fruit from the backcountry. "Timothy Daugherty! I saw that! That apple does not have your name on it. Put it back right now. Gently please!"

Ten-year-old Timothy looked sufficiently chastised; however, Elizabeth knew better. Under that contrite expression he was plotting how he would talk his way out of this. It wasn't that he was starving. With his father managing the building of the new nail factory up the road, his family had the funds for whatever they desired here in the mercantile. It was the challenge that drove Timothy. He wanted to boast to his friends that he'd given "old Miss Morley" the slip and had gotten away without her realizing she had one less piece of fruit to sell.

His best friend and cohort, Lucas Slater, stood shoulder to shoulder with him and, by the looks of him, was also hiding an apple behind his back. He, however, concerned her. His mother, Martha, struggled to put food on the table for him and his sister ever since her husband passed on suddenly a year ago.

Timothy scowled and tossed the apple back in the crate.

Elizabeth winced. That would be a bruised— and therefore unsellable—piece of fruit. She mentally counted to ten. Deep breath in, deep breath out, letting the briny scent of the harbor fill her lungs. Better that than saying something she would regret. It would be so easy to retort with a sharp word. Too easy. And then wouldn't she be one step closer to being the sour old spinster she vowed never to become?

"Don't you have schoolwork or something you need to be doing?"

"Naw. It's Saturday."

"I am well aware of the day, young man." It was the day before Sunday—when after church she would sequester herself inside to be proper. A day she was coming to hate for all that it forced her to be alone when everyone else had families to enjoy. Usually she would work on her quilting, although even that pastime had dulled of late. She had made several quilts and given them away, but wouldn't it be wonderful to have a reason to make a special one to keep?

She pressed her lips together. Wasn't she sounding bitter all of a sudden? Better to be grateful for what she had—a roof over her head, sustenance, her health. She put a smile in her voice. "Perhaps you'd like to earn that apple… and a few more…by doing some chores for me."

Timothy wrinkled his freckled nose. "Ugh… I got enough chores at home. Don't need no more."

"Don't need *any* more," she corrected gently.

"That's what I said!"

"Well, then…" She turned toward the other boy. "Lucas? How about you?"

Startled just as he was returning his own stolen apple, Lucas jumped and scraped his fingers across the edge of the barrel. He winced and examined his thumb.

"Here. Let me see," Elizabeth said, reaching for his hand. Two splinters pierced the skin and had settled below the reddened surface. "I'll get my drawing salve…and needle."

She found the items behind the counter and returned to Lucas. His eyes grew large when he saw the needle. "I remember my mother doing this for me when I had a splinter." Her throat tightened at the image of Mother tending to her minor hurts over the years. Oh, how she missed her.

At Lucas's anxious expression, she pulled her thoughts back to the present situation. "It will hurt much less to have the piece of wood ease out than it did going in. I promise. Just hold still for me."

He braced himself, trying hard to be brave, but still he squirmed under her attention. When the splinters came out, she spread the salve and tied a small cloth bandage around the injured thumb. "There now. Have your mother look at it tonight."

"Thank ya, ma'am." He shuffled a bit with his feet and avoided her gaze, his face a bright red.

"You're welcome." Amused at his obvious embarrassment—was it from being caught red-handed with the apple or because she'd held his hand?—she found herself studying him. His dark tousled hair could use a combing. For that matter, his clothes could stand a cleaning.

"Isn't your mother taking in laundry now?" she asked.

"Yes'm."

Like the cobbler who didn't have shoes for his children, it must be the woman didn't have time to wash her own family's clothes…or have the energy once her other work was done. Elizabeth sighed. Her knack for details was a good thing to have in running the mercantile, yet it unfortunately came with a negative side—the tendency to be altogether too critical of others. She would make up something for Lucas to do—perhaps sweeping or dusting—even though the store was as clean as could be. Then he could take home a sack filled with apples for his family.

Lucas shot a look at Timothy, who had started backing away.

Timothy cocked his head, indicating they should go.

"Can't stay today," Lucas said. "We're goin' fishin'." And with that, he bolted out the door with his buddy. They each grabbed a fishing pole that they'd left leaning against the store's outer wall and jumped off the boardwalk. The motion dislodged the wedge that propped open the door and it swung shut with a loud bang. The shelving display of colored glassware rattled at the disturbance.

Elizabeth stepped to the entry and propped the mercantile door open again with the wooden wedge and watched the two race across the dirt road to the open area beyond the old jail. Just before scooting out of sight behind the building, Timothy reached into each of his bulging back pockets and pulled out two apples, handing one to his cohort. Amused, Elizabeth blew out a short breath. At least it wouldn't weigh on her mind about Lucas being hungry.

Something pressed against her ankles. Patches. She reached down and picked up her cat, scratching him behind the ears as she cuddled him to her and continued to watch the two boys. They headed for the small strip of sandy beach where they rolled up their pant-legs and waded into the water to throw in their lines. September, as a rule, was warm enough for wading, but another month and it would be too cool to fish that way. Still, she envied them their freedom. It had been years since she walked barefoot on the beach and dug her toes deep into the soft sand.

A cool sea breeze teased a tendril of hair that tickled her neck. She tucked the strand back up in her loose bun. It was a cursory repair that would be down again in another half hour, but by then she would be closing the mercantile and how she looked to her customers would be the last thing on her mind.

Across the way, in front of her alterations shop, Mrs. Flynn stopped rocking in her porch chair and waved.

Elizabeth raised her hand in response and then lowered it slowly when she noticed a scruffy-looking rider down the main street of town. Something about him seemed familiar, but with his back to her, she couldn't place where she'd seen him. The way he sat his horse reminded her of someone. With one last glance toward the boys, she turned and entered the mercantile.

Twilight offered Tom Barrington the anonymity he craved as he rode his horse down La Playa's main street and silently took in the changes in the town. Twilight, and the fact that his month's growth of facial hair and well-worn clothes made him look every bit the dusty itinerant. Not far from the truth. He'd lived in the shirt and canvas pants long enough they'd lost their itch and then regained it. How—he didn't want to contemplate too deeply.

He reined the Major to a stop before Rose's Hotel. Through the front windows the warm glow of lamplight beckoned hospitably. His first order of business, once he'd seen to his horse, would be a bath and a shave. After traveling for the past three weeks he could scarcely stand to live with himself. He dismounted, taking care to put his weight on his right leg, and looped the reins around the front post. The Major pranced sideways and then pawed at the ground. "Easy now," Tom said quietly. When he was sure his horse had settled, Tom climbed the steps and strode through the front door.

A short, balding man stood behind the high counter, took his information and handed him a room key and a folded note. "Mr. Furst left this for you. Northern California, you say? Seen any Indian action?"

Tom had, but long ago he had learned to keep things to himself. "Some," he murmured. Upon reading the message he relaxed slightly. Sam had received his wire and would meet with him later that evening. He had just enough time for a bite to eat after taking care of the Major.

"May I see to your horse?" the clerk asked.

The livery was probably in the same place. And in a town this size, if it wasn't, he would soon find it. "I'll take care of him."

"Suit yourself."

He slipped the key and the note into his inside vest pocket and headed back outside. The Major snorted at the weeds at the base of his holding post, sending up a small cloud of dust. He stomped one foreleg, the motion jarring his muscles up to his shoulder. He had seen a lot of action over the years. A new place, a sharp sound, and his horse could easily break into an all-out dash down the road and be three miles to the foothills before anyone noticed. For three weeks, Tom had used his saddle as a pillow and slept close by, sensing calmness in the horse when he was near. Wouldn't happen tonight. He was done in. The lure of a soft, clean bed was more enticing than camping out on stacked hay bales near a skittish horse. Once settled, Tom hoped a full feed bucket and a warm stall would soothe the Major's disposition.

The livery was the same, inside and out, as it had been when he'd been posted here in the army. The town had changed some—construction had commenced on what looked to become a large building on the outskirts of town. Other than that, some businesses had left—most notably the bank. Couldn't blame 'em. Nothing much happened in a town this size. Seeing as it was Saturday night, a few regular customers were in the small saloon, but all in all, it was still a quiet, isolated place compared to just about anywhere else on earth but the desert. Heck, if he remembered correctly, even the main road to San Diego washed out on a yearly basis. Nothing like that to keep a town to itself.

He sure hoped Mr. Furst, Sr. hadn't wired Sam the minute he'd left the main bank in the city. He'd like to say his piece before Sam completely shut him out and refused to listen. During the ride south he had asked himself how he would handle it if neither man would talk to him. Hadn't come up with any answers. Guess if it came to that, he'd know what to do.

He stabled the Major, gave him an extra helping of oats and headed back to the hotel. He should wash up a bit and shave before meeting Sam. As he neared the building, he could smell the beginnings of supper cooking, the scent of onions and garlic and fish floated on the breeze, intertwined with the briny odor from the harbor. After hours in the saddle, the walking eased the pain in his leg, so instead of going directly into the hotel's restaurant, he headed down to the water's edge.

Miniature waves lapped against the pilings of the wharf—the sound relaxing him further.

A light flashed overhead, bouncing off the low clouds. Adrenaline shot through him. Instinctively his hand wrapped around his gun handle. He hesitated…and then exhaled, feeling foolish as he remembered. He'd seen the beam of light before—the lighthouse at the end of the peninsula. Skittish? Heck, he was worse off than the Major.

Across the harbor in Old Town, lamplight flickered, the same as it did in the adobe and wood homes scattered along the roadside and up against the base of the ridge behind him. It seemed peaceful, but peace in his line of work was more often than not an illusion.

He reached in his pocket for paper and tobacco and rolled a cigarette, the motion smooth until he realized his hands shook. Disgusted with himself, he tossed the paper and pinch of tobacco into the shallows. What was he doing here? The military couldn't use him anymore except behind a desk sorting papers. What made him think he was different than anybody else in his line of work that this had happened to?

Was he getting too slow for this kind of work? He wanted to squash that thought even as it sprang into his head—just as he had the past fifty times he had considered it. He knew plenty of men older than his thirty-one years who still handled fieldwork. To hear them talk they did all right. However, they weren't crippled. It was his injury that ruined everything and made him a has-been.

But then he remembered Jeff Cranston. His own injury was nothing compared to what had happened to his partner, whose body now rested eternally. He swallowed hard. *Leave it. Nothing good comes from digging up the past.*

The past… He took a long look at the quiet street, for the first time letting his gaze roam past the small bank building, past the dark jail and the old Mexican custom house, until he came at last to the mercantile. The store windows were dark, as he expected, yet above, on the second floor, a soft glow lit one window. Who lived there now?

Four years ago it had been Miss Elizabeth Morley and her brother. He'd never gotten along with her brother, but he sure remembered her. Prettiest deep brown eyes he'd ever seen along with her rich, coffee-colored hair. She was taller than most women, slender and graceful to a fault. The day he had walked into her store and first laid eyes on her he'd been hard-pressed to find an intelligent word to say. He had fallen under her spell even before they'd shared that kiss, but once that happened he knew she was the only one for him. He thought for sure she felt the same way.

Anyone worth his salt could see she was a catch back then. She could have had her pick of any of a dozen officers in the army. They all thought she was something special, yet they'd all given up the minute that dandy from the city started hanging around her doorstep. He'd been the fool to keep coming around. Maybe that's why he wasn't officer material—it took him longer than most men to admit defeat whether it was chasing down criminals or when it came to matters of the heart.

Guess in the end money talked louder than any feelings she had for him because he wasn't gone four weeks before he heard she had up and married that rich fellow. Remembering the letter he'd posted was an embarrassment now. He had explained why his contingent had had to light out in the gray light of morning, but more than that, he'd gone on for an entire second page about making plans for when they'd see each other again. Likely by the time his letter made it here from Texas she was already set for her wedding. One thing was certain—she sure hadn't bothered to send a reply.

Even thinking of it now set up a slow burn in his gut. He should listen to that and leave things alone. That chapter of his life had closed a long time ago. Over. Done. It was a frustration that the entire ride south from Sacramento he had been unable to avoid thinking about her. The closer he got to La Playa, the stronger the images of their time together returned. Likely because this was the first time in years he was back in this small town.

His stomach grumbled, reminding him he hadn't eaten anything since two cold tortillas he'd saved from his breakfast at that cantina along the San Luis Rey River. He turned toward the hotel and then paused, looking once more down the main street of town toward the mercantile.

She wouldn't be there. He knew that. Why did he feel this compulsion to see for himself? Was it for old times' sake? Which was a maudlin emotion he should abandon right now. Or was it to torture himself over the fact that she was gone and married off? She was probably living in some big fancy stucco house in San Diego now with a passel of children.

"Aw…hell…"

He wouldn't be satisfied until he saw for himself. She wouldn't be there…but maybe whoever owned the place now would have word on what had happened to her.

Chapter Two

The sun had set when Elizabeth descended the stairs to draw the shades and light the stove. At the base of the stairs, Patches rubbed against her skirt, butting his head against her ankle to remind her that it was suppertime. "Don't you worry. I'll find someone to take good care of you while I'm away." A frisson of excitement raced through her as she thought about the look on Gemma's face when she saw the supplies for her new school. Her friend would be overcome by the outpouring of generosity from the small community here.

Elizabeth moved to the stove and filled the kettle with water. Stuffing kindling and old brown wrapping paper into the stove, she struck a match to it. "Just to take the chill off."

Oh, my. She gave herself a mental shake. Here she was talking to her cat. Again.

Bells tinkled as the front door opened.

"We're closed for the day," she called out absently without looking up. A body should know one didn't do commerce so late in the day. Who would be wanting something at this hour?

"Ma'am?"

Odd how a voice could stay in a person's memory forever. The deep tone sent tremors to the ends of her toes. She nearly dropped the kettle. As it was her hand shook violently. A vision flashed through her memory of the stranger she'd seen riding through town earlier. Now she could put a name to that form. Tom. Tom Barrington. Elizabeth stood frozen to the spot, unable to move for a moment. Then she glanced up.

Despite the thick dark mustache and scruffy beard hiding most of his face, she recognized him. It was his eyes. The blueness that had been so striking all those years ago was still there. His shoulders were broader than she remembered, and his frame taller, leaner, as though he'd lived hard without a lot of the finer comforts. That barely registered. She'd given up on ever seeing him again and now here he was standing before her. She could scarcely remember to breathe.

He stood in the doorway, black Stetson in hand, waiting for permission to enter the store farther. So clearly did the image come to her of the last day she had seen him standing there in his soldier blues that she drew in a shaky breath and set down the kettle. He wasn't wearing a corporal's uniform now, but a dark gray leather duster. His clothes had a layer of grit on them at least a half-inch thick. The wind off the ocean had tousled his dark brown, nearly black hair until it was completely lacking its parting on the side—or perhaps he no longer kept it as he once had when he was in the military. He looked surprised to see her—perhaps even shocked.

"Elizabeth?"

How many times had she hoped he'd walk back through that door over the past four years? One hundred? Two hundred? She'd imagined all sorts of scenarios. He'd rush in and sweep her off her feet. She'd run to him and throw her arms around him. Always, always, the dreams had ended in a deep kiss. Of course, that had been when she'd thought he'd return for her upon receiving her letter. That hope…that dream…had died years ago. And, unlike Lazarus, it would not be revived. Four years was too long to wait for anyone.

Oddly, the thought flashed through her mind that she was glad she hadn't yet changed from her day dress as she so often did once she shut up the store for the night. Usually she anticipated the removal of her corset at the end of a long day much as she imagined a horse reveled in the loss of his cinch and saddle. For now, the laced binding under her dark plum-colored skirt and bodice held her upright and firm. Perhaps she had enough layers on to feel sufficiently armored against his charm now.

After all, he was the one who had left *her*. Without word, without a care for what she'd thought they meant to each other, without asking her to wait for him or taking her with him. He'd been a scoundrel…and she hated him for it.

Well, at least she'd learned a thing or two since then. She had grown stronger after the initial hurt when she'd found out he was gone and wasn't coming back. And she was strong enough to face him now. More than strong enough, even if her knees did feel a bit wobbly.

She swallowed. "Mr. Barrington." The sound of his name came firm and cool. "I assume it is…'Mr.' now by the way you are clothed. Not 'Corporal.' Not 'Captain.'"

"'Mr.' is fine." He ducked his head under the door frame and stepped farther into the store. The door swung shut behind him with a solid whump. He didn't even jump at the sound. In fact, he appeared a bit dazed as he looked at her, almost as though he were seeing a ghost. "What are you doing here?"

His question baffled her. Where else would she be? "I'm not sure I follow…"

He huffed out a breath but still eyed her warily. "Same here."

The timbre and cadence of his voice hadn't changed and she recalled with a sharp pang how at one time she had loved its sound. He spun his hat slowly by the brim as the silence lengthened uncomfortably between them.

Her pulse picked up. "You're looking well," she managed to say. He did look well. She couldn't quite get over how he'd filled out in the years since she'd seen him. Irritated at herself for feeling even the slightest twinge of physical reaction she rested her hands on the countertop and intertwined her fingers, glad to have the solid wood between them to steady her.

His gaze swept down to her hands.

She thought he frowned, but she couldn't be sure under all that scruffy beard. "I must admit I'm surprised to see you at all. It's been so long." She was rather pleased with herself. She had spoken coherently even though her insides were dashing to and fro.

"I just got in from up north. Near Stockton. Thought I'd take a look around, check out the changes." He broke eye contact, finally releasing her from his hold, and glanced about the store—a cursory, uninterested look. "Hasn't changed much."

"Things are near the same here—except, of course, the army is gone."

"Heard that happened right after I left."

"For a while things were tough. Businesses left. But now the new nail factory is helping turn things back around. The men building it often use this store and the Fursts are reopening a small branch of the bank here, which will be good for the area." She didn't want to talk about the town or the nail factory. She wanted to know where he'd been and what he'd been doing since she'd last seen him. All the polite inanities meant nothing to her in the face of that. And yet…why should she care where he'd been? He'd left her and by the sound of it was only here on a whim. She began to wish he'd just go, just leave her in peace. She didn't need his brand of tormenting.

"You been working here all that time?"

She shrugged slightly, still confused at his question. "Of course."

The kettle whistled.

Startled, she jumped, having forgotten about the tea. Relieved to have something to do, she turned back to the stove and grabbed a quilted pad to protect her skin, and then slid the kettle off the burner plate.

"I don't see a ring on your finger. What happened to that rich fellow?"

Still facing the stove, she absorbed the import of his words. He thought she had married? Then he didn't know? Her mouth dropped open before she covered it with her hand and turned quickly to face him. "I…I never married Preston."

He pulled back as though she'd slapped him, an incredulous look on his face "Never? What the deuces happened?"

Why was he suddenly angry with her? She was the one who had been spurned. He left *her*! In the middle of the night he left her without a word! "You have no call to raise your voice at me, Mr. Barrington."

Rapid footsteps sounded outside the door and her neighbor, Mrs. Flynn, barged into the mercantile. The interruption punctured the air of discord that had grown between the two of them. Elizabeth exhaled.

Her heavyset neighbor was huffing like she'd run a race rather than just walk across the dirt road. The woman glanced sharply at Tom and then back at her. "Oh, my. I didn't realize you had a visitor. I had a bit of extra stew, dear. Thought you might like it for your supper." She raised the item in her hands—a dish covered over with a heavily embroidered towel.

The bright innocence in her expression didn't fool Elizabeth. Apparently she had seen Tom enter the store and wanted to find out what was going on. "Mrs. Flynn, this is Mr. Barrington," she said, trying to muster up a more gracious attitude. "He has just come to town and didn't realize I close the store at dusk."

Tom glanced from Mrs. Flynn back to her, sizing up the situation. It was unseemly for a man to be present in the store after hours unless it was family. Her reputation could be called into question. His jaw tensed as he slid on his hat and tipped the brim to Mrs. Flynn. "Ma'am." He turned back to Elizabeth, his blue gaze stormy. "Sorry to interrupt your evening *Miss* Morley. I'll just take my leave." He strode out the door.

She sank into the nearest chair. Truth be told,

she was grateful for the reprieve. His question hammered inside her with no answer. Why had the man thought she married Preston? It didn't make sense, not after the kiss they'd shared. How could he think she would go and marry someone else after that earth-shattering kiss?

Her neighbor's eyes were alight with anxious speculation. It wasn't every day that the town spinster was caught alone with a gentleman caller. She wouldn't be surprised if Mrs. Flynn had this spread faster than a fever all over the village by tomorrow. She groaned inwardly, realizing the looks she might have to endure at church services tomorrow morning. If only she had thought to keep the door wedged open. At least that would have made everything more socially acceptable. As it was, Tom's entrance had completely flustered her.

"Nothing untoward happened," she said irritably. For goodness' sake, she was a grown woman. And this was her store. Her house.

Mrs. Flynn set the covered dish on the counter. "I understand, dear. I just thought you might need my help with an uncomfortable situation. I was on my way over when I heard raised voices."

That stopped Elizabeth. "You interrupted… because you were worried?"

Mrs. Flynn readjusted her wire-rimmed glasses on her button nose and peered down at her. "Of course. You live alone. Someone has to watch out for you. And I know your mother would appreciate it."

"Then thank you. I didn't mean to sound ungrateful just now."

The older woman fussed with the placement of the towel over the bowl, trying to keep the steam and heat contained. "Did you know that man, dear?"

Elizabeth sighed. "Once, a long time ago."

"He's rather gruff if you ask me. And unkempt."

Her appraisal sparked a memory, making Elizabeth relax her grip on her frustration. "You should have seen him in his army blues. He was quite dashing."

She ignored the woman's sudden renewed interest and rose, walking over to the counter and the bowl of stew. The aroma of onions and cooked meat wafted up. She wasn't hungry in the least. Not now—now that she knew Tom Barrington was near. "Thank you for this. It smells delicious."

"You are entirely welcome. I'll…just be going, then."

"Good night, Mrs. Flynn."

Elizabeth waited for her to leave, and then shut and latched the door. Through the crack between the shade and the window frame she peered out the window and watched her neighbor enter her house. Exactly how long did the woman intend to look out for her? Until she herself was ninety? Her brother…Mrs. Flynn…they meant well. In their way, they made her feel safe. She loved La Playa, loved the harbor and the people. Truly, she did. But lately the town seemed to close in on her in the same way that the air could feel heavy before a threatening storm.

She walked to the stove and poured the hot water from the kettle over the tea infuser while her thoughts centered on all that Tom had said. He thought she was married! All this time! For all these years! It was so improbable. Could that be why he had never answered her letter?

And now, what did it mean that he was back? He had given no reason for his being here, and since he'd believed she was married, it certainly wasn't to see her.

Would he return? Would she see him again? He might come back—although judging from his past record she didn't know why she should believe that. Slowly, the tightness in her chest eased. Perhaps the question she should be asking herself is whether she wanted him to. Just thinking that way made her stomach churn. No. Definitely no. It would not be for the best.

"Come on to the house." Sam Furst tilted his head, indicating Tom should follow him. Tom descended the hotel's steps and together they walked past the livery. Neither spoke until Sam stopped before a house that was easily the largest one in the small town. An aged picket fence surrounded the two-story clapboard house and matching carriage house.

"Watch your step," Sam said when he opened the gate for Tom to pass through. "Got a few loose bricks that need repairing." Sam led the way, unheeding of Tom's slight hobbling and slower gait. That's how Tom wanted it. No concessions.

When he entered the house, Tom heard a woman speaking in a cultured tone somewhere down the hall and out of his sight.

"Amanda is in the kitchen," Sam mouthed quietly. He ushered Tom into the small private library off the hall and shut the door. "She has taken it upon herself to ready this house for me to inhabit again. We haven't been here in years—ever since we moved to the city."

Tom wanted to ask how his sister was doing, but thought it best to see first how Sam handled the meeting. If he was tense and...hostile, Amanda would be that and more.

As Sam lit the lantern, Tom removed his felt hat and took in the changes that a year had wrought on the man.

Furst had put on weight. Nothing that would slow him down. His face was slightly fuller— fleshed out—as though he didn't get much time to be out of doors now that he'd entered the banking business. His light brown hair had been cut short recently and his small mustache and goatee, although thin in areas, had been trimmed to a tidy length. His clothes looked to be brand-new and a bit on the large size. Maybe, like this new job, he was counting on growing into them. He looked more the part of a banker now—stable and moneyed. Sam removed his hat and with his other hand smoothed back his short, pomaded hair. With the motion, his jacket parted, revealing a silk vest with a chain and watch fob.

Sam didn't extend his hand—not that Tom had expected him to. Too much water under the bridge for that. The last time he had seen him they weren't on the best of terms so Tom figured he should address him formally.

"Thanks for seeing me, Mr. Furst."

Sam hesitated a second—as if the title were still new to him—but then motioned to the wingback in front of the cold fireplace while he sat down in the chair opposite. Tom moved to sit and Sam followed his every move, sizing him up with his gaze. "I thought that injury would have healed by now."

"It has as much as it's going to." He hoped that wasn't a point against him in collaborating with Sam.

"I wouldn't have recognized you. You always have been a chameleon."

Tom rubbed his beard, thinking maybe he should have shaved for this meeting, although he doubted a small thing like that would put him in the Fursts' good graces. Besides, maybe he once was a chameleon but no longer. It had been hard enough to blend in with his six-foot-four-inch frame, but now the catch in his walk made it even harder. It made him slow…and awkward at times. A person could pick him out of a crowd, which was not a good thing for someone who was a field agent.

Sam's eyes narrowed. "I thought you'd gotten

out of this type of work. Last I heard the government let you go."

So Sam had been keeping tabs on him. Interesting. "Just took a hiatus. Had to let my leg heal…" And a few other things he wouldn't go into.

"But you are not with the government?"

"No. Not any longer. My choice." The desk job they insisted he take hadn't suited him.

"I am surprised the agency sent you."

Tom didn't blink at the rub. "I *am* the best man for the job. Wells Fargo knows that." He'd been running down thieves and criminals for years—particularly gold thieves. He knew how they operated and was usually one step ahead of them.

"I suppose so…now that Cranston is gone."

On hearing his partner's name, a shaft as cold as an icicle sliced through him. Sam probably didn't need to know that he had asked for this assignment. First, Tom needed to prove to himself that he still had it in him to manage an operation, but more than that, he needed to atone for Cranston's death. He owed it to Cranston, and to Amanda, his widow.

"Just so you know…when Amanda heard it might be you they were sending she wasn't happy."

"Guess that's understandable, considering things." Considering their past. He had never expected to talk with Sam or his family again. His showing up here was a reminder of their loss.

"In the event she walks in on us…you've been warned."

Tom nodded. "Understood."

"Did you stop at the main bank? Talk to my father?"

"I tried to," he answered honestly. "He refused to see me." He raked his fingers through his hair. He didn't need Sam's blessing or permission. He could do what he wanted to do without it. Yet if all went well, he'd be helping the Fursts and maybe atoning somewhat for his partner's death. So why did he feel like he was in front of a firing squad?

Sam studied him for a minute, his fingers steepled in front of him. Likely he wondered if he should follow his father's lead. Tom just hoped he'd keep an open mind. Finally Sam lowered his hands. "All right. Here's what I know."

Now it came to it. Tom leaned forward.

"A month ago there was a robbery in Bakersfield, similar to the one we had recently in Clear Springs. They tried running the ore down the mountain in the dead of night like we did and still ended up getting waylaid by the crooks and losing ten thousand dollars in gold bullion."

"They've got someone on the inside," Tom said immediately.

Sam drew his brows together. "How can you know that?"

"They were ready. At night. Doesn't take much to deduce."

Sam sighed. "Well, then go ahead. What's your take on things?"

"Wells Fargo is aware of all you just said. They think it is likely the same group of thieves. Their ploy was successful, which makes Wells Fargo believe they'll target you again. They'll gain a certain arrogance in succeeding. Criminals do. And the fact that you are so close to Mexico makes it all too easy for them to slip over the border and disappear."

Sam listened, but then pulled back, his gaze clouding over. "I just can't get past why the agency sent you after what happened. Because of you, my sister is a widow."

The barely controlled emotion shook Tom up. He had known, even though it had been an entire year, that he would encounter anger. Still, Sam's attitude made him feel all over again how unworthy he was to be alive when Cranston, Amanda's husband, wasn't. "I'll get the job done, Sam. If anything, I have more at stake in the outcome than any other field agent."

Sam let out a sigh. "Guess you have something there."

"Believe me, no one wants this more than I do. I don't care how messy things get."

Sam clasped his hands over his stomach and blew out a breath.

Tom could tell he wasn't getting through to him. "Let me put it another way. Wells Fargo hired me. Not you. I answer to them so I am going to do this whether I have your cooperation or not. Without it, there is more of a chance I won't be successful and you may lose more gold. If we work together things will go smoother. We can collaborate and figure out a few moves that keep us ahead of any robbery."

Sam snorted. "Persistent, aren't you?"

He was still on shaky ground. That wasn't a yes from Sam, but at least he was able to joke about it a little. "I know what I have to do and thanks for the vote of confidence."

"You're welcome." Sam huffed, still tense. Then slowly he relaxed his shoulders. "However, I agree. We do have to work together."

Tom waited. This entire meeting was awkward as they both tried to assess where they stood with each other.

"You've got nerve, Barrington, showing up here after all that has happened," Sam finally said. "But then maybe that's exactly what is needed in this situation."

Nerve had nothing to do with it. What he had was nothing to lose. He was through living his life in the shadows like an injured dog, the way he had for the past year. Losing his partner had eaten at him until he barely recognized himself.

"I tell myself there was no way you could have prevented Cranston's death," Sam said. "Given the same circumstances, I might have called it just like you did. Still doesn't mean that I can accept what happened."

Whatever had made Sam say that much, Tom was grateful for it. At least they were talking. "I don't expect you to. I wish it had gone the other way." He could commiserate and tell him that not a day went by that he didn't regret what had happened. He could still see his partner crumpling to the floor, still see the shock on his face as his life bled out. They had orchestrated any number of scenarios to make sure they each had each other's back, just not the presence of a little boy who should never have been on that train car in the first place.

"But it didn't," Sam stated. "And along with Cranston, Amanda's life was destroyed."

Amanda blamed him, but no more than he did himself. Surely she hoped he would have died instead of her husband. It was the number one reason he didn't want a wife or family with the type of job he had. It wasn't fair to them. He'd talked to Cranston a number of times before the man married, trying to dissuade him from getting hitched. His warning had fallen on deaf ears. And now it had all come to pass. Being right didn't make it any easier to swallow.

"I heard she had a girl."

For the first time, Sam smiled. "Lacy is a little over a year old now." He stood and paced the length of the small room twice, then came back to stand in front of him. "All right, Tom. It is obvious this is personal. I can't help but think I'd want to do the same thing if it were me. Meet me at the bank first thing Monday morning. I'll have your stipend and we can hash out any further details then."

Tom stood. It felt as if the first obstacle had been overcome. After the ride south, his horse needed another day of rest and so did he before heading into the backcountry. "Fair enough, but I want to leave immediately afterward. I need to get an idea of the lay of the backcountry."

Chapter Three

Pastor Warner's sermons usually held her attention, but this morning Elizabeth couldn't concentrate one wit on his words. She found herself checking the pews behind her, scanning for Tom's presence. When she didn't see him, she wondered why she even hoped he might attend services. The thought exasperated her. Her brother would call her naive and foolish, and in this instance, she would agree with him. When Tom was posted here, he would attend services with the others from the fort. It was a way for them to mingle with those in the community and also a way to escape the daily sameness at Fort Rosecrans. But now he was no longer in the military and he certainly didn't have a stake in anything in La Playa.

As the pastor droned on, Elizabeth's thoughts drifted back to when Tom had been posted here in town. The memories of him came back as vivid as though it were yesterday. Especially the last time she'd seen him.

It had been near the end of the workday, that day in late July. The daylight lingered long after the last customer had left the store. She had yanked a bolt of fabric out from under the stack of other bolts and spread it on the table, thinking that the creamy white cotton would be perfect for pillow cases. It was for her trousseau and it was one thing she knew would be appreciated if only by her. Preston had stopped by earlier and listened with a disinterested expression at her idea for crocheting edging out of the same color thread and adding pink rose florets for further decoration. "Feminine nonsense," he called it. Her brother had chuckled condescendingly and the two of them had left for a drink at the saloon. Those two, she had come to realize, were cut from the same cloth. She remembered that the thought had bothered her.

Earlier that morning, Terrance had accepted his birthday present—a deep reddish-brown shirt she'd sewn with embroidered initials on the pocket. She'd known by his expression he didn't care for it. When had he become so difficult to please? Seemed all he liked were personally tailored suits from that Marston's store in San Diego. How could her sewing hope to compete with that?

It was a relief that he had chosen to spend the evening with his lady friend in the city. After the shirt fiasco, she wouldn't have known what to do to celebrate his birthday. He had even set aside the cake she'd baked, saying he'd taste it later. And then he'd left for San Diego! A day-old cake was preferable to a few more moments with his sister!

A knock sounded at the doorpost. She should have closed the door after the last customer but the summer day had been so warm that even her thick braid had felt like a heavy blanket lying down her back.

"Miss Morley?"

At the sound of Corporal Barrington's deep voice, delight had spread through her. This was a surprise! He'd said he had duty. Smiling inwardly, she smoothed the fabric once more and then turned to the door.

"Permission to enter requested, miss."

He looked gallant standing there in his blue uniform, his yellow bandanna fluttering at his neck from the light evening breeze. The uniform set off the blue in his eyes so perfectly.

She remembered wondering if there was a special event at the fort that day. Earlier a few gunshots had gone off, equally spaced such as would happen in a ceremony. She grinned at his use of formal address. "Hello…Corporal. You are quite late. I don't know if I shall give permission or not. I was just closing up."

He glanced into the store, ducking his head as he swiped off his blue cap and stepped just inside the entrance. "It's quiet in here. Where is your brother?"

"He's celebrating his birthday in the city."

He raised a brow and said in a conspiring manner, "So you are…a woman…alone?"

She nodded, a giggle bubbling up. "That doesn't mean you have permission to enter. I don't allow miscreants in my store."

"Miscreants?" He teased her with a wounded look and then pointed at her feet where Patches rubbed against her skirt. "You allow that cat in… I'd say I rate better than a cat."

She picked up Patches. "He's not just any cat. He's my expert mouser." She rubbed her cheek against the smooth orange hair on her pet's head. "What is your specialty?"

"Why I can shoot a flea off a rabbit at fifty paces."

She laughed softly. "There is no way you can prove that claim, Corporal."

He grinned. "No way to disprove it, either." Then he straightened, all amusement evaporating from his countenance and a tender expression entering his gaze. "I can't believe how much those brown eyes of yours sparkle when you laugh."

It was the first time he'd ever said anything so personal…and been serious about it. Although sometimes she'd catch him looking at her and she would wonder if, maybe, he was thinking those kinds of thoughts. But then, they never spoke to each other about it. This was a bit unusual. "What is it, Tom?"

"Something came up today. I want you to celebrate with me. Are you free?"

She lowered Patches to the floor. "Certainly." Picking up her light pink shawl, something to keep her arms covered properly in public, she slipped it over her shoulders and then stepped through the doorway, pulling the door shut.

He waited on the steps. "I have something special planned. No questions, all right?"

"I thought you were on duty this evening."

"I got permission to take a few hours off."

He took her arm and led her to the pier where

the water lapped at the pilings and the half-submerged boulders. He was quiet during the short walk.

"What's going on?"

His blue eyes twinkled in a devilish grin. "No questions. Remember?"

A medium-size rowboat bobbed at the pier. He started down a short ladder, stepped into it and steadied her as she followed in her long skirt. She sat down in the bow, tucking her skirt around her ankles, while he settled on the wide wooden board in the middle of the boat. Behind him, he had stored a large basket that he'd covered with a thick blanket. From it the tantalizing aroma of fried chicken wafted over to her. Beside the basket, an armload of kindling and wood had been piled on the floorboards.

"A picnic?" She was charmed. Then she realized she'd never seen him in a boat. "Do you know how to row this thing?"

"I've had a trial voyage. Practiced a good five minutes."

"And I can trust that we won't capsize?" she said.

"With my life, miss. I won't let you go under."

"Well, that is encouraging, Corporal." He was a good swimmer. She'd spied him once with a few other soldiers in a race across to North Island.

"No whitecaps. The water is smooth this evening." He frowned at her then as if remembering himself. "Didn't I say no questions?"

She smiled, enjoying the teasing. "And I'll be back at a respectable hour?"

"Absolutely. Your reputation is my main concern."

"Imagine that."

She was quiet after that and leaned back against the boat, enjoying the tug and glide of the boat that hinted at Tom's strong muscles as he pulled on the oars. The evening breeze cooled her skin—now so much cooler than it had been all day. She sighed, contented with how the day was ending after the unpleasant start with her brother and Preston.

"So, we are celebrating something. Hmm. Is it your birthday?"

He shook his head.

"That's a relief. If it was, that would mean you shared it with my brother."

"At the sour look on your face, I'm suspecting that that would not be good."

"Definitely not good."

"And you are asking questions again."

"Well, you are always so quiet about yourself. For instance, besides not knowing your birthday, I know nothing about your family. Do you have sisters or brothers? What about your parents?"

He stopped rowing and let the boat glide. "I did. They're gone now. My father was a sheriff in Tucson. My mother ran the house and painted landscapes, but mostly took care of her two men. No siblings." He pulled on the oars again. "And that is all you are going to get for now. We have a celebration happening."

In his short, clipped response she'd noticed his use of past tense. She had the distinct feeling that she would only dampen the mood by pursuing more information about them.

They reached the shore of North Island and Tom jumped out into the shallow wash. He tugged at the boat, scraping it up on the sand until she could alight without getting herself wet. He assisted her first and then grabbed the wood.

They didn't really need a fire considering the day's warmth, but it did make the picnic more special. A jackrabbit raised its head and stared at the flames for a second and then hopped away. She spread out the blanket on the beach and sat down. From here she could see a few whitewashed buildings in Old Town and also in La Playa. The strong smell of kelp that had washed up on the sand traveled on the breeze and mixed with the scent of burning wood from their fire.

Tom retrieved the picnic basket from the boat and plopped it onto the blanket. He sat down beside her and a spare grin slanted across his face. The small fire crackled and sparked, warming her face and hands, the light flickering and dancing in his gaze.

Her heart fluttered nervously. This was the most alone she had ever been with him. She felt safe, of course, but she also felt an intimacy unlike anything she'd ever experienced. Before, they'd been surrounded by other soldiers or her friends from church. This was different. His slightest shift of position, his gentle tug on her shawl to pull it back into place on her shoulders, all seemed so much more special alone like this. She placed her hands in her lap and waited.

"I was promoted today," he finally said. "I am to be Corporal First Class under Lieutenant Cranston. We are going to be honed into a special team."

A glow of happiness for him filled her. "But this is wonderful! It's what you've always wanted! You've been waiting for this to happen."

He beamed self-consciously. "It was taking them so long to notice that I thought they had passed over me. They said they liked my sharp-shooting and the fact I can tell the good guys from the bad guys." He tilted the basket her way, offering her first pick of the chicken pieces.

"I imagine it is a wonderful opportunity." She hesitated a moment, thinking about what it might entail. "And perhaps dangerous?"

"Just about any other assignment is danger-ous compared to this quiet post."

"Your father would be proud," she said tenta-tively, hoping for a little more insight into who Tom Barrington was.

"I hope so." He seemed to contemplate her for a moment, then looked back at the fire, concen-trating on the glowing flames. "I'm not the law-yer he wanted. Once he was gone, we couldn't afford school. But I'm doing something that will make a difference. Something that will bring justice."

When he said the word *justice*, the look on his face made her pause in taking another bite of food. He looked determined—and in a way almost vengeful. Her eyes burned with the quick welling up of tears. She reached over to squeeze his arm. "He would like that," she said softly.

A soft orange sunset fanned across the sky and colored his skin with a deep tan. He swallowed hard, staring at her hand. "The minute I heard, all I could think about was telling you. That's all that mattered. You look… You take my breath away, Elizabeth. Every time I see you…from that first day in the store."

She blushed, aware of a similar feeling every time she looked at him. Handsome, broad-shouldered and tall—the sight of him did fascinating things to her insides.

"Are you still seeing Preston?"

Dismayed at the change of subject, she let go of Tom's arm. For some reason, she couldn't meet his gaze. "He comes by. Lately it seems that Terrance monopolizes his time more than I do. My brother hangs on his every word. I heard them scheming up a new business venture just this morning."

Tom's brow furrowed. "Instead of paying attention to you? He's a fool."

"No," she said with a tolerant smile. "He's a nice man, but sometimes I wonder what drew me to him in the first place."

"Money. Prestige. Those can be powerful."

"At times I feel that I am just a proper decoration on his arm," she blurted out, and then stopped talking. Whatever was going on was between her and Preston? She wasn't engaged, but she had the feeling he was heading in that direction. It was just his way to be methodical and sure. Unfortunately, that made her feel as if she were one of his business acquisitions.

"But you love him."

She stopped short, surprised Tom would say such a thing.

At her hesitation, a slow, warm smile broke across his handsome face. He tilted his head slightly to the side, studying her. "Good. I wanted to be clear about that."

Her heart began to pound. She was unable to look away, captured easily by his gaze. She gripped tight to the ends of her shawl and wrapped them closer. "Wh…why?" She felt as if she were slipping down a deep chasm.

He shifted his hips and moved closer. "Because I don't like competition." He splayed his fingers on her upper back, drawing her toward him. Firelight flickered in his eyes and suddenly she was much warmer. He had never kissed her before, although sometimes he had looked at her and she knew he wanted to by the way he studied her mouth. That look made her pulse race, but this…this was so much headier.

His lips touched her skin beneath her ear in a soft, warm kiss. Slowly he trailed his lips to her neck under her jaw. He paused for a second—which to her seemed like an eternity—and then with purposeful intent, his gaze still on hers, he pressed his mouth against hers.

The horizon seemed to tilt on its edge and for a moment her breath ceased movement in her lungs. She flushed all over—and then, as she exhaled, a sigh of contentment followed.

"I want to be first in your life, Elizabeth," he murmured against her lips. "I need to be first."

"You are," she breathed, albeit a bit shakily. First kiss, first...

Apparently that was all the encouragement he needed. Tom deepened the kiss. The sparks and crackles from the fire blended into the touch of his mouth as light exploded through her. He teased the seam of her lips with his tongue until she opened her mouth.

Now a new sensation careened through her. Her pulse raced and she melted into a puddle of fire and feeling. She'd never experienced anything so all-consuming. Her bones turned to butter, soft and pliable. She gripped the brass buttons on his uniform, drawing him nearer, reveling in his strength. She feathered her fingers through his hair at the base of his neck, cupping her palm on his warm skin. She wanted him closer.

"Ah, Elizabeth. Had I known..." he murmured into her ear, sending delightful shivers throughout her body. He circled her with his arms and pressed her gently to the blanket.

The first shards of impropriety pricked her conscience.

She froze, tense.

He stopped kissing her immediately. "What is it?"

"We need to stop." She pushed against his chest. When he moved away, she wiggled away from him. Sitting up, she dragged in a big breath and adjusted her shirtwaist and skirt. Her skin felt hot and tingly—and she knew it was not from the picnic fire.

"Are you all right?" he asked.

Shaken, she wanted to say. Shaken beyond anything she'd ever felt—at him, at herself. "I'm fine. Perhaps, though, we had best start back."

He sat up, took a deep breath and raked his hand through his hair. For a moment it seemed he wanted to say more but he only nodded and then began returning the napkins and dishes to the wicker basket. He popped up to his feet and carried the basket to the boat.

When he came back, they shook out the sand from the blanket.

"The wind has come up," he said. "You'd better wrap this around you."

He helped her into the boat, tucked the blanket around her gently and shoved off, rowing back across the channel as the purple twilight faded away into night. Stars sprinkled the sky with pinpoints of light all the way to the horizon at the sea. He was so quiet. She wished she knew what he was thinking. Her own thoughts were in turmoil. Was it the same for him?

"Tom…I…"

"It's all right," he reassured her. "I should get back to my barracks, too."

In town, the road was a gray ribbon in the twilight, leading out of town. Shadows darkened the boardwalk in front of the store. Across the way, Mrs. Flynn turned up the wick on the lantern in her parlor, letting the light shine out through her front window and onto the road.

At the mercantile's door, Elizabeth turned to him before going inside.

He pushed aside a strand of her hair, tucking it behind her ear. Something new shone in his eyes…a tenderness she hadn't noticed before. She wondered if he could see the same thing in her. She raised up on her toes and kissed him on the cheek. "Congratulations on your promotion. I'm so proud of you."

He stopped her from pulling away with his hands on her shoulders and drew her back to him, wrapping his arms around her once more. "I don't want to let you go."

She huffed out a breath. "You have to. They've already played taps."

"I know," he breathed into the crook of her neck.

"I'm not going anywhere. I'll see you tomorrow."

He looked at her and the intensity she saw in his eyes overwhelmed her. "That's not what I meant."

"I know," she whispered. Over the summer her feelings had grown stronger with every innocent moment they'd shared. And now all pretenses to deny her true emotions evaporated. She loved him—and wanted him to know it. "I love you, Tom Barrington."

At her confession, he hesitated a moment, and then bent down to kiss her long and thorough. She closed her eyes, absorbing the warmth of his lips, enjoying his soft touch.

"I'm on duty tomorrow, but I'll come afterward."

She opened her eyes and smiled up at him. It was a promise. "Tomorrow."

That had been the last time she saw Tom… until now.

It was painful to ponder what had happened all those years ago. She had blurted out her feelings and the thought of it embarrassed her now. Tom had gone to seek his future and never wrote, never tried to contact her. He'd obviously enjoyed the summer on the water and then moved on. It was futile to wish things had been different. He hadn't cared enough to stay—or ask her to go with him.

She tightened her jaw. It may have taken a while, but she had learned her lesson well. She would not be making a fool of herself again. Not ever.

With surprise, she realized that people in the pews surrounding her had risen and were singing the ending hymn. Quickly she rose and joined in, hoping no one had noticed her lack of interest in the sermon.

After the service, Elizabeth descended the whitewashed steps of the church, while at the same time tying her straw bonnet ribbons under her chin. The day was sunny but cool, so she tugged her heavy ecru shawl about her shoulders and then glanced toward the hotel. On the wide porch stood her brother, nose to nose with Sam Furst in what appeared to be a very heated discussion by the way Terrance was using his hands and leaning into the conversation.

Tall and thin, with dark brown hair and eyes the same as hers, it was nonetheless curious how different Terrance was from her. They might look similar and both have ambitious natures but that is where it ended. Her brother's personality veered vastly different from hers. Even his sense of humor was nothing like hers. Where she preferred witty anecdotes and puns, his tended to the coarse and at times rather banal. She certainly didn't understand him. He glanced over just then and noticed her approach. Straightening, he waved impatiently for her to hurry up.

She eyed the disgruntled expression on his face. Whatever the topic between him and Sam, he certainly wasn't happy with what he was hearing. It looked as though he was more than ready for her to join him.

In the hotel's restaurant, her brother chose a favorite table in the center of the room. She had asked him once why that particular table and he answered that Preston had once recommended it. It was so that he could see and greet people all around him at nearby tables. Sitting near the wall would give him only half the area. She suspected an opposite motive—he wanted people to notice he was there. Plus, a few times she'd been aware of him eavesdropping on conversations at nearby tables. She'd thought to caution him on it, but then held her tongue. It wouldn't do any good to say something. He wouldn't listen to her, anyway.

As she settled into the chair, smoothing her midnight-blue dress over her knees, a man with a thatch of dark brown hair at the table just beyond Terrance caught her eye. She inhaled sharply. Tom sat not ten feet away—alone with an empty plate and full cup of coffee in front of him. He tipped his chin up, acknowledging her, his gaze steady and unnerving as always.

She realized, suddenly, what was different about the way he looked from last night. He had shaved and put on a fresh shirt, so that now without the scruffy beard she could clearly see the contours of his face. He had definitely matured—not an ounce of boyish flesh that she remembered remained. Everything about him signaled strength and manliness. Tiny lines fanned out near each eye—the kind that happened from laughing a lot or perhaps squinting in the sun. She rather thought it was the latter. It wasn't fair that he had grown even more handsome since the last time he'd been here.

When Terrance eyed her with a curious expression, she smiled a bit too brightly, distracted as she was by Tom's presence. One moment she wished he would just disappear and the next she hoped he would come join her. How could he sit there so casually oblivious to all that they had been to each other? Of course, it no longer bothered her. It happened too long ago and she had learned…oh, yes…she had learned from it. The others in the restaurant would not be getting an eyeful today.

Apparently her brother hadn't noticed Tom. Considering how things had gone in the past between the two, it was probably a good thing. And as it was none of her business why Tom was in town, and he obviously wasn't here to visit her, she had best ignore his close proximity other than to be pleasant should the need arise. With concerted effort, she turned her attention to her brother, who, she realized, was dressed particularly sharp. In the next second, she realized why.

"A new suit?" she asked. "From Marston's?

Does this mean you have decided to run for the city commerce board?"

"I thought about what you said a few weeks ago. You were right. If changes are to be made that will affect my business, I want to be in on the decision-making."

She had encouraged it only to keep him from pressing her about moving to the city with him and helping him with his business—a discussion that surfaced more and more often now that his business was up and running. She hoped instead that he would marry and start a family. If she wasn't going to have a family of her own, at least she would be able to dote on nieces and nephews.

A serving waitress stopped by their table and took their orders. Dinner consisted of yellowtail fish and boiled parsley potatoes—a staple and one well-liked by the Sunday crowd. She pushed her food about her plate, taking a bite now and then while Terrance droned on about the Chinese abalone and shrimp fishing going on in the area. She could barely concentrate on what he was saying. Each time she looked up, she couldn't keep from glancing beyond Terrance, and each time Tom was watching her. She lowered her gaze immediately, but still felt a flush of warmth rise on her cheeks. He simply filled the room with his presence.

"The supplies you ordered have arrived," Terrance said. "They'll be on the Wells Fargo Stage for the Tuesday run."

Her brother's words registered after a moment. "The supplies?" She had ordered them months ago. "That's wonderful. I received word from Gemma just this week. The schoolhouse is nearly finished."

She toyed with her china cup, smoothing her finger around the rim, hoping Terrance would go along with her plan to visit Gemma. She could just imagine the delight on her friend's face when she first opened the crates of supplies and she wanted to be there to see it. Terrance didn't like change—especially change that he didn't instigate and might affect his income in any way. He would shove a laundry list of reasons at her why she shouldn't go, and since half of the store was his, he did have a right to be a part of the decision. "As a matter of fact," she said, "I would like to visit her…and take her the supplies myself."

Terrance paused from stuffing a forkful of slaw into his mouth. Slowly he put his fork down. "I don't see that that is necessary."

She leaned forward. "I'd like to be there when she first sees everything. I want to see the expression on her face."

"Just who do you expect to watch the mercantile? I certainly can't."

She pressed her lips together. Of course that would be Terrance's first concern. Always practical. Always economical. But he had a valid point. Who would watch the store? And there was her cat to consider. Left on her own, Patches would be easy game for coyotes.

She tapped her fingers on the tabletop, considering her limited options. "Otis Ferriday? Mrs. Flynn?"

With a wave of his hand, Terrance dismissed those two suggestions as unsuitable.

"Why not? What wrong with one of them? Mrs. Flynn has even availed herself of the order sheets and dusting once or twice when I wasn't feeling well."

He ticked them off on his fingers. "Otis Ferriday is older than dirt and just as rumpled. He doesn't instill trust. Mrs. Flynn will gossip with everyone who stops in. We'd lose business because of her overactive tongue."

She sat back in her chair, stunned to hear him speak so harshly right out in the open where anybody could hear. She leaned forward, lowering her voice to a whisper. "I cannot believe you said that here in front of everybody! These are my neighbors! Besides hurting business…it is rude!" They were his former neighbors, too.

His expression of disdain let her know that her shock didn't faze him. "Is Miss Starling even expecting you?"

"Well…no. But that's part of the fun. I…"

"Then it won't matter if you delay until things are better planned," he said, interrupting her. "You can't travel alone, and as you know I am too busy to accompany you, especially for such a frivolous trip."

Elizabeth frowned. Here she was just barely warming up to the idea and her brother was dashing cold water on it. She wouldn't want him along, anyway, with such an attitude.

"I will be perfectly safe on the stagecoach. It is only one long day's travel. I would stay for a week at most. I've not had a holiday since…" She stopped short. She hadn't had a holiday—not a real one—since taking on the mercantile full-time after their father died.

Terrance pressed his lips into a thin line. "Elizabeth. You haven't thought this through. You do realize my appointment to the city council will occur in four weeks. I could use you in the city, helping run things at my store there. Besides, a trip is just too expensive right now."

"This from the man who just bought a new suit," she hissed. But perhaps he was right. They would have to pay someone to watch the store and it sounded like Terrance had been counting on her help. She sighed. She hated to let him down. Maybe it was poor timing. It began to feel that way now.

"Why is it even necessary? A note, along with the crates, will suffice."

"I was the one who rallied the community and gathered the money for the school supplies. I was the one who ordered them. I want to be the one surprising Gemma." Maybe it was selfish, but that was how she felt. As the sinking realization that she really shouldn't go settled over her, she pushed away from the table, no longer interested in finishing her meal.

Her mother's dying wish was that they do their best to keep the family together. She and Terrance had both held Mother's hand and promised, but lately Terrance made it so difficult to keep that promise, especially when he stubbornly refused to budge on certain issues.

The excitement of only a moment ago evaporated as quickly as it had occurred. She placed her napkin beside her plate. "Thank you for the dinner...and for seeing to the supplies. I suppose whether I'm there or not, Gemma will still be happy to get them."

Terrance pulled his money clip from his inside vest pocket, preparing to pay the bill. Behind him, Tom moved his head slightly, drawing her attention until she met his eyes. Wonderful. He probably overheard the entire conversation. Wouldn't that be just perfect?

Without preamble, he pushed his chair back, making a loud scraping noise, and stood, unfolding until he towered over the both of them. He took a minute to meet Terrance's gaze before settling on hers. "I don't mean to interrupt your meal, but seeing as how you are done, I'll say hello." The corner of his mouth came up in a spare lopsided smile that did funny things to her inside. "Didn't get that far yesterday."

"Good afternoon, Mr. Barrington," she said, feeling her brother's scrutiny as she spoke.

"Well, well," Terrance said in his smoothly oiled voice. "This is a surprise. What brings you to town, Barrington?"

Tom broke eye contact with her and faced her

brother, the half-smile dissolving into a thin, straight line. "A job."

Then his gaze slid right back to her. Heat flared in her cheeks. She was sure every set of eyes in the restaurant must be concentrated on them. What in the world did he want?

"Then you won't be in town long?" Terrance asked.

She felt the press of her brother's hand against the small of her back, signaling it was time to go. Curious how Tom would answer him, she planted her feet firmly in place.

"I haven't decided. It depends on a few things."

"Sorry we can't stay and join you," Terrance said, pushing her more insistently.

"That's all right. I actually prefer to eat with friends."

She drew in a sharp breath. Why was Tom deliberately taunting her brother?

"Well. Good luck on that."

The tension running beneath their words puzzled her, like a taut cord of leather made stronger by a soaking. Where was all this animosity coming from?

"Perhaps Miss Morley would like dessert? It is 'Miss,' correct?"

He knew she wasn't married. What was he getting at?

"I'll walk her home afterward."

All civility dropped from her brother's aspect. "I can walk her home myself. She doesn't need anything from the likes of you. Understand?"

Tom stepped into the space between the tables, successfully barring the path with his body. He narrowed his eyes to slits, his jaw tense. "Understand? As a matter of fact—yes. I'm beginning to understand a heck of a lot. I don't believe you gave the lady a chance to answer."

So much for not making a scene in front of everyone in the restaurant! She was sure that all eyes were staring at the three of them. Mutely she shook her head.

"Another time, perhaps." He took his time stepping out of the way.

She remembered to breathe, and then somehow made herself move forward toward the door. Her cheeks had to be cherry red they were so hot.

Terrance hung back. She couldn't hear what he said to Tom, but she knew that tone of voice. It wasn't pleasant being on the receiving end of it.

Yet it seemed that Tom's words and attitude

had done everything to antagonize Terrance when all her brother had been was polite. Well—perhaps until that last bit that she couldn't hear.

She stepped onto the porch and clung tightly to the wooden railing. For a moment she let the ocean breeze cool the heat emanating from her face. This was a different Tom than the one she remembered. Before, he'd been fun and forgiving of the differences between himself and her brother. This Tom was in all ways a self-possessed man, not taking any aggravation or intimidation from another and able to hand it out if necessary. Had he been like that before and she simply hadn't noticed? She didn't think so. What had changed him?

Terrance took hold of her arm and accompanied her down the steps and toward the mercantile. She stumbled, trying to keep up with his long, brisk stride. Her satin hat ribbons whipped across her face and her skirt tangled around her. She wanted so badly to look back to see if Tom remained on the hotel's porch. She turned her head ever so slightly…

Terrance tugged her around with a firmness that bordered on pain. "He's there. No need to look."

They stepped up onto the boardwalk in front

of the mercantile and Terrance unlocked the door. "Well, sister. It's time you and I had a little talk."

Inside the mercantile, Elizabeth jerked from Terrance's grasp and rubbed her arm. Her heart pounded from seeing Tom and then being half dragged down the street by her brother.

"What, may I ask, was that all about?" she demanded.

Terrance scowled as he removed his coat and hat. In one swift motion he threw them with such momentum over the straight-backed chair that they continued on to the floor. "Well, that was unexpected. And by the way Barrington spoke, apparently you knew he was in town. How long has he been here?"

Elizabeth stopped rubbing her arm. Was he accusing her of something? She walked over to pick up his hat and coat, smoothing the latter carefully over the chair's back. "He stopped in last evening."

"No wonder he was so casual with you. What did he want?"

She stiffened. What business was that of Terrance's? "He didn't want anything. He seemed as surprised to see me as I was to see him. We barely spoke past acknowledgment of each other before Mrs. Flynn interrupted us."

He paced the length of the store, rubbing the back of his neck and mumbling. "Great. This couldn't have happened at a worse time."

"What do you mean?" It wasn't like him to be so agitated. She moved to the counter and removed her gloves and her bonnet and waited for an answer.

He barely acknowledged her words. "Last I heard, the military released him. I didn't think he would have the nerve to show his face around here again."

"Why ever not?"

He met her gaze. "It was a dishonorable discharge."

That caught her attention. She immediately stiffened. "Dishonorable! No. I can't believe that. He would never…"

Terrance snorted lightly. "It's been a long time since he lived here. Circumstances, good or bad, change a man."

"No. Not that much. Not Tom."

He dismissed her words with an irritated wave of his hand. "You are quick to come to his defense, considering how he treated you in the past."

"I'm not coming to his defense…I just cannot fathom that he would do anything deemed dishonorable." Everything about Tom in the military had screamed justice.

"Like I said, a man can change."

She realized suddenly that her brother had not shared any of this with her at the time. "You knew they let him go and didn't tell me?"

Terrance did not seem to hear her. "I wonder who he is working for now." He stopped pacing and looked at her as if she could supply the answer.

Slowly she removed her shawl and hung it back on the peg. She didn't know anything about Tom's job here, and whatever she revealed her brother would try to twist and turn to his fortune. He'd always been that way. It didn't seem her place to say anything. If he wanted to know more, he should ask Tom. "Why are you upset, Terrance? I'm the one he left. I'm the one who had to face things before. Not you."

He swallowed, his expression a curious mixture of speculation and worry. Then his shoulders relaxed. "I don't want to see you hurt. That's all. What he did before took you years to put behind you."

He had always blamed Tom…and she was

tired of it. "That was as much due to what Preston did as it was due to Tom. Preston nearly ruined this town when he pulled out his backing. That wasn't Tom's fault at all."

"No. It was yours."

She refused to feel any guilt, although Terrance tried his best to blame her. In her heart she knew that she'd made the right decision. With Tom, she had realized what love was for the first time and she couldn't go back to the watered-down affection she felt for Preston even if it did mean giving up the man's fortune—something her brother couldn't seem to understand. She felt that way even though in the end nothing had worked out as she had hoped. She had learned to adjust, learned to live with her choice. She had moved on. Terrance was the one who wouldn't let it go. "It wasn't my fault and I wish you would stop saying that. I made the right decision for me. It's in the past and it's over."

"That's just it. You are different whenever Barrington is around. I don't like it and I don't trust him around you. He's not good enough for you."

She knew what he meant about being different. She felt it inside herself. It seemed that Tom was the only one who kicked up emotions and nerves that ran shallow beneath her surface. In the intervening years she'd had opportunities to be courted, but had always rebuffed her would-be suitors—finding gentle excuses as to why she wasn't interested. Tom overshadowed everyone and everything for her—he always had. And now even the thought of him back in town caused a reaction, a tightening in her gut. She hated the sharp, anxious sensation that had taken up residence inside. It would not control her. She would not let it. And yet she hadn't been able to stop thinking of Tom since he rode into town.

"I don't know why you are worried. He's not in town to renew anything with me. If that were the case he would have contacted me years ago after I wrote to him. Like he said, he's here about a job."

Terrance eyed her as if he wasn't sure he believed her.

"In my limited experience, any job he takes has precedence over any other part of his life. He'll be gone in no time and without a second thought toward me, I assure you. You have no need of concern."

"Like before."

She pressed her lips together, the thought painful despite the passage of years. "Just like before." She couldn't afford to let down her defenses. Not for a moment. Tom was the wind and she could no more tie him down than she could a cloud.

"Good. Then we understand each other on this because I don't want him around you." A muscle ticked in his jaw. He pulled out a chair from the table and sat. "Now, let's get down to business."

A leaden weight sat like a jagged rock in her stomach as she walked to the counter to get the store ledger. Every Sunday after their dinner, just as it had been with Father and Mother, they went over the past week's receipts. She remembered Mother saying once that Sunday was supposed to be a day of church and rest, but her words had fallen on deaf ears. Father kept right on checking the books. And now with Terrance managing his store in San Diego, Sunday was his one chance to go over the records together. In the past year, Terrance had become even more diligent at double-checking her figures, as if he were looking for ways to squeeze more money out of the little store.

He opened the ledger to the start of the month, scanning the neatly recorded figures. He made notes on a separate piece of paper where she had already listed a few items to reorder.

While he assessed what needed replacing, she stood by the counter and studied him. He used to tease her. When she wore her hair in pigtails, he used to tug them to irritate her. All that was long ago. Over the years they'd grown apart—his ambition for social standing and wealth such a different approach than the things she cared for. Anymore, they seldom saw eye to eye. He was her brother, and she cared about him, and she wanted to keep her promise to her mother. Yet she wondered, at low times, if he really cared much for her at all.

In some ways, once he moved to the city, things became better. They weren't with each other day in and day out. He could no longer criticize and judge her and she no longer had to worry about measuring up to his standards—at least not daily. Now only on Sundays.

And today, well, he must be concerned for her considering the way he spoke of her not getting hurt by Tom again. Inwardly she sighed. There was no need for worry on that account. What happened between Tom and her had occurred too far in the past to revisit.

"How are the small coffee grinders selling?"

"Must we talk about business today?"

He raised his gaze from the ledger in front of him, using his finger to keep his place in the book. "We do this every Sunday. I need to know what's going on here to make good decisions for both stores."

She thought that interesting on one level because she was the one who managed this store; he just double-checked her figuring. "Is it enough for you? Running the store in San Diego?"

"I'm working on plans to expand. And, as I mentioned, running for a seat on the commerce board. Never hurts to be the first to know about new property."

"No. I suppose that's a good idea." However, it wasn't what she meant at all. She tried to explain herself more clearly. "I'm not talking about business. I mean… You never talk about having a wife or family. Don't you ever feel lonely at times?"

He huffed and leaned back in his chair, obviously amused by her question. "A wife? Children?" His smirk held an ugly condescension. "Tethers? No. At least, not while I'm building my business. Later on?" He shrugged. "Maybe. A son would be nice to pass the business on to."

His words sliced through her. Children weren't tethers. A family wasn't something that pulled you down. And yet even before she'd asked she had the premonition he would feel differently than she did.

"Now, if you don't mind, let's get back to the coffee grinders."

She did mind actually. He didn't seem to understand the concept of an afternoon off. "Three out of the five are sold. Mr. Cornwall wants one. They were an excellent idea."

He hunkered down again over the book for the next ten minutes, his muddy-brown hair falling forward over his forehead.

Finally, he folded his notes and tucked them in his pocket. He stood, shoved his arms into his new coat and plopped his derby on his head. "Do you have last year's ledger?"

The request was an odd one. "In the back room."

"Will you get it for me?"

She nodded and turned to do his bidding. What was going on?

In the storage room, she opened an old trunk against the wall and removed the top ledger. There was one for every year her family had owned the mercantile, twenty in all. She returned to Terrance and handed him the book.

"Will you be back before you leave town? I'll put the kettle on for tea."

"Not today. I want to return to the city before dark." He tucked the ledger under his arm.

Always busy. Always in a hurry.

"Elizabeth…since I'm campaigning for office, I'll expect your support."

"Of course." She agreed quickly, delighted that he had asked. Then she realized he hadn't asked—he'd told her. "What would you have me do?"

"I'm not talking about signs and flyers, although I do want your help there, too. It is important to keep up appearances. To do that, I really need you to move into San Diego and run my store there."

She lowered her shoulders. "Terrance, we've gone over this territory before."

He quickly held up his hand. "I realize you prefer this town. Why? I don't know. But you've done a fair job here of turning this store around from the brink of loss. It's sustaining itself now, often with a growing margin of profit. It's time to sell and get it off our hands for good."

"You are pushing this again? Why?"

"I told you. I need help with my store. And…I

need the money from this place for my campaign."

"But, Terrance! You've taken fifty percent of the profits from here for the past three years! Don't you have enough to campaign on your own or hire someone for your store?"

"I put all that money back into my place. It's not available for a campaign."

She folded her arms in front of her. "I don't want to sell."

"You're being sentimental. This place is just wood and nails."

"It is more than that, and you know it." This was the family store. Her legacy from her mother and father...and her livelihood.

Exasperation filled his countenance. "Granted, you've had a good run here but things happen. And—" he hesitated slightly before continuing "—you may not have a choice."

A chill went through her. This was new. She rubbed her upper arms and moved closer to the woodstove. "What do you mean—'things happen'? What has happened?"

"Things are a bit tight with the bank right now."

Why was the bank even involved? Unless... "Terrance. What have you done?"

"Nothing for you to worry about."

"This is my store, my responsibility, my… livelihood."

"It's not *your* mercantile." The look in his eyes was flat, unemotional.

"Oh, Terrance. What have you done?" She suddenly felt ill and slowly lowered herself into the chair. It couldn't be that bad, could it? He'd bought a new suit, after all. Still, he'd done things before without consulting her. She took a deep breath. "I think I have a right to know. How *tight* is it?"

"They want the store."

Shock gripped her. "What!"

His brown eyes hardened. "They want the building to cover the loan I took out four years ago."

She couldn't believe it! After all her hard work to save the store. Sleepless nights and doing without, long hours and loneliness over the past four years. She'd saved it only to have her brother plunge them into debt?

"So that's why Sam stopped by two days ago." At the time, Sam had been so pleasant. The snake! All the time he'd been planning to sweep the rug right out from under her. How could he do this? How could Terrance have let this happen?

Yet even now her brother had tried to make her believe that she would be helping him, that it would be her decision to move, all in an attempt to save face. Apparently he hadn't counted on her digging in her heels.

"That's why you need last year's ledger. That's why you and Sam were arguing this morning. You weren't going to tell me, were you? If I hadn't refused, you would have made me believe I was doing it for your career."

Terrance shrugged. "I'd hoped you would see things my way and move to the city. It would have been less...emotional...that way. You wouldn't have needed to know any of this."

She no longer wanted to hear him. This was *her* store! She was the one who cared about it and the people she served. Yet, from what he said, it was futile to argue. Numbness started at her feet and crept up and over her. She rubbed her forehead. "If what you say is true, then how much time do I have?"

"A month." He took hold of the door handle again, preparing to leave. "So you see, your desire to travel comes at a poor time as well as Barrington's unwelcome appearance. I'll talk to you more about all this next week when I have figures from the bank. Oh…and Sam may contact you to sign papers."

"That's the real reason you didn't want me to leave town—so I'd be around to manage the sale, around to sign papers and start packing," she said dully.

His brown eyes held no compassion, only a slight irritation that this had to be talked about at all. He really didn't care that he'd upended her entire life…that he'd hurt her. "No need to start packing yet. There will be time for that later. Sell as many items as possible—but only lower prices fifteen percent at most. It will make the final inventory go faster."

"I see you have it all figured out." She was proud of her composure. On the inside she felt overwhelmed. It must be the numbness helping. All her worries that had revolved around Tom Barrington suddenly seemed shadowy and vague compared to the very real loss of her livelihood.

Chapter Four

Tom stood on the hotel's wide porch a long time after Elizabeth disappeared into the mercantile. Considering the loud bang when Morley shut the door, Tom wondered if the entire building might implode. In the end, however, it stood strong.

No doubt Morley had a few things he was worrying about right now. Would he try to hide them from Elizabeth as he had in the past? Tom wouldn't be surprised. The rat had sure hoodwinked him for years. If Tom had not returned to La Playa and learned for himself that Elizabeth had never married, Morley might have gotten away with the lie. Now that Tom knew, he wondered what to make of that information.

He had a good mind to hang the man out to dry.

It became apparent, as he sat at the table and listened to the conversation between them, that

Elizabeth wasn't spoken for. At least, it didn't sound like it by the way she talked of her trip to Clear Springs. He had wanted to pin Morley then but something held him back. Maybe it was his years of training and gathering all the facts before acting. He'd wanted to listen longer and see what else he might learn.

And he'd learned plenty.

The first being that, for some reason, Elizabeth felt compelled to seek her brother's approval to do the things she wanted. Why? She was her own woman and could make her own decisions. Did she actually believe her brother was looking out for her? Or was she doing everything for him out of sisterly love?

He'd nearly lost his coffee when he'd overheard Morley had political ambitions. 'Course, all that he'd done to Tom was on a personal level. It probably wouldn't matter squat in thwarting his bid for office. Heaven help the unsuspecting public. Morley didn't give a fig for Elizabeth's plans. He had his own vision of "the future according to Terrance," and he wanted her to kowtow to it. What she wanted to do in her own life wasn't important.

Things just didn't add up and that bothered him. But what could be gained by him poking his nose in now? He couldn't change the past—couldn't bring back the years they'd lost. She had told him she loved him once. A man didn't forget a declaration like that. And he thought he had loved her. It had been so new a feeling to him and had barely rooted and started to grow when he received that letter from Morley saying she'd gone ahead and married. What would have happened if those feelings had had air to breathe and room to grow? Would their love have thrived? Or would the stress of his profession have worn it thin until it finally frayed and died? Or worse—would it have put Elizabeth in harm's way?

He remembered the look on his mother's face as she watched her husband die in front her, and he remembered feeling so helpless to stop any of it—his father's death or his mother's pain. He couldn't knowingly put anyone else in that position, especially not someone he cared for. That seemed to him the opposite of love. The truth of it was, the only difference between then and now was that he was much better at his job. He had honed and perfected his skill at shooting until he never missed. He would get the draw so fast he usually didn't have to shoot at all. After this job, Wells Fargo would have him moving on to do another one and then another.

He hiked his hip on the porch railing and watched the town folk go about their lazy Sunday afternoon. Again, the thought struck him as it had the evening he'd entered town that the place was about the most serene he'd ever encountered. Two boys, one looking suspiciously like the little boy he'd seen that morning in the hotel hallway, stood at the end of the pier and threw stones into the water. They looked carefree, each one trying to outdo the other with the distance of their toss. Three fishermen sat nearby on barrels and talked in their native language—possibly Portuguese? Every once in a while they'd each take a draw on their pipes and blow puffs of white smoke over their heads. Down by the water on the small strip of sand, a little girl walked with her father. She had her pinafore gathered up into the shape of a bowl to carry her collection of seashells.

Peaceful.

He glanced once more at the mercantile. He could see why Elizabeth might like living here. He wondered what he'd say to her when he caught her alone. He wanted to find out what had happened—from her own mouth—since he'd last seen her. It was water under the bridge now, but still he was curious. The problem with asking questions is that turnabout was fair and she'd probably have some of her own for him that he didn't want to answer.

He could walk away. That would be the easiest route to take. Just get on his horse and ride out of town. Let Wells Fargo send somebody else.

His gut rebelled at the thought. There wasn't time. And besides, this was personal. He had to do this for Cranston and the Fursts. He was here to make things right and atone for his partner's death. Which meant seeing that the thieves were behind bars for good or more preferably hanging from the highest tree.

And yet he still could not shake the premonition that he was supposed to be here in La Playa, too. That he had unfinished business with Elizabeth. The sparkle had gone out of her eyes. It was the one thing he remembered liking the best about her—the way her pretty brown eyes sparkled when she was happy. He'd do just about anything to see her that way again.

In her living quarters over the store, Elizabeth paced the length of the room, her mind whirring with all that Terrance had revealed. This was serious. Somehow she had to find a solution. She didn't want to leave La Playa. She'd grown up here and loved the town and the people.

She tossed her Sunday gloves on her bureau, the action ruffling the most recent letter from Gemma. What a mocking salute to all their hard work. Four years ago when she had been in a fix with the mercantile, Gemma, with her quick, inquisitive mind, had helped get her through the worst of the situation, no thanks to Terrance or Preston or anyone. If only she were here now. It upset her all over again that Terrance didn't want her to visit Gemma.

Although she already knew the contents of the letter, she picked it up and read it again, if only to derive a small amount of strength from her friend through the love and caring behind the words.

Dear Elizabeth,
I hope this letter finds you well.

I have decided to stay with Molly Birdwell—an older widow here in Clear Springs. She takes in boarders since her husband passed a few years ago. I believe this will afford me the greatest degree of liberty while I teach here.

The schoolhouse is in the final stages of completion and should be ready by the time you receive this letter. Although the children will have benches at first, it is my hope to have individual desks eventually. There is a dearth of supplies—pencils, slates and such—but the blackboard sits waiting to be fixed to the front wall of the room and the glass panes have arrived for the windows.

I am giddy with anticipation of the coming year. Although this profession wasn't my first choice, it will be a good one. I'll be making young minds grow—not a bad legacy if I do say so myself.

Elizabeth smiled, hearing Gemma's voice in her mind.

I am missing you, dear friend, especially the intense discussions we shared in our Shakespeare's Reading Circle. I hope you were able to keep that going after my departure. I wait eagerly for the arrival of my next letter from you and news of the happenings in La Playa.
Your friend,
Gemma

Unfortunately, without Gemma's engaging wit, the reading group had died a quick death.

Oh, how she would love to talk with Gemma now. She was the closest thing to a sister Elizabeth had ever had in the few years they'd known each other, and the only person Elizabeth had ever confided to about Tom when her heart was breaking and then when it was healing. Gemma had listened without judgment or condemnation. She'd listened as a friend—something Elizabeth had needed desperately at the time. If only she were closer. If only she could visit her.

Yet, how could she leave the store? Who would watch it as well as she could? Certainly not Terrance. He'd sell it out from under her and hope to make a profit in spite of paying off that stupid loan. And now...now she had to be here to sign the papers. She might as well sign away her heart. She fought the urge to crumple up Gemma's letter in a sudden fit of frustration and instead smoothed it out on her bureau. She would get through this just as she had all of her other disappointments.

She plopped down in her rocking chair and rocked back and forth, mulling over her situation, barely aware of the squeaky, familiar sound the chair made over the worn floorboards. There had to be an answer to this dilemma. If she just thought it through, something would come to mind that would save her from losing her store.

This place was the only security she had. She mustn't lose it.

Her chest tightened with past memories of working beside her mother and father at the store, sweeping the boardwalk, making the signs for the sale items. She had tried so hard to keep her promise to her mother to keep the family together, but if Terrance was not going to do his part, then she just didn't know that she could continue anymore. It seemed it had all been one-sided.

From where she sat, she stared at her traveling bag peeking out from beneath the bed ruffle. A layer of dust coated the leather handle, turning it from brown to a light gray, and making the imprint CA Malm & Company nearly unreadable. It hadn't been out from under the bed in years. The handle hung from its hinges in a mocking smile, taunting her that she would never use it—would never take a chance at anything remotely exciting again. Angry with that thought, she rose and walked over to the bed. Using the toe of her shoe, she shoved the peeping case back under the frame until it knocked against the wall and was completely out of sight.

"Elizabeth?"

She froze. That sounded like Tom's voice.

"Elizabeth. I know you are in here. We need to talk."

He was inside the store!

She exhaled a shaky breath and walked to the top of the stairs to peer down the stairwell. Tom stood there on the merchant side of the counter, hat still on his head, looking up at her.

"I'll be outside." He spun around and headed toward the door.

For a moment she just stood there, unsure what to do, ambivalent after her talk with her brother. She wasn't afraid of Tom…but if what Terrance had said was true… What had he done to be dishonorably discharged?

The front door creaked open. "You have until the count of ten," he said in that deep baritone voice of his. "If I don't see you by then, I'll be coming in and we'll talk inside. I'll even come upstairs if it will make it more comfortable for you, although that would give your neighbor even more ammunition in her arsenal of gossip.

"One…"

She stiffened. Mrs. Flynn! That definitely would not do.

"Two."

She gripped the railing—

"Three."

—and hurried down the stairs.

Chapter Five

Tom waited on the boardwalk by the large sign that read Morley's Mercantile, the letters painted in dark red with yellow edging.

"Four."

He hoped she wasn't mad at him for the restaurant situation. He hadn't meant to embarrass her with her brother like that. Morley just always brought out the worst in him.

The day had turned bright and sunny after the morning fog bank rolled back. A large bumblebee zoomed past his head and buzzed over the purple flowers in the flower box under the store window. He had left his duster in the hotel room and now took the time to roll up his shirtsleeves.

"Five."

The scrape of a shoe sounded and suddenly Elizabeth appeared at the door. She stood there in her dark blue Sunday dress, nervously tucking a wayward strand of hair into the braided knot of rich brown hair at the back of her head.

"Figured your neighbor would prefer us out here."

"You understood that well last evening. Mrs. Flynn does tend to keep an eye on the mercantile."

"And you."

"Yes. And me." She darted a glance across the street to the house with a sign in front that said Tailor Alterations and then back to him. "What is it you want, Mr. Barrington?"

He sighed. So she was still calling him by his proper name. "I'd like some answers."

"Well, I'm afraid that I am fresh out of answers. What did you want to know? Whether I sell tooth powder? Or—" she glanced at his bum leg "—Epsom salts?"

He frowned. She hadn't been touchy like this before. What was going on? Was it because of Terrance? Or had the situation in the restaurant bothered her that much?

She dropped her shoulders and closed her eyes for a moment. "That was mean. I'm afraid I am upset about a few things happening at the moment, although that is no excuse to be rude."

"It takes a bit to rile me. I think I can handle a little, uh, spirit."

She didn't comment, but she did cross her arms over her breasts. An interesting move when it wasn't the least bit cold.

"I saw your brother take off. Figured it was safe to stop by."

"Safe?" she said with soft derision. "You aren't afraid of Terrance. The two of you were nose to nose at the restaurant. If we had been there any longer, I was sure to have to step in to curtail things."

"Then let's just say I didn't want him in the way. Like I said, I want to talk to *you*."

She met his gaze. "What is it you want to know, Mr. Barrington?"

It was awkward, facing off like this in front of the store. "Will you take a walk with me?"

She immediately tensed and then shook her head tightly.

"All right, then…" He sighed. It would be here. Now. "Guess I'm still wondering why you aren't married. I asked you yesterday but we were interrupted by your overly friendly neighbor. I want to know what happened with that rich fellow." He had been a man of means. Someone who could care for her well above and beyond what his army pay could afford back then. The man owned several businesses, if Tom remembered right. Whereas Tom had been lucky to have a horse at the time.

"Whenever I thought of you," he continued, "I saw a passel of kids at your feet. Can't believe I was so far from the truth. Guess you've been right here at the store all along."

She raised her chin slightly—brief, stiff.

And by the closed look on her face, he knew something wasn't being said. Likely the mention of children. She seemed like the type who'd want a family. "What about now?" he asked. "Is there someone?"

She hesitated a moment, and then shook her head with a small, tight motion.

"Well?" he said, hoping she would talk to him. He didn't want to have to drag it out of her.

"You know, all that happened a long time ago," she said with a touch of rancor. "I believe the statute of limitations has expired. I've put it behind me."

He about choked on his spit. That sure was an interesting way to tell him to stay out of her business. She was sharp as a prickly pear this morning. Maybe he'd been too personal for her. "Actually, since I've had the feeling that you hoodwinked me, I consider I have a right to know."

"*You* have a right to know!" Her eyes suddenly flashed fire. "After you left in the dark of the night without even a word?"

Well, at least he'd gotten her talking to him.

Her feathers obviously ruffled, she rushed on. "The only word I received was when I sought out your Sergeant Potter and demanded to know where you were. That was three days after you had already left for Timbuktu or wherever was so necessary. And may I just say that seeking out your sergeant, in a fort teaming with curious soldiers, was extremely humiliating."

"Guess that would be a mite uncomfortable." She was angry as a wet cat. Maybe it was time they straightened a few things out. "Look. Let's get one thing straight. I'm not a man who writes to married women, and as far as I knew you got married a few weeks after I left."

She clenched her hands into fists. "You honestly think I would do something like that? Marry someone else after the things we said to each other? After that kiss?"

So she hadn't forgotten their last night together and that kiss. Her furious expression had him questioning his delivery of the news. Maybe he should have gone about this differently. Guess it was too late now. "I received a letter that said you were married…and on your honeymoon."

That bit of news stopped her. "It was a lie!"

He huffed. "Ah…yep. I see that now."

"Who would have…?"

"The letter was from your brother. He said you had married Preston Reynolds."

She stumbled backward and he stepped toward her, worried she might tumble off the edge of the boardwalk and right on down to the dirt road. He grabbed her arm but she quickly shrugged away and grasped the four-by-four post that supported the roof like it was a lifeline. "*My brother* sent you that? *My brother?*"

The horrified look on her face told him everything he needed to know. She hadn't been involved in the least. The letter was all Morley's doing.

He nodded once, giving her a minute to absorb the information. "And just so you know, I did mail a letter off explaining why I was gone. A letter that apparently you didn't get."

"You did?" Utter bafflement replaced the look of shock.

It was a lot to take in. At least she wasn't all out of sorts toward him now.

"I suppose it could have gotten lost and never arrived," she said slowly, half hopefully.

"Could have." He waited for her to think it through.

"You think that was Terrance, too?"

He wouldn't disabuse her further about her brother. That was for her to figure out. "No way to know unless you ask him. But even then... would you trust his answer?"

After contemplating that, she shook her head. "So all this time, all these years, you've believed I was married. No wonder I didn't hear from you."

She put her hand to her brow and stared down the road. The wounded hurt in her eyes was hard for him to stomach. It would have been easier to handle if she were angry about the news. At the moment, she looked so disillusioned he couldn't think of much to say. "Like I said, a lot to wrap your head around."

"It is, but I suppose it really doesn't matter now. It happened a long time ago and we've both gone on with our lives."

Did she really believe that? Or was she trying to convince herself because there was nothing either of them could do about it now?

On the other side of the livery, her brother

emerged from the Furst home and glanced toward the mercantile. Although it was too far off to see his expression, he obviously had seen them because he started toward the store at a strong, rapid stride.

"Guess he's not happy about my being here. You know…Miss Morley…although I can't condone what your brother did, there is another way to look at this. Maybe he did us a favor by nipping things in the bud. I didn't know it at the time, but where I was going, what I ended up doing…there really was no room for a woman in my life."

Innumerable emotions swam in those big brown eyes, but mostly he saw the hurt. He wanted to be honest with her, to tell her that their acquaintance had been more than friendship to him. Yet it was true what she'd said. It was all in the past. Dredging up old feelings and old hurts wouldn't accomplish anything today. He just wanted the truth laid out between them as best it could be.

Something shifted in her eyes. He could tell the moment she shut him out.

"Well, we will never know now, will we?" she said.

"I don't mean to cause a rift between you and

your brother, but I do want things to be clear between us."

"Oh, they are clear now. Quite clear."

"Good. I'm heading out tomorrow on a job. I'm not sure when…or if…I'll be back this way."

She drew back farther within herself. "Then you have your answers, Mr. Barrington."

Near the hotel, Morley turned the corner toward them. "Wonder what kind of hullabaloo will commence once he arrives," he murmured.

Elizabeth watched her brother approach. "I prefer to avoid another scene like the one we had in the restaurant and I have things to do so I'll bid you good day." Calm and cool as could be, she turned with a small flounce of her skirt and entered the mercantile, closing the door softly behind her.

If that don't beat all. He hadn't expected things to end like this. More likely a fistfight with her brother was his idea of an agreeable outcome. He would have been all right with that…if it meant he could have talked a bit longer with Elizabeth.

Tom stepped down from the boardwalk as Morley arrived, thinking to say something about the cards being on the table and the truth now out, but then he held his tongue. Terrance would stew more if he was unsure what either of them knew…and perhaps Elizabeth would have the upper hand.

Without a word, Morley strode past him and into the store, shutting the door.

Tom waited. Listening. Just to make sure he didn't hear raised voices. Just to make sure Elizabeth didn't need him. He made himself comfortable, sitting down on the step. When, after five minutes, no raised voices emerged from the store, he ambled down the road to the hotel.

Elizabeth expelled a shaky breath as Tom strode away, watching through a crack in the drawn shades, unable to take her gaze from him. Her stomach was in knots. *Knots.* She spread her palm over her midsection and took a deep breath, hoping to unravel them. The things he'd said playing over and over in her mind. *Terrance had done him a favor! No room for a woman in his life!*

At least this time she'd managed to keep herself a step away from his charm. Perhaps it was a bit of self-preservation on her part. She didn't think she could bear a repeat of the anguish she'd felt when she learned he had left before. This was much better. There were no expectations to be dashed on either side. No promises. He hadn't said anything about *wanting* to come back. Apparently she just didn't inspire that in him or any man. Granted, she hadn't been very warm to him. Perhaps it was time to accept once and for all that it was her destiny to go through life alone.

Her brother hadn't said a word when he strode inside. He'd looked hard at her and then headed to the back storage room. She found him on his knees, rummaging through the chest, inspecting more ledgers and stacking the ones he wanted on a small stool.

"Is he gone?"

"Yes."

Terrance lowered the chest lid. "What did he say?"

"We talked about letters…and you. Why did you write Tom and tell him that I married Preston four years ago?"

He rose to his feet, a resigned expression on his face. "He told you?"

"Everything," she said.

He pressed his thin lips together for a moment before answering. "I doubt that."

"Why did you do it? Why did you feel the need to interfere at all?"

"It was for your own good. You were making a mistake and too innocent to realize it."

"So it seems."

"You're not angry?"

"Of course I'm angry. I'm actually livid. Yet how do I make sense of something that you did years ago?" Somewhere the feeling sat banked and controlled and pushed down on the inside. Why she acted so calm at the moment baffled her. Her chest was so tight she thought she might scream. Perhaps she was in shock, completely, utterly in shock.

"At the time, I thought it best."

"Perhaps for you. You wanted a direct link to Preston and his position and money."

"You would have, too, if you gave him a chance. The minute Barrington showed up, you quit considering Reynolds. He wasn't even a close second."

"So you manipulated us."

He frowned. "Your greatest asset is your beauty and you were squandering it on Barrington. It was my place to look after you and you were making a stupid mistake. Letting you back out of your situation with Preston wasn't doing that. You needed someone with the means to support you. Barrington couldn't—not on a corporal's pay. You were better off without him. I mentioned that quite a few times. You just didn't want to hear it."

Her brother was a master at twisting facts to make him sound better. Now he made it sound as though it were her fault! "So it had nothing to do with the money you stood to lose. The money Preston had invested here in town and in that land in the city where you wanted to build your store?"

He didn't answer.

"You had no right to play with my life!"

"I had every right! You were ruining your life and, for better or worse, I am your brother and I will look after you. That doesn't mean I have to explain myself to you."

She was flummoxed. He truly believed he was acting on her behalf! "And the letter I gave you to post to Tom? What of that?"

"That gave me his address."

Her heart took another blow. "You didn't send it. You haven't once given me a choice," she said dully, looking about the floor at the scattered papers and ledgers from the chest. "And now the store. My store."

The tips of his ears reddened at that. "I'll make you a cup of tea."

His offer surprised her. He seldom reached out to her. "And that will take care of everything?"

"It sounds like something Mother would do."

Dumbfounded at his rationalization of his actions, she couldn't answer. He really didn't care about her feelings at all.

He walked through to the front customer area of the store, probably to get away from any further tirade from her. She bent down to pick up the papers. As she gathered them, she noticed one in particular and moved it to the top of her pile. The legal jargon made her head spin. Were they ownership papers? Glancing through them, a kernel of hope pushed up through the frustration she'd just endured.

Gemma would be able to see right through this type of wordage to the essence of the document. Gemma could look at a tin of talcum powder and find something buried in the small print. Perhaps she could find a way to free her from the bank lien and retain the rights to her store?

She walked out to the front area and confronted her brother. "Better than a cup of tea," she said calmly, moving the kettle off the burn plate. "I expect you to take me into the city today. Tuesday, you will get me on the Wells

Fargo coach along with the supplies. I am going to see Gemma. For once I am going to do something that makes me happy."

He frowned. "What about the store?"

"I will leave that up to you. Your choice. Either go across the street while I pack and see if Mrs. Flynn will manage it for a week…"

He scowled. "Or?"

"Or you can close it."

Chapter Six

The bank's door was ajar when Tom arrived the next morning. He let himself in. The place was tiny compared to the Furst Bank in San Diego and bore little resemblance to the shiny brass teller stations and gleaming wood and marble that he'd seen there. No one stood behind the one teller window.

"Mr. Furst?"

"In here."

Tom followed the sound of Sam's voice to a small office toward the back of the bank. A desk. A tall file cabinet. A heavy safe. Tom cataloged the objects mentally—especially the money safe and the security bars on the back window.

Sam sat behind his desk, riffling through a stack of papers. "Still getting organized. We're not officially open yet. Ah, yes." He found the file he was looking for and set it aside before leaning back in his chair and focusing on Tom. He didn't offer a seat—or a smile—but steepled his fingers together as he spoke.

"The last robbery came as a complete surprise. The fact that two of the mines were shut down at the time made the haul minimal compared to what it could have been. So my question is, do you think it's Hodges?"

Just hearing that man's name made Tom's stomach clench. "He's still incarcerated up in Fresno. It's not him."

"His gang? It was lucrative for them until he got caught."

"Hard to say."

"All right," Sam said slowly, mulling over things in his head. "I want to be clear on something if we do this. Your job is to get the gold shipment through safely to the main bank. Nothing else. That is the position the bank is officially taking. That is the reason we contacted Wells Fargo for help."

"I understand." Sam's interest was in the bank's name and stature. The public had to believe a bank was secure enough to hold its own against the criminal element. If the newspapers got word of a second botched assignment, people might decide to pull their money out, believing the bank couldn't protect it. Still, in Tom's mind, all that was secondary to stopping the thieves.

"Another thing," Sam continued. "I want Craig Parker informed. He's the law in Clear Springs—the sheriff. He's new. If I need to contact you, I'll send a wire through him."

"Fair enough. I'll keep him abreast of the situation as it plays out but I don't want to involve him in the actual transport. I'll need him more as backup."

Sam snorted. "You really do want to do this on your own."

Let Sam think what he would. Tom knew the real reason. He wasn't about to risk another man's life ever again. He listened while Sam detailed the current situation further and explained the regular routes, along with the number of men involved to protect the gold, and the days and the times. It would take careful planning to keep a step ahead of the thieves…and not let anyone get killed in the process.

"When will the next shipment be ready to move?"

"In about a week."

Which meant he had to get up to the mines and scout out the terrain now.

Sam opened his desk drawer, moved a few papers and pulled out an envelope. "For expenses. I don't want you worrying about food or stabling your horse. This should be enough to hire extra help if you feel it's necessary."

Tom stuffed the envelope into the pocket inside his vest. "Appreciate it."

"Anything more I can do for you on this end?"

"Not that I can think of. I'll check in with Parker as soon as I arrive." He thought for a moment. He didn't have anything but his horse. There was no one to contact other than Wells Fargo if something should go wrong and thinking that way might just jinx the entire operation.

Tom walked to the door. He paused, remembering that the door had been ajar when he first entered. "You might not want to be here in the bank alone. Anyone could take advantage of that fact."

"In La Playa?" Sam said with a hint of derision, following him outside. "Quietest place on earth. Good people here."

"A place like this makes for easy pickings."

Sam sobered immediately, considering Tom's words. "Duly noted, Barrington."

As he untied the Major's reins from the post and thought about La Playa, Elizabeth's face flashed before him. He glanced over at the mercantile. He needed a few supplies yet. The door was open, which meant the store was open for business.

"If something…" He swallowed, not sure he wanted to reveal anything to a man who halfway expected him to fail, but it seemed Sam was the only one he could say anything to, the only one who would get word about him other than Wells Fargo. "If something happens to me…" he plunged ahead. "Let Miss Morley know."

"Elizabeth?" Sam raised a brow. He looked from Tom to the mercantile.

"Seems she was vexed with me a few years back when I left and she didn't hear I was all right. I don't want that to happen again."

"All right, Barrington."

"Talk to you in a week."

Sam stuck out his hand for a shake. "Good luck."

Surprised, Tom shook his hand. "Thanks."

He had a few supplies he wanted to pick up for the journey before he left town, so he led his horse across the road and tied up again in front of the mercantile. When he entered the store he found Mrs. Flynn behind the counter.

"Hello…again." He looked about the store. "Where's Eliza—Miss Morley?"

She bristled at his slight. "Out of town, young man. Now…is there something I can help you with?"

He removed his Stetson. "No offense meant, ma'am. Just surprised to see you here instead of her."

That seemed to soften her some.

"I could use matches, bullets, jerky…coffee."

She bustled around the place like a whirling dervish. While she checked into bins and boxes gathering the items he wanted, Tom wondered about Elizabeth. Had Terrance dragged her away? He couldn't quite imagine that. She'd been too upset with him. Then he remembered her words at the restaurant about visiting somebody. Is that what she was up to? He hoped so. He hoped she was finally doing something for herself.

"Anything else?"

He added a few licorice sticks from the jar on the counter.

Mrs. Flynn smiled at that. "A sweet tooth." She tallied up the cost, then loaded the items into a small box. "It appears you are leaving town yourself. Safe travels, young man."

"Thank you. Don't suppose you could tell me where she went?"

"Well, I can't say much, but since you seem to know each other…I believe she is in San Diego. Her brother accompanied her there yesterday."

"Thank you, ma'am." He slipped his hat back on and paid for his supplies, then carried the box to his horse and transferred the supplies to his saddlebags. He was disappointed. He would have liked to see Elizabeth one more time before leaving town. Heck, he would have liked to see her a whole lot more than just once, but it would have just muddied up the leaving. And he had to leave. He had to know once and for all if he could still pull off a job…especially this one.

Besides, who was he kidding? Elizabeth didn't know him anymore, just like he didn't know her. It had been four years and they'd been years chock-full of changes. He wasn't the man he used to be. Nowhere near it… He wished he could tell her some of the things he'd done and the interesting places he'd been. He wished he had the time to figure out why she held herself so all bound up and tight now. But he didn't have that kind of time allotted to him. He sighed. Better to get his thoughts back on the job at hand. When he returned with the gold, he'd be taking it to the main bank in the city. Not anywhere near here. His life after that was difficult to envision. Guess he wanted to make sure he came out of it all right first. Anything beyond that seemed impossible to contemplate.

He mounted and reined the Major to the road leading out of town.

Tom headed due east through the valley. It was one of those days where the lack of haze made it so bright a body could hardly see in the shadows. The sun played havoc with his vision as he rode the Major along the river. Water trickled over smooth rocks that were exposed now in the fall of the year. A few deep pools filled with fish pocketed the riverbank. Sagebrush and scrub oaks bordered each side of the water.

Every once in a while a rabbit or lizard would dart out in front of his horse and he would have to steady the Major with a quick word and a reassuring pressure to his flanks. Tom tried to memorize the terrain and scout out any areas that might potentially hide those intent on stealing a wagonload of gold.

He doubted that the thieves would accost the

wagon this close to San Diego. There were too many small ranches—too many people scattered through the valley. With few places to hide, they'd be hard-pressed to make a getaway. No...if they were smart, they'd do their job farther up on the mountain and then race for the border of Mexico.

By early afternoon he reached Knox's Corner in Big Box Valley. There he gleaned a bit of information from the stationmaster. Two men were involved in the attempted holdup—a young skinny kid, and a tall man that liked to use big words. Both had sacks over their heads. Not much to go on, especially since just about every kid went through a skinny string-bean phase.

He started up from the valley floor along the Old Mussey Grade, riding past small fields of wheat and orchards of grapes and avocados. The higher elevation supported a wider range of vegetation. Pine trees and manzanita started to appear. Here a man could take cover, shoot at the driver of the wagon and make his getaway.

He did a modest job of keeping his thoughts on business during his ride, but once in a while without preamble something would remind him of Elizabeth—a certain clear birdsong, the scent of wildflowers. Toward evening when he started searching for a place to stop for the night, he gave up the fight.

By the time the sun set he was forty miles from the mudflats of Old San Diego and the air was so clear the setting sun was an orange ball in a sky of pink and blue over the ocean. He set up camp on the southern bank of a stream, and after dining on the jerky he'd bought at the mercantile and a biscuit he'd talked off the cook at the hotel, he stretched himself out, head on his saddle, and watched the stars come out and let his mind wander. Of course it wandered right to *her*.

She sure wasn't easy to forget—not that he ever had completely. At the restaurant he'd held his breath, half expecting her to show some of her old spunk and defy Terrance, but it hadn't happened. He wondered if she was in the city with her brother, or if after learning of her brother's deception she'd had the gumption to visit her friend, after all. For his part, he'd kind of like to think of her waiting for him in La Playa, maybe even pining a little. Wouldn't that be something? But the way she had held herself most of the time—all stiff and starch—led him to believe it would be false reckoning on his part. More like a pipe dream.

Things were different now. They'd both gone their own way years ago. And they'd done all right despite that brother of hers. The thought of Terrance's interference still left a sour taste in his mouth. And after the man's pompous words at the restaurant warning Tom to steer clear of Elizabeth, Tom felt a need to make sure he had his comeuppance. Maybe he'd look into that once he was finished with this job. Maybe he just would.

Her brother had out-and-out lied four years ago. Tom wasn't sure what had happened to the letter Elizabeth had sent, but he remembered the one he'd received from Terrance telling him Elizabeth was happily married. He couldn't figure out why the man would lie other than the fact that Tom wasn't rich like Preston. Maybe Terrance had had a side deal going on that he was afraid would fall through. Elizabeth had mentioned Preston pulled out on some of the business dealings in town after she'd backed out of the marriage plans. Had things been even worse than she'd let on? He'd left town just like Morley had wanted and Elizabeth had remained—caught in his web.

He blew out a long slow breath, thinking about yesterday. Elizabeth had pulled away from him mighty fast when he'd rushed to grab her and keep her from falling. And she'd colored some. Even after all this time, she was still such an innocent in so many ways. He liked that about her. Trouble was, it made her no match for that brother of hers. It was a fact Terrance wasn't looking out for her best interests.

As Tom drifted to sleep he blocked those disturbing thoughts from his mind and considered one more appealing, such as all that rich coffee-brown hair of hers and what it would look like if loosed from that tight coil. He thought about how he might go about it—slowly, one hairpin at a time—and darned if he didn't catch himself smiling just a little.

Chapter Seven

⁂

The team of six horses strained to pull the Wells Fargo Stage up the steep grade toward Nuevo. The wagon master urged them on, shouting and encouraging and snapping the reins until finally they crested the incline and came to a level patch of road where the beasts could forge ahead at an easier pace. Another hour and they would stop at the halfway point, to water and change the horses. After hours of riding, Elizabeth would be ready to stretch her legs.

Across the seat from her sat a young married couple heading to Clear Springs to visit the husband's family. After visiting with her for the past hour, they now held hands and spoke in whispers to each other. Elizabeth envied their happiness. It simply glowed throughout the entire coach. A bump would jostle them closer together and the woman would giggle while her husband caught her closer to his chest. They were ever so polite, but she could tell they wished they were alone together. As the coach barreled on, she stared out the window, fixing her eyes on the passing meadows and fields and trees, in order to give the couple a modicum of privacy.

The increasing warmth of the day as they traveled farther inland and away from the natural sea breeze, along with the rocking of the stagecoach and the rhythmic pounding of the horses' hooves, served to lull her into a sleepy state. The couple across from her notwithstanding, it was impossible to keep from thinking about Tom. Since his return to La Playa, thoughts of him permeated everything she did. Finally, she gave in to the overwhelming desire to rest her head against the high leather cushioned seatback and consider Tom.

My, but he was a handsome sight. Just the thought of him—lean, tall, tough—made her sigh. She smiled to herself, amused at the thought that she preferred a rough-and-tumble kind of man compared to someone like Sam Furst or Terrance. Tom was all strength and sinew and muscle—now more than ever. Had he broken any other hearts in the intervening years since hers? She hoped not. She wouldn't wish that hurt on anybody. And truth be told, she couldn't stand the thought of him with another woman.

She wondered who he was working for now and realized it must be someone in La Playa. Was it Louis Rose, who owned the hotel? Or the man who was building the nail factory? Those were the two most prominent men in town. The rest were hardworking fishermen. A few merchant vessels still stopped at the wharf, but all in all, most continued on to San Diego where a larger clientele awaited their goods and a higher price could be negotiated. The only other man she would consider hiring Tom was Sam Furst.

Really, she didn't care who had hired him. She was simply glad she had seen him once more and so relieved that he had cleared up what had happened between them. Although she could no longer distance herself by using the excuse that he was a cad and had played her false, at least she now knew the truth. To think that she might have gone her entire life believing her brother was an irritation she simply couldn't abide.

But what was it Tom said yesterday? That perhaps Terrance had done him a favor? His words had stopped her blood cold. She had loved him! All those years ago her heart had broken in a million pieces and it had never healed. Yet Tom thought in the end it worked out for the best. How could that be? How could being forever separated from the one you love be right?

She must face the fact that once Tom did care for her, but not enough to make a life together. He didn't love her. It was his job and his life apart from tethers that he loved. She grimaced, remembering how Terrance had used that word. Maybe some men were just made that way. It seemed to be her misfortune to be drawn to that kind of man.

Well, bully for both of them...especially Tom.

As unobtrusively as possible, she swiped away the moisture in the corner of her eye and sighed. Her life had turned upside down in the matter of days. Who knew what tomorrow would bring, but at least today she'd kept a smidgeon of control over her own life. After all this time...she had left him.

According to the shadows from the tall pines, it was just after noon when Tom rode into Clear Springs. The town was far different from La Playa. La Playa still had a few solid old adobe buildings and the jail that gave the village a Spanish air and a feeling of permanence.

Here in Clear Springs, the buildings had the slapped-up look of a boomtown that was still booming. On one side of the wide main dirt road he rode by a livery, bank, restaurant and dry goods store. And on the other side a saloon, law office and jail, a bakery and hotel and another saloon. Down one side street he noticed a grocer's and down another was the assayer's office and another hotel. A few residences stretched farther down the street. One even boasted a pretty picket fence around a small front patch of flowers and garden. Most likely that was the banker's.

Everything looked new. The wood on the buildings hadn't had time to weather all the way. Paint—when used—was fresh on the boards. From a mile off he'd heard the constant pounding of the stamp mill. The noise it made crushing the gold ore out of the rocks reverberated down into the valley like thunder. Now that he was here, it sounded like it was right on top of him.

He dismounted in front of the law office—a wooden, clapboard building—and tethered his horse. He stepped up on the boardwalk, his boots pounding out a distinct pace on the worn wooden slats. The door to the jail stood wide open, allowing the crisp autumn air to blow through the main room. On the back wall, which was void of windows, a large map of the area had been nailed. To his left a jail cell with iron bars took up half the room, and to his right stood a large desk, behind which sat a man watching him quietly size up the place while he sized up Tom. He stood when Tom entered.

"What can I do for you?"

"Name is Tom Barrington. I'm looking for the sheriff."

"You found him."

The large man stood an inch shorter than Tom. His solid build had Tom thinking of a steer he'd once wrestled. Like the steer, he didn't think he'd best this man, either, especially not now with his bum knee. Parker appeared to be close to his age with dark blond hair clipped short.

Tom had a rule when he met new people. Call it self-preservation. He preferred to play things close until he knew whether he could count on a man or not. Tom would make up his own mind whether he'd let the man in on any details. Didn't matter what Sam thought of him. Just because he wore a badge didn't mean he was the smartest man in the town. Also didn't mean the man could be trusted. Tom had learned that lesson the hard way a few years back.

"Name's Parker. Craig Parker," he said, shaking Tom's hand. He motioned to a chair across from him. "Have a seat."

Tom removed his Stetson and sat down. "I'm here to make sure the next shipment of gold ore heading down the mountain gets to the bank."

Sheriff Parker cast a quick look toward the door, rose from his seat and walked across the room to shut it. "I received a telegram from Mr. Furst yesterday. Been looking for you. Have you done any of this kind of work before?"

"Some with the government. Mostly in Nevada and Colorado."

"I'll help any way I can. The robbery has got the mine owners more than wary about their next shipment."

"I can understand that. There's always someone looking to bypass hard work themselves and steal someone else's earnings."

"It was a first for around here," Sheriff Parker said as he sat back down behind his desk.

Tom nodded, acknowledging the fact that the thieves likely had the mine owners in an uproar the same as the bankers. "I heard you were new to the area. How long you been here?"

"Two months."

"Picked up any information you can share?"

The more the sheriff talked, the more Tom questioned whether he'd been right about his hunch in the first place. It didn't sound like this was a robbery masterminded by one of Jack Hodges's gangs. Some of the key things didn't add up. Still, a lot of the information from the sheriff matched what he'd gleaned from the stationmaster about the two thieves.

"Anyone hurt?"

"No. Seemed to be a fairly cordial exchange."

"At gunpoint?" Tom asked dryly.

"The driver wasn't much for heroics, which likely saved his life. Oddly enough, he said the man who robbed him acted like a gentleman— his language and mannerisms."

"Did he get a good look at him?"

"No. The man had a flour sack over his head with holes cut out for the eyes."

Parker stepped behind his desk and rummaged through a drawer. "I have a small map of the area. It shows the mines, the roads, the Indian trails around here. It's crude, but it might come in handy."

Tom took the paper and examined it. Sam had given him a map of the actual route the shipments would take. After looking over Parker's map, Tom folded it and stuffed it into his inside vest pocket. "Thanks. Sam mentioned that the next shipment would go out sometime this week."

The sheriff nodded. "We won't decide the exact time and day until just before it happens."

"Good."

"All this makes me wonder why they'd even strike the same place again. It's like they are tempting fate, just asking to get caught."

"Seems that way, but men like this believe that they are so smart they can get away with it. It's part of the thrill. Sometimes they're right. Sometimes they're wrong. This time…it's going to be wrong. From what Furst said, they didn't get much gold the first time. One of the mines had shut down for repairs and another was flooded from heavy rains. That had to make them angry."

"Right," Parker grunted. "With both of those mines back up and working, the output of ore will make for a larger haul."

They talked a bit longer, piecing together the information they both held on the thieves' habits. Finally Tom rose.

"Got a place to stay?" the sheriff asked. "There's a room behind the jail here. Has a cot. A small stove. You're welcome to it. Not big. But serviceable and fairly warm."

Tom shook his head. "Too close to the law. No offense," he added quickly.

Parker grinned. "None taken." He rubbed his jaw. "I have it. Mrs. Birdwell. She takes in boarders now and then. Has a place just off the main road to the east of the livery. I can introduce you." He slipped on his hat, ready to walk out the door.

"No. Thanks, anyway. Nothing against the woman, but wherever I stay carries a risk if someone gets wind of why I'm really here. I saw a hotel up the road. Does a man run that?"

Sheriff Parker assessed him again. This time more slowly. "That's Adolf Green's place. Guess you know what you're doing."

"I'll be visiting the mines and assayer's office over the next few days and talking to the men there. I'd appreciate it if you'd back up my story that I'm evaluating the mines for a corporation that wants to invest. I'll hang out at the saloons a bit, too. That way I may hear something that will give me an edge."

"Sounds like you have your work cut out for you. Just remember I'm here to help."

Tom shook hands with the sheriff, liking the man's firm grip. "I'll get back to you in a day or two after I see the lay of the land."

When he stepped from the law office it was nearly dark. He had a good feeling about Sheriff Parker. The man was solid in his job and in the things he'd said, which made Tom inclined to trust him. He looped the reins over the Major's head and led him down the road to the smaller hotel. The next building beyond the hotel happened to be the saloon. That worked to his advantage. Nothing like a community watering hole to find out information, especially if it was someone here in town who was leaking information to the thieves about the where and when of the ore transports—or was himself a thief.

The desk clerk, a thin, white-whiskered gentleman with more hair on his face than on the top of his head, looked up from his ledger when Tom strode in. After learning how long Tom planned to stay he went over the rules…

"One week's rent up front.

"Breakfast at seven. Dinner at five o'clock sharp. My wife makes the meals and they're not fancy but they're filling. You're on your own for the midday meal.

"No female company allowed in your room.

We don't tolerate shenanigans. There's rooms at the saloon for that sort of thing if you're going to ignore the Good Book."

"Sounds fine," Tom assured the man. He handed over a week's rent compliments of Sam.

Mr. Green counted the money carefully, pocketed it and then led him to a room at the back of the house.

"Bathroom's at the end of the hall," he said from the door, handing Tom a room key. "Supper's in an hour."

He dropped his duffel bag on a hardwood chair. "I'll stable my horse and be back to eat."

"Suit yourself."

He contemplated the stalwart man as he led the Major around the corner to the livery. He'd met many men like him over the years. Things were either right or wrong. It kept things simple. A person knew where they stood with a man like that. Nothing murky or gray. He liked that about the man even though he knew life wasn't like that. Things were never that easy to figure out. In his line of work, the men he came up against didn't live by a moral code or have a sense of honor, but they'd sure turn someone else's code against them. That's how his father had met his death. He hadn't expected a bullet in the back from someone who he considered a friend. In a way, Cranston's death had happened like that, too, only it had been Tom's hesitation, worried he would shoot the young boy Hodges had held in front of him, that had put Cranston in harm's way.

It helped to think of Elizabeth. It had been for people like her and his mother that he first signed on in the military. He would make the world a safer place—a better place. Elizabeth saw the best in people. That's what had drawn him to her at first. It was that spark of goodness inside her and her belief that all people were basically good—or desired to be. Unfortunately, that spark had burned a bit too brightly for her brother and slightly out of focus. He sure hoped her eyes were open now so she could protect herself.

He unsaddled his horse and rubbed him down, his thoughts still on Elizabeth. She was different with this last visit. Except for a brief smile or two, she had held herself apart. Rigid. It was like she was being careful about everything and everyone—especially him. He sighed. Guess people change. He just didn't want her changing. She'd been near-perfect before—fun and spontaneous in a gentle way. He didn't want the world wearing her down like it had him. He hoped clearing things up between them had helped.

After he had settled his horse, Tom left the livery to start back to the hotel for supper. He paused for a moment to take in the descending twilight. The scent of pine filtered through the dry evening air. The saws at the mill had ceased their whirring and the five-ton stamp mill had stopped its constant hammering for the day. A rise in volume of voices from the direction of the two saloons in town indicated that business at both had picked up.

Then he heard a new rumble far off like the roll of thunder. The sound built, growing louder until he made out the sound of horse hooves striking the hard earth. Many hooves. In a matter of minutes the relative quiet was interrupted by the appearance of the Wells Fargo Stage as it rounded the corner pulled by six horses. They came to a stop amid a cloud of dust in front of the livery.

Good thing he had stabled the Major before the added confusion of the stage horses. He climbed the steps and entered the hotel.

Chapter Eight

Elizabeth stepped carefully onto the boxed steps positioned at the stagecoach's door by the driver, Mr. Brenner. She held his hand for balance since her legs were woefully in need of a good stretching after riding for the past three hours. Stepping aside, she allowed the driver to assist the other travelers.

"After this," she said to the young woman, "I cannot imagine a coach trip across the continent, no matter how comfortable the leather thoroughbraces might be."

The man who'd sat across from her for the journey tipped his hat. "Don't forget what I told you about Mary's cooking if you eat at the hotel, miss."

"I won't," she assured him. "And thank you."

Mr. Brenner climbed above and one at a time handed down her traveling bag along with belongings for the other travelers. Taking the moment to look down the main street of Clear Springs, she came to a cursory assessment. It looked…a bit wilder than La Playa…judging by the number of saloons and the men loitering outside them. But there was a bank. And a restaurant. And the aforementioned hotel.

A heavyset man stepped from the livery and helped Mr. Brenner unload the two crates. The liveryman grunted as he set one down in the dirt. "What in tarnation have you got in here?"

"Supplies. For the new school," Mr. Brenner answered in her stead. "This is Gil Jolson, Miss Morley."

"Hello, Mr. Jolson," she said. "Where may I keep them until I can see to their transfer to the school?"

Mr. Jolson straightened and wiped his hands on a work rag. "My livery is fine until you are ready for them. No one will bother them there. Sure didn't expect a woman to arrive with them. You fixin' to teach, too?"

"Oh, no. I'm just here for a visit. I've come to see Miss Starling."

He thumbed over his shoulder with his meaty hand. "Got a room at Widow Birdwell's. Let me know when you're ready to move the supplies.

You are welcome to use one of my wagons. No charge."

Grateful for his help, she was nonetheless surprised at his generosity toward someone he didn't know. "Why, thank you, sir."

"Doin' my part. That's all. We need a school here. Only way for the community to grow and me to stay in business—especially with some of the mines closing up." He turned back to the crates. "Brenner? Give me a hand, will ya?"

The two men picked up a crate and carried it between them into the closest corner of the livery. They did the same with the second one, stacking them. Then Mr. Jolson set about unhitching the team of horses to stable them for the night.

Once Elizabeth was assured the supplies were stored safely away, she sought out Mr. Brenner. "Would you mind directing me to this Mrs. Birdwell's? Perhaps I can let a room there for my visit."

"Be happy to." He picked up her traveling bag. "Gil? I'm gonna walk Miss Morley to Widow Birdwell's place. I could use the stretch. Be back to help directly."

The liveryman waved them both off. Elizabeth followed Mr. Brenner around the corner and down the road. Her stomach rumbled. She sure hoped she'd be in time to join Gemma for supper and that this Mrs. Birdwell wouldn't mind an extra mouth to feed at her table.

She shuffled through a carpet of fallen leaves with the sound of acorns crunching beneath her shoes. Living by the water all her life, she had only heard about the change of seasons, but here it happened! The air was drier, crisper and colder as the sun set and the tall pines scented the night. In the distance, a coyote yipped, starting up a chorus of noise as others joined in. A vague prickling sensation tickled her neck. She scrunched her shoulders and glanced around. Surely it was the eerie sound of the coyote and nothing more. She tried to shake off the feeling. Ahead, a soft yellow glow beckoned from the front window of a cabin. She quickened her steps to catch up with Mr. Brenner's long strides.

When they arrived at the small house, her guide rapped unceremoniously on the door. "Molly? You in there?"

"Who's making all that racket?" a high-pitched voice called out from inside.

"Got a customer for you if you've got the room."

The door flew open and a short, round woman

with snow-white, frizzy hair stood in the entry-way. "Land sakes, Vern. You're loud enough to wake a hibernating bear!"

"Got a customer."

"Well, I see that." She looked over Elizabeth with her clear, baby-blue eyes peering through wire-rimmed spectacles.

"I'm here to visit Miss Starling for a few days if you can spare the room. Is she here?"

"Oh, she's here all right. You from down by the coast?" At Elizabeth's nod, the woman continued. "Come right in. She'll be right glad to see you."

After thanking Mr. Brenner, Elizabeth followed Mrs. Birdwell down the hall to a small room in the back. She plopped her traveling bag on a straight-backed chair.

"I 'spect you're tuckered out from that ride. It's been a while since I rode the stage, but I remember having bruises in places I never knew I had 'afore. You just settle in now. I'll bring water for the pitcher so you can freshen up. I'll have supper ready in another bit."

"That sounds wonderful." She opened her travel case and removed her slippers and night-gown, and then placed her comb and brush on the bureau. She thought it odd, in such a small cabin, that Gemma hadn't appeared.

Her hostess came back with a full pitcher of water. "Had some warming on the back of the stove."

"Ma'am? Is Miss Starling here?"

"I expect her any minute. She stopped over to the Tanners to help young Benjamin with his arithmetic. Said to expect her for supper."

Elizabeth smiled her thanks. She walked to the window and pushed the curtain aside. The pale light of the half-moon winked through the branches of the pines as the wind rustled the trees.

It was all so very different from La Playa. How had Mrs. Flynn managed these past two days at the store? That woman had certainly been around enough years to know all that Elizabeth did and she'd certainly appeared excited for the chance to do something new with her time. A week wasn't that long. Barring anything unforeseen, things should go well. Had Tom stopped by the store again? Or had he already left on his new assignment? Did he even know that she had left town? And if he did know— would he care?

She closed the curtains and turned to wash

up, pouring a generous helping of water into the basin. She squeezed out the excess water from her washcloth and smoothed it over her face. Her skin tingled. Glancing into the small wall mirror, she was caught by her reflection. Something was different. It was the oddest sensation. Instead of simply washing away the grime from a day's worth of traveling, it was almost as though she was washing away the dust from La Playa. Her eyes looked brighter. Her skin had a glow she'd not seen before.

Excitement that she'd suppressed during the journey on the stagecoach suddenly bubbled up inside. She felt lighter, as if her worries on the harbor had remained there or perhaps fallen away during the ride east. Was it…hope? She pressed her palm against her stomach, wanting to capture the unusual feeling and hold it close.

"Elizabeth? Elizabeth!" Gemma peeked in the partially opened bedroom door and then swung it open wide.

Her wide-eyed expression of astonishment satisfied Elizabeth at once that her journey had been well worth any bumps or bruises. And… she giggled! Surprised at the sound, Elizabeth clapped her hand over her mouth.

"I…I can't believe you're here!" Gemma cried out and rushed toward her. "When? How?"

"It's a good thing you are happy to see me. It would have been awkward otherwise."

"Well, heavens, yes, I'm happy!" Gemma hugged her tightly. "I never thought you'd come this far from your precious store. Your reason for that will be interesting to hear. You don't know how I've missed you!"

Elizabeth gave her friend a squeeze and then stepped back, holding her at arm's length. "Oh, but I do. La Playa hasn't been the same since you left." Gemma looked positively radiant. Her eyes sparkled with delight and her cheeks were pink—likely from the cold outside.

"Did you come on the stage? You'll be staying awhile?"

"A week if that will work for you."

"That is not near long enough. I want to hear everything about La Playa. Some days I even find myself wondering about Mrs. Flynn." She slipped her arm through Elizabeth's. "I'm famished and the smell coming from the kitchen is calling me. Perhaps we can talk over supper. Molly will want to hear any news you bring, as well. You will like her."

She held back for a moment, the slight tightening of her arm keeping Elizabeth from heading down the hallway. "And later, when you are ready to tell me, I want to hear the real reason you are here."

The real reason she was here? Elizabeth blinked and avoided her friend's gaze, wondering how she'd answer. Was it because of the supplies? It had been at first. That was before she'd learned of the mercantile's impending sale.

Or…was it Tom?

Celebration! Grand Opening of the Schoolhouse! the sign promised in bright bold color. And then lower, in smaller script, the details— Saturday night…bring dish to pass…music and dancing.

Gemma wrinkled her nose at the odor of turpentine. "Ugh. This is strong. I need fresh air." She flung open the door to the small shed that stood on the back of Mrs. Birdwell's property and then finished wiping her paint-splattered hands on an old rag. Critically, she checked her work once more. "The blue-and-yellow contrast was a good idea. The words stand out much better."

Elizabeth grinned. "I learned after years of

practice at the mercantile. Now, where is the best place to put these so that people will see them?"

"The café, I think. In the window. And the bank has a board for community postings. People look there every time they walk by the bank."

"Perfect." Elizabeth surveyed them critically once more. "They are almost dry. If you'll take yours to the bank, I'll take mine to the café. I remember seeing it when I arrived—straight across from the livery. At least I know where that is."

Gemma smiled. "I'm glad to be sharing this with you. It makes it all the more fun."

Touched by her words, Elizabeth gave her a quick hug. "That's why I came." She hadn't… and wouldn't…burden Gemma with the other things going on in La Playa that had spurred her hasty departure. She had successfully avoided it last night when Gemma probed her after supper.

Gemma examined her sign once more. "I think these are dry enough now. Let's get them to their respective places and then I'll meet you at the livery. We can see about getting a carriage to transport the boxes to the schoolhouse."

"Actually…they are crates."

"Crates?" Gemma's green eyes opened larger. "Just how many supplies did you bring?"

"Not telling," Elizabeth teased. "I want to see your face when you open the *crates*." With that, she picked up her sign and headed toward the house to get her shawl.

When Elizabeth arrived carrying her bucket of supplies from the hardware store and her sign, the Butterfield Café had seen the breakfast crowd come and go. The lingering odor of bacon and sweet rolls scented the air. A wizened old man, still nursing his cup of coffee, looked up when Elizabeth entered. She nodded to him and then sought out Mrs. Kuhn. According to Gemma, she was the owner's wife, and the one to see about placing the sign. She found the woman wiping down a back table in preparation for the noon customers that would soon arrive.

"You're welcome to place the sign in the window," Mrs. Kuhn said in answer to her query. "It's a good thing you're doing. Folks around here need that school for their young'uns."

"I hope you will come and enjoy the evening. You and your husband."

"Any chance to socialize is a welcome event. I could bring rolls and my homemade jam."

"Mrs. Birdwell mentioned you made jam. She is talking about making a few pies," Elizabeth said.

"Oh, she is? Pies, you say?"

Elizabeth could see the thoughts spinning in the woman's expression, even as she turned back to her humming and tidying.

Walking over to the large window that fronted the road, Elizabeth stood the sign on the sill and wedged it against one of the panes so that the words could be read from the road. The morning sun beat against the glass, warming it considerably compared to the crisp fall air outside. She only hoped the new paint didn't melt right off and smear. She took a moment standing there to warm her hands.

Someone's shadow fell across the sign and Elizabeth glanced up. Staring back at her from the other side of the glass was the steely gaze of Tom Barrington. With a swift intake of breath, she straightened, knocking into a kerosene lantern hanging near the window. The chimney teetered precariously. Despite the sharp burning pain in her scalp, she had the wits to grab the lantern and steady the entire thing.

It simply couldn't be!

She peeked through the window again, just to double-check that she wasn't mistaken. But there he was, standing with his back to her now, a dark red bandanna at his neck showing just above the collar of his dark gray leather coat. His black Stetson sat forward on his head in a no-nonsense tilt, and by the tightness in his jaw from this angle he wasn't amused at seeing her.

She put her hand to her brow. What was he doing here? Is this where his next job was? How ironic it was for her to have left La Playa, believing she was distancing herself from any reminders of that place, and he had traveled here. How absolutely ironic.

She wasn't prepared for him. Back home she had her store, her friends and the intangible support of a daily routine. That sameness, that comfortable routine, kept her as steady as the rising and setting of the sun—cocooned in a comfortable cloak.

Here it wasn't like that. Here she felt off-kilter and a little bit fragile. He must never know how he affected her.

Across the road, Gemma drove a light one-horse buggy through the livery doorway and headed her way. Wonderful. Just wonderful.

Bravado was all she had. She gathered up her courage and straightened her shoulders. Taking a deep breath and then letting it out, she marched through the door.

Before she could speak Tom nodded, tipping his hat brim. At the same time, Gemma called from the small buggy, pulling back on the reins to slow and finally stop her horse in front of the restaurant. "All set, Elizabeth? Molly made a basket lunch." And behind her, Mrs. Kuhn opened the shop's door, held out her bucket of supplies and called to her. "Miss Morley? You forgot this."

She felt torn three ways from sideways and chose the easiest reply. She turned and took the bucket from Mrs. Kuhn. "I'll need those if we're going to get the schoolhouse ready by Saturday, won't I? Thank you." The woman nodded and slipped back inside the café.

"Ready to go?" Gemma looked askance at her.

Elizabeth felt Tom's gaze on her as she tugged her shawl closer around her shoulders and then stepped over to the buggy.

"Gemma? This is…"

At a muted shake of his head and a warning look, she stopped her introduction.

"Up you go," Tom said quickly, whipping the bucket from her grasp. With a strong hand beneath her elbow and then to her waist, he assisted her into the conveyance and tucked the bucket at her feet. "Good day, miss."

He headed down the boardwalk.

Stunned, feeling as though she couldn't quite grasp what had just happened, she plopped down on the seat beside Gemma. Her arm radiated his heat where he'd touched her even though it was through the layers of her sleeve and shawl. She had fairly flown into the buggy under his strength. As she stared after him, slightly mesmerized by his form—the broad shoulders, the slim hips—she realized that the hitch in his walk seemed less pronounced, almost to the point that Elizabeth wondered if she'd imagined it in La Playa. Whatever the injury, it certainly did nothing to diminish his strength, nor her reaction to him if the rapid beating of her heart was any indication.

"Wasn't that nice?" Gemma said, watching him walk away. "I wonder if he lives around here. Maybe he will come to the dance."

Chapter Nine

Tom kept walking until he was sure he was out of Elizabeth's line of sight. It was the movement of the sign in the window that had caught his attention. Before he knew it, he was staring into Elizabeth's face—wide-eyed and stunned. They had both been caught off guard. What the heck was she doing here?

He needed a moment to gather his wits. Had it been anyone else he could have handled the meeting just fine. He closed his eyes, remembering the feel of her waist under his hands as he helped her into the buggy. It had set his fingers to tingling. She was such a slender thing.

Hearing the jostling of a rig, he pulled back into the recessed doorway of the bank building. The younger woman seated next to Elizabeth was talking incessantly. Her distraction wasn't enough to keep Elizabeth from glancing down the side street looking for him. He huffed out a breath. She was probably more curious than angry at the way he had acted—at least, he hoped more curious than angry. The bright sunlight, dappled with shadows from the trees and building, would make it difficult for her to see him.

He'd left her with more questions than he'd intended, but in the middle of Main Street was not the place to have a heart-to-heart. But he did need to talk to her. Soon. He couldn't have Elizabeth spouting off that he was ex-military or that he had a past different from the one he'd manufactured in order to gain more information. He had to do something about her. *Now.*

He strode back the way he had come and ducked into the livery. Saddling the Major took all of two minutes. The horse seemed to sense his urgency. A fine tension radiated from his withers. "Easy, boy," Tom murmured, taking the reins and leading him out to the street. As keyed up as he was, he didn't want to draw attention to himself. In full view of anyone who might be observing, he took the time to double-check the cinch strap and stirrup length and rummage through the contents of his saddlebag. Then he mounted and kept the Major to a steady walk heading opposite the way the women had gone. He tipped his brim to an older man exiting the dry goods store. Even though he kept his horse to the same slow clop, inside his heart pounded and all he could think about was catching up to Elizabeth.

The moment he was clear of town he urged his horse into a gallop, veering west through a copse of tall pines and then along the edge of a meadow, circling back to the north only after he'd traveled a safe distance out of view. He reined in behind a granite boulder where he could see the ribbon of dirt road stretched out half a mile in either direction. There he listened for the sound of their buggy.

He hadn't formulated any plan of action. In the field, planning and execution had always been his strong points. Just showed how much Elizabeth's presence skewed everything for him.

A high-pitched giggle alerted him. He could hear the women talking before he saw them driving the wagon over the rise in the road. He tightened his grip on the leather reins. Four hundred feet. Three hundred. He leaned forward. Two hundred. The Major pranced sideways, skittish. One hundred. He pressed his knees into the horse's flanks and the Major bolted out onto the road directly in front of the wagon and skidded to a stop. Rocks and gravel spewed under the horse's agitated, prancing hooves.

The dark-haired woman screamed and dropped the reins.

Elizabeth grabbed them up and pulled back to stop the carriage before they collided. "It's all right, Gemma."

Tom rode up beside her. He tipped his hat to Gemma, who had stopped her ear-piercing noise at the end of her breath.

"Just what do you think you are doing, terrifying us like this?" Elizabeth demanded, and stood up in the buggy to tower over him.

"We need to talk." He ripped the reins from her hands and tossed them to Gemma. In one quick motion, he scooped Elizabeth onto his saddle in front of him. The other woman's eyes widened and she looked to be gathering another wail of a breath.

He looked hard at her. "Stop!"

She clamped her mouth shut.

"I'll bring her back soon as I've had my say." With that, he reined the Major away and, with Elizabeth cushioned in front of him, galloped off.

He wanted to get far enough away that he

could speak freely and without concern of someone coming or going on the road. He headed toward a stand of trees, then veered north, making for the cover of the scrub oaks and large boulders along a creek bed, where water rippled through the wash.

The sudden gouge into his gut surprised him. "Oopf."

"Stop. Tom. Stop right now and tell me what is going on or so help me I will punch you again." She did it again, anyway.

He growled. "Cut that out!"

"You scared my friend half to death and now you've left her thinking the worst. With any luck, she'll have the sheriff after you."

He'd like to see that, considering he knew the sheriff. He thought it best not to mention that to Elizabeth. She looked angry enough as it was.

"I told her I'd bring you back." But he slowed the Major to a walk and considered her words. Guess he hadn't thought things through, but when it came to Elizabeth it seemed like his common sense wasn't as common as it should be. He pulled back on the reins.

"All right. Get down." He braced as she grabbed his arm and slid slowly to the ground, his left knee throbbing with the extra work.

She stepped away and straightened her dark green skirt and shirtwaist, and then waited for him to dismount. Her one foot tapped like she was stewing up a storm, the short squat heel making an impression in the weeds bordering the creek.

He glanced up from her busy foot, taking note of the arms she'd crossed over her chest and the ready-to-explode expression on her face under that pretty straw bonnet of hers. Maybe the best tactic would be taking an assertive stance. "Just what are you doing here, Elizabeth? You were supposed to stay in La Playa." The words came out rough—like he was accusing her of something. Well, he was! At the restaurant she had told Terrance that she wouldn't be leaving town.

"Supposed to stay?" she countered. "Why does my coming and going have anything to do with you?"

"Just figured you'd stick to your words. You said that you couldn't leave your store. That there were too many things holding you there."

She gasped. "You were eavesdropping!"

"Kind of hard not to hear in a room that size."

"You had no right…"

He was handling this all wrong. For some reason, he just couldn't get on the right side of her.

He removed his hat and raked his hand through his hair. Having her here complicated everything. Having her here looking as pretty as she was made it worse. Her expressive eyes had always captivated him. Why couldn't she have grown fat and ugly over the years instead of more beautiful?

"For your information, I'm here on holiday. It's been wonderful…or it was all the way up until today at the bakery when you acted like you didn't even know me."

He scowled. "It appears that's true. I don't know you. Suddenly I find you a day's ride east of where you are supposed to be."

The Major shied away from him. Guess he had raised his voice a bit. Elizabeth looked indignant standing there, hands on hips—indignant and self-righteous and stunning. What was it about her that got his blood up? Whatever it was, she was like no other woman he knew.

Slowly, her stance relaxed. She lowered her shoulders and studied him with those big brown eyes of hers. "This has to do with your job, doesn't it?"

He resettled his hat on his head.

Her brow wrinkled. "I'm right, aren't I?"

"Close enough." What the heck was he going to do with her?

"What exactly do you do, Tom? You've never once told me. All I know is that you are…or rather were…a very accurate shot."

He studied her, wondering how much he should reveal. "I do whatever it takes to get the job done."

She pulled back. "But that sounds like it could be illegal."

"It could, but it's not. Not the way I work."

"Tell me, then," she demanded.

He would have been amused if the situation hadn't been so serious. Things fell close to the line between legal and illegal in his line of work but he'd never crossed that line. Guess she really didn't know much about him anymore.

"A lot is classified, but I guess since I'm not working for the government any longer I can mention some parts. When I left Fort Rosecrans I rode east to Fort Yuma with my new detail. We met up with some others—ten soldiers altogether—and we went through special training with some fancy rifles and guns. Those rifles were more advanced than any I had ever seen before. Then our orders took us to El Paso where a stand of renegade Apache were attacking the ranchers." He glanced at her, wondering how much she'd like knowing or if things like this made her squeamish. "My specialty detachment was called in to stop them."

Her attitude had softened slightly as he spoke and now she asked, "Did you? Stop them?"

He nodded. "After that, the government sent us to Colorado where a group of men had sabotaged the railroad. The president was coming through and it was my job along with a few others to keep him safe."

"The president of the railroad?"

"No. The president of the United States—President Grant."

"Oh," she said, straightening and looking somewhat impressed. "I couldn't believe you were doing something against the law."

Where had she heard that? He'd worked beside a few men that had come to the conclusion they could make more money on the other side of that line and switched sides after a year or two of working in the field but he'd never done it. "I've known men that would, but it's not me."

She looked a bit relieved at that news. "I have to ask…did the army let you go?"

"No."

"Then it was your decision to leave."

"That's what I said."

An embarrassed flush stained her cheeks.

"Guess you heard differently."

She nodded.

He imagined that bit of information had come from her brother…or maybe Amanda. He could see either one saying things about him, blaming him. "I wouldn't be too shocked about that. People pass on information that suits them. After my injury healed some, I was offered a desk job. I tried it for a few months. Hated it and left it."

She splayed her hand against her chest and exhaled. "I'm so relieved to hear that. I couldn't bring myself to believe that you were dishonorably discharged. You've always struck me as a man with a keen sense of justice." She looked down for a moment and seemed to be gathering her thoughts, then looked him in the eyes. "You have always wanted more. And look at you! You are doing what you set out to do… You are making a difference."

She probably didn't know what it meant to him to have her say that. The fact that she remembered his dreams from so long ago and acknowledged them… "That was always my plan, right up until this." He slapped his injured leg. "Now…I guess we'll see."

"About that. I was cruel the other day. I'm not usually like that. I am sorry for what I said. Can you…" she began tentatively. "Will you tell me what happened?"

He didn't like talking about it so he said as little as possible that would satisfy her. "Shot in the line of duty. Happened a year ago."

"Shouldn't it have healed all the way by now?"

"It has."

"Oh." She looked momentarily disconcerted.

"A surgeon in Carson City took care of it. I doubt another doctor could do better."

"You favor it. Does it hurt much now?"

"Enough."

The corners of her mouth pinched in. "And just what does that mean?"

"I'd say enough to keep me humble. Can't move like I used to and I hate that." The memories plagued him at times. He hated being awkward…slower than sludge…when once he had depended on his quickness for his life. "But the pain is only a dull ache now and only if I'm on it too long."

She glanced about the area.

"What are you doing?"

"I'm looking for a boulder, of course. So that you can sit."

He took hold of her upper arm to regain her attention. "I can take care of myself. Look. You're right about me doing a job. If you know what's good for you you'll head right back to the coast the way you came. Since I doubt you will do that, I'll ask you not to say anything to your friend, at least for now."

She squinted against the sunlight as she looked up at him. "I don't know, Tom. Gemma's my best friend. She'll certainly want answers. How can I not say anything?"

"Folks here have no idea that I worked for the government and it's best that they don't. I can't say how things are going to play out and the less either of you are involved, the better."

She didn't comment—or agree. Just stared at him, the sunlight playing on her face, the wind teasing her hair and causing short tendrils to dance. This was the closest he'd been to her in four years. He swallowed hard, and then dropped his gaze to her lips, remembering the kiss they'd once shared. A pang of longing seized him. If he kissed her now, would she welcome him as she once had—drawing him in with those soft, generous lips of hers? He swallowed and forced himself to glance away from her—anywhere but at the sweet temptation of her mouth. If only things could be different. He exhaled and let go of her arm, finally admitting, "I don't want you caught in the middle."

Her expression softened. "You're serious."

"I figured it was obvious. Why else would I do anything as crazy as carting you off just now?"

That seemed to set her back some. She swallowed. "So you are worried about my safety."

He'd said enough. He wasn't going to admit anything more. "I need to get you back." He turned to his horse and flipped the reins over his head, preparing to mount.

"But how will I know if something happens to you?"

Her question stopped him with one foot in the stirrup. He lowered it to the ground. She sure was turning the tables on him. Instead of securing her promise to secrecy as he had started out to do, he was slowly revealing more than he wanted. But with her question, she'd revealed something, too. She still had feelings for him. Maybe not the warm fire she'd once had. Maybe now it was only a candle. But something was there. It hadn't been snuffed out completely. At least, not yet.

"You won't."

Her mouth dropped open at his callous reply. "What?"

"You are not even supposed to be here. I hadn't counted on you in the mix of any of this."

She stiffened. "Believe me, I do not intend to get in your way."

He could live with her frustration. What he couldn't live with would be her getting hurt. Like his father. Like Cranston. He took hold of the Major's reins and swung up on his horse, silently cursing his awkwardness in front of her. Again he offered his forearm to her to grasp. "It's for the best. Now that we have settled things, it's time I took you back. Mount up."

Silently she did as he commanded, taking hold of him and, as he lifted her up behind him, throwing her leg over his horse. She wiggled into position, her body molding to his as she slipped her arms around his waist. The soft press of her breasts against his back played havoc with his thoughts. How could it feel this good, this perfect, after so many years?

He pressed his knees to his horse's flanks. Memories tortured him as he rode back to the buggy. Thoughts of her riding with him along the beach with her arms circled around his waist and hugging him tight, the weight of her head resting softly against his back, trusting him like she once had. It made him wonder what would happen if he picked up where they'd left things between them all those years ago. Would she allow it?

But the realization grated inside—it was for the best. Things were different now. He wasn't the man he once was. He had a bum leg and a bum life. Until he could make amends to Cranston's memory there was no room for anything...or anybody else.

"What is going on?" Gemma demanded the minute Tom had deposited Elizabeth back into the buggy and reined his horse away. "You owe me an explanation, Miss Elizabeth Morley."

Elizabeth's emotions were swirling to the point she wasn't sure she could answer her friend coherently. She opened her mouth...and then shut it again, shaking her head. "I'm not sure myself. There's too much...I really want to tell you, Gemma, but he asked me not to say anything."

"Well, I like that! The man drags you off and

scares me nearly to death and I'm not allowed to know why? I want to know." A very disgruntled Gemma flicked the reins and urged their horse into a slow trot.

Elizabeth was grateful for the steady roll of the small conveyance and the chance to gather her wits. Tom had been as surprised to see her as she to see him. It had bothered him enough to kidnap her!

Just what did that mean? If her presence here in Clear Springs had simply been a nuisance he would have ignored her or perhaps made sure never to run into her during his "job." He'd said he didn't want her in the way, which was a far cry from meaning she meant anything special. With his sense of obligation he'd feel that way about anybody—any acquaintance. Recalling how he had burst out of the brush along the road like a highwayman had her heart racing. My, but he could sit a horse handsomely!

A short distance farther Gemma stopped the buggy in front of a whitewashed clapboard, one-room schoolhouse. Although still stewing over Tom's words, Elizabeth tried to drum up enthusiasm for her friend's project as Gemma escorted her through the small building, explaining her plans and dreams for the place. Rough-hewn pine benches, the shorter ones to the front of the room, stood in rows on each side of the center aisle. A slate board rested on the floor behind the teacher's desk and Gemma explained how they needed to have that set high against the wall—a project too unwieldy for two women. Every once in a while, Gemma would look at her a certain way and Elizabeth knew she was exasperated with her…and very curious.

They donned aprons and settled each to their own bench and began sanding the wood to a smoother finish. It wouldn't do to have the children sporting splinters on the first day. The physical exertion helped ease Elizabeth's tension, even though every once in a while she caught Gemma watching her with a contemplative expression.

When they finished with the benches on the west side of the room they broke for a light meal.

"I'm so glad you are here to help," Gemma said. "It would have been impossible to be ready otherwise."

Her friend was being careful to keep her conversation focused on the work—too careful. Gemma was usually quick to speak her thoughts and Elizabeth began to feel guilty about not being as honest. Gemma deserved answers. She rubbed the dust from her apple with a cloth handkerchief and then sliced it in half, holding out a half to Gemma.

"It's Tom Barrington," she admitted.

Gemma straightened, more alert now. "Tom from years past?"

"The same."

"Am I right in suspecting that he is the real reason you are here?"

"No!" The denial came instinctively to her lips. Then, unsure, she allowed, "Yes…maybe. Oh, I don't know, Gemma. I just don't know anymore! But it is pointless. It is all pointless." Just hearing Tom's name brought up a hopeless yearning inside. A yearning that was, of course, futile. She would never let herself be hurt the way he had hurt her before.

Gemma watched her closely. "Why didn't he acknowledge you back in town?"

"Honestly, I think seeing me simply stunned him."

Gemma tilted her head and gave her a flat look. "I run into people I haven't seen for a while. Ignoring them and then turning around and running off with them hasn't ever crossed my mind."

The image that brought to mind evoked a

chuckle from Elizabeth. "When you put it like that, it does sound strange. I suppose it's complicated, but it has everything to do with his job."

Gemma waited for her to continue.

She lifted her hands and shrugged hopelessly. "Which he won't tell me a thing about. He just said that I was in the wrong place at the wrong time and he wished I wasn't here." She hadn't realized until he had deposited her in the buggy again that all he'd said about his job was what he'd done in the past. None of it pertained to what he was doing in Clear Springs now.

"Then it must be dangerous. Something against the law. He's guilty about something."

Elizabeth couldn't believe that Gemma would jump immediately to that conclusion, but then realized she'd done the same thing. *"Whatever it takes to get the job done."* No—she would not believe he'd be part of anything unlawful. Especially after all he'd done in the military. "It sounds like some sort of a field agent."

Gemma arched a delicate brow. "And he doesn't want you involved…"

"It's not like that," Elizabeth hurried to say. "He's not like that. You are getting the wrong idea. He would say the same for you or Mrs. Birdwell, too."

"But he wouldn't kidnap either of us just to explain things."

"No. Probably not. He's not the impulsive sort." She stopped short, questioning it now. "At least, I never thought he was. I wonder if I ever really knew him at all?"

"Perhaps he is only impulsive…when it comes to you," Gemma said softly, with a speculative look.

Elizabeth rubbed her brow, musing out loud. "No. There hasn't been anything between us for a long time. Honestly, I don't know what to think anymore."

"Did you know he'd be here when you decided to visit?"

She wanted to laugh—which in this situation was a sure sign her emotions were on edge. "That's just it. Ever since I ordered the supplies I hoped to accompany them here on their arrival and surprise you. Terrance kept thinking up reasons I shouldn't, reasons I needed to stay in La Playa."

"That sounds like your brother."

"Well, he did try to squash all my enthusiasm for the trip. He told me I was being selfish and that I hadn't thought things through."

Gemma shook her head and sighed.

"I know, I know. But I promised Mother to try and get along with him, remember?" Elizabeth looked about for the sanding block she'd been using, preferring to avoid another lecture from her friend about Terrance. Gemma had never liked the fact that so many of Elizabeth's decisions were swayed in her attempt to keep a close relationship with her brother. She found the sanding block and attacked the next bench with renewed energy. "Then Tom showed up. And I found out that everything I'd thought had happened four years ago when he left…was a lie."

"A lie!" Gemma's eyes widened.

Elizabeth explained the letters to her and only felt renewed anger at her brother for all the manipulations he had done and all the hurt feelings he had caused.

"And yet, Mr. Barrington didn't come to see you. He came about a job and then just decided to see who ran the mercantile now. I wonder who he is working for there in La Playa that would have ties here in Clear Springs. Knowing that would help."

"I wondered that, too. He didn't say, only that the less we know, the better. But I'm sure it is nothing against the law. I've never met a man with more ambition, it's true. But he was and I'm sure still is on the right side of the law, believe me."

"You still care about him a great deal, don't you?" Gemma suggested softly. "I can see it in your face."

"It doesn't matter whether I do or not," she said quickly.

"Why do you say that?" Gemma knit her brow. "Of course it matters."

"No. He said that he realized after he left and started his new job with the government that he had no room for a woman in his life. He believes things worked out for the best, after all."

"Humph! He may say that, but his actions say something else entirely."

Elizabeth hit the bench with the sanding block. "All I know is that I'm twisted up in knots whenever he is near. It's all so frustrating! This was supposed to be a holiday and now look at it! I don't know whether I'm coming or going."

"Perhaps this is a good thing," Gemma said, thoughtfully watching her. "You could use a little shaking up in my estimation. For the past four years you've been doing the same thing day after day to keep that mercantile running."

Elizabeth started to disagree, but Gemma

held up her hand. "Now hear me out. I don't mean anything bad by what I'm saying. The routine is soothing and safe. You know what to expect and you know how to deal with anything that comes up. Everything tidy. And then Mr. Barrington comes along and turns everything on its ear." She cocked her head slightly to one side, an amused smile playing across her face. "Your life has suddenly become quite interesting."

Elizabeth drew in a breath. Today had been exciting and disturbing enough. She couldn't imagine that she would want it any more *interesting*! "Well, all I know is that it is very uncomfortable. Add to that Mrs. Flynn being so nosy lately, and then Terrance taking out that loan on the mercantile…"

Gemma straightened. "What? Terrance took out a loan? You hadn't mentioned that."

"Yes…and the bank is calling it in. They want to take the store as payment—or at least that is what Terrance said. I brought the papers with me. I had hoped you could read through them. You might be able to find something to help me. I certainly couldn't."

"Of course! I'll look at them tonight after supper. You know, I'm not surprised. He barely lifted a finger to help when Preston left. It was as if he hoped you would go under."

Elizabeth stopped sanding and swept her hand over the bench. Smooth now. Good. "He was buying his place in the city then and trying to get that up and running."

"Yes. And ignoring all your troubles like the plague when he could have been helping."

Elizabeth recalled wondering why he wasn't helping her more, but any time she considered that he might not care or might have other plans that didn't include her she had become uncomfortable. So much so that she'd pushed it from her mind.

"Where did he come up with that money for his new place, anyway? I'd like to know that."

Gemma's criticism of Terrance always made Elizabeth dig in her heels. "He received a sizable amount from Father's estate."

"He did?" She raised her brows. "Funny how none of that money came to you."

Elizabeth frowned.

"Oh, Elizabeth!" Gemma said with affectionate exasperation. "You have always been quick to come to his defense."

"Of course. He's my brother."

"You are hopeless. Underneath all that practical exterior, you have such a soft heart. Terrance does not deserve having you for a sister."

"Well…he is angry because I won't budge on selling. And probably because I found out the truth about the letter he wrote to Tom." Growing amused now, she added, "And because I came to see you instead of minding the store."

Gemma stared at her a moment and then burst out laughing. "Good for you! Your stubbornness is what saved that mercantile in the first place. It might be just the necessary ingredient to do it again."

Elizabeth's smile grew larger. Then, in a moment of lucidity, she realized that all this had come about the minute Tom Barrington had walked back into her life.

Chapter Ten

Tom stretched out on the small bed in his hotel room, his fingers laced together behind his head. The dark red curtains at the window rippled softly as the cool night breeze buffeted them while next door at the saloon the tinny notes of a poorly tuned piano floated up to him. Tomorrow night, he told himself, he'd avail himself to a shot of whiskey and listen to the locals but not tonight. He was tired. With all the traveling he had done over the past week, he figured he'd sleep like a bear in hibernation the minute his head hit the pillow, but sleep wasn't coming and he knew the reason why.

Every time he closed his eyes he saw Elizabeth. First she would appear like she had today—her hair falling from a loose knot, her face flushed and annoyed—and then slowly she'd fade into the Elizabeth he had left four years ago, the one with a pink glow to her cheeks and her pretty brown hair falling softly over her shoulders and down to her waist. And always there was that impish sparkle in her large dark eyes. He stared at the plaster ceiling and tried to wrap his thoughts around the fact that she was here in Clear Springs and much more a vibrant woman now than the sweet girl he'd left four years ago.

All these years he'd been angry, thinking she'd shucked him off like a too-small cloak so that she could have a fancy, highfalutin life—one that he could never afford to give her on his corporal's pay. He had pictured her sipping tea with the ladies of San Diego, putting on airs and generally being a snoot. And all the while, she'd been in La Playa, tending to her store. She hadn't married. Not ever.

He thought back to their last day together. He had been ordered to give a shooting demonstration with Crebs and Sandell before Captain Webber.

"Fine shooting, Corporal," the captain had said when he was done.

"Yes, sir. Thank you, sir." He stood at attention before his superiors and wished he'd taken the time to spit polish his boots. There hadn't been any notice, any explanation, of what this was all about. He'd only been asked to display his targeting ability—the one thing that had set him apart from the others in his company stationed at Fort Rosecrans.

"He'll do well." The portly captain had turned to Sergeant Potter. "Handle the details. See that he's ready." The man turned and walked down the hillside toward the barracks, leaving Tom with his sergeant.

Ready for what? He turned to Potter. "Sir?"

"You are being promoted, Corporal. You'll have new orders once things are ironed out in Washington."

After waiting for this moment for the past year, Tom could scarcely believe it was finally happening. "Sir?" he repeated, still trying to absorb the news.

"Lieutenant Cranston is now your commanding officer. You will report to him from now on."

Tom knew a little about Cranston. The man might be from back east and a West Pointer but Tom liked what he'd heard about him.

Potter thrust out his hand to shake. "Congratulations."

"Thank you, Sergeant. I'm still a bit surprised."

"Webber is putting together a special contingent of soldiers. It's not just your target practice that caught his eye. You have a head for strategy and thinking on your feet. Those talents have been noticed."

Potter wasn't one to hand out compliments. "Sounds like a great opportunity—one I've been hoping for."

"You earned it. You stick with that officer and you two will go far."

Tom's chest swelled with pride. After starting years ago on the bottom rung, he was finally advancing. Maybe he could make his mark. He had ideas. Good ones. And he had heard that Lieutenant Cranston respected those who spoke up. That wasn't the case with most of the other officers.

This might be his chance to prove himself. He'd never be a commissioned officer like Cranston, but it sounded like he was being singled out for something important, which is why he had joined up in the first place. He wanted to make his mark and make a difference. And in doing all that, he wanted to make his father—at long last—proud of him.

Suddenly he was full of dreams that were

being realized! He had to celebrate! And he had to tell Elizabeth. To do that properly he needed a few hours off. "I...I'd like to let someone know."

"Can't say that I blame you. I've seen her. I think every other red-blooded male in this army post has noticed her, too. Don't know what she sees in you."

He started at the gruff criticism, but then caught the twinkle in Potter's eyes. Sarg? Teasing him? This day just kept getting better!

Potter relaxed his shoulders. "Go on, then. Take the rest of the day off, but be in by taps."

"Yes, sir!"

And he sure had celebrated. He had rowed with her across the harbor to North Island, built a small bonfire and opened up a bottle of wine. He'd kept her out until the stars came out and he heard taps being played over at the base. He hadn't wanted the evening to end. If he'd only known that it would be the last time he would see her he would have changed a few things. He would have told her how he felt—although that kiss they shared should have gone a long way to doing that. That kiss had changed everything for him. With that kiss he had realized he loved her.

In the end it hadn't mattered. In the end she

had gone ahead and married that Preston fellow. And Tom had come to hate her for it.

Only…all that had been a lie.

Where did that leave them now?

This job was important to him. It had always meant more than a simple paycheck. The money was necessary to live, but the reason he had stuck with being a field agent had to do with making his small corner of the world a better place to live, to grow, to thrive…and to stop those who got in the way of that. His father, his mother…and now Cranston deserved that. They were no longer here to do their part, so he had to step up even more.

After Elizabeth, he had vowed never to get involved with matters of the heart again. He shouldn't have let it get as far as it did with her the first time. He'd seen what it did to his father—he'd lost his edge and died for it. Mother had all but faded away once she'd lost her husband. And so he had focused on his work—solely on his work. It was lonely at times, but it was enough.

Until today.

He'd practically kidnapped Elizabeth. He hadn't thought…he'd just acted, ignoring all the warnings ricocheting through his brain. He might as well have a bright sign on his chest that labeled him a fool. He couldn't deny it any longer. He'd never stopped caring for her, never stopped wanting her. She filled his waking moments with the hope of seeing her and his sleep with dreams.

He had to get control now. He *would* get back on track because if he continued in this vein he'd end up no good to anyone—not even himself.

Bright and early the next morning, Tom spoke with each mine supervisor and met the two men who would ride along to protect the gold ore down the mountain. He spent a few minutes with each of them to get a feeling as to their experience and their personalities. He wanted steady nerves and quick reflexes. Unfortunately, in his position, he didn't get to choose them himself, so he had to trust that the supervisor who did the choosing was proficient in the task. A technicality, but a big one if it meant his life.

Toward noon, he rode back into town, his eye on the sky overhead. In the time he'd spent inside the mines, clouds had blown in from the coast to shadow the mountains. He hoped any rain would hold off. He had plans for the afternoon to survey the Wells Fargo route to the north. A downpour would ruin the travel but likely he'd still do it.

For now, he wanted to speak with the local assayer—mostly to get an idea for the man's character and standing in the community. If the man had lived here any length of time and was liked by the locals, he would know what was happening in town. Likely would know more than the new sheriff. Tom might learn something.

The land office was located on the opposite side of the main street than the sheriff's office and saloons, and down a block. The door stood ajar. Tom approached, fingering a small chunk of quartz and gold in his pocket.

He stopped with one foot up on the boardwalk when he heard a raised and angry voice coming from inside the building. He held back to listen rather than barge right on in.

"You might as well quit bringing me this dirt, Farnsworth." This voice came from a man older and more relaxed than the other.

"You knew what was going on and kept it to yourself!" Young and likely impulsive, Tom assessed.

"You and your brother should have talked to me before buying that claim. It's half underwater and been played out for more than a year.

My advice to you is to find another spot…head somewhere new."

"I don't have any money to try again."

"Maybe you should have thought of that before throwing in with your brother. He's not the bright one of you two, but he sure bamboozled you."

"He's blood."

"I figure I did you a favor. You will be smarter from here on out."

A moment later, a slender young man stepped into the doorway. He wore a red plaid flannel shirt, tucked neatly into his jeans. His boots could use a decent burial by the worn holes along the sides. Straggly, dirty blond hair hung to his shoulders. His hands tightened into fists and angry frustration filled his gaze as he focused on Tom for a moment. Then he turned and walked away.

"Are you coming to see me, mister?" The same man who'd barked to Farnsworth stepped into the open door and eyed Tom. He was tall and thin with red bushy hair. The most notable thing about him was his large red handlebar mustache and lamb chop sideburns. A telltale redness on his cheeks made Tom think he either had the start of mercury poisoning or he imbibed a bit too freely of the ready alcohol in the town.

Tom started toward him.

"Come on in. Name is Bart Noble." He stood aside as Tom entered and then closed the door. "What can I do for you?"

Tom handed the small rock to Noble. "I want this checked out."

As the assayer sat down on his tall stool behind the desk and started analyzing the gold in the rock, Tom surveyed the two rooms as unobtrusively as possible. The room he stood in had Noble's desk and stool, along with a long table chock-full of bottles with solutions for chemical and analytical work on the gold. On Noble's desk was a scale with weights and measures. The one thing that caught his eye because it just didn't seem to fit an office like this was a framed poem on the wall. A quick look in the second room revealed a small table with a bottle of brandy and two glasses, a chunk of cheese in a bowl and a heavy iron safe.

Noble glanced up, narrowed his eyes for a minute and then motioned to one of the chairs. "Have a seat. This won't take long."

Tom walked over to the other chair in the room and sat down.

Noble's shirt and suspenders had small stains, likely from the solutions he'd used. He had on brand-new black boots—buffed to a dull sheen. And the gold chain and watch fob he wore didn't look too tarnished, either. He pulled a magnifier from the middle drawer of his desk and held it up, peering through it at the small quartz that was shot through with a small vein of free gold. "You pick this up around these parts?"

"North of here." He didn't want to be too specific considering the rock had come from Nevada.

Noble set the magnifier on his desk. "Most of the big veins around here have been mined out and the mines are shutting down their operations."

Tom shrugged. "I had heard that."

Bart eyed him shrewdly. "I hear there is someone visiting the mines. Is that you?"

"Most likely."

"Not much goes on around here that I don't get wind of. Just what are you looking for? Maybe I can help."

"Information, mostly. The men I represent want to know if there is any chance of pulling out more gold if they alter some of the methods and go deeper."

"And if that's the case are they are willing to invest?"

"Maybe. I'm just reporting back to them. They'll decide based on my report and other information. They are interested in the entire operation from start to finish—with the gold in the bank." He shifted forward and indicated the rock. "This is my own little discovery."

"I see. So you are not from around here."

"No. Up near San Francisco."

"Your name?"

"Barrington. Tom."

After running the rock through a short series of tests, Noble handed it back. "Well, Mr. Barrington, I can't say it's worth much more than three dollars. It's got good color. Better than I've seen around here in a while."

"Three dollars," Tom said. "That'd be plenty for some men for something easily fished out of a stream."

"The streams are played out around here. I've seen enough go through this office that something this small wouldn't generate much excitement."

Tom paced the small office, rubbing his chin as if in deep thought. "Can the bank cash it out for me?"

"They could…or I could."

That made Tom pause. Seemed to him that would be a conflict of interest.

Noble noticed his hesitancy. "If you're worried I might not give you a fair price you can try the bank or head down to San Diego. Furst Bank deals with the gold that comes from the mines." He snorted softly. "Although…they haven't had much luck lately."

"Why do you say that?"

"It didn't make it down the mountain last time. With that being the case, they might offer you more than my quote."

Tom stuffed the rock in his vest pocket. "Thanks for the tip but I doubt anyone accosts me for a measly three-dollar rock unless they are desperate. How much do I owe you?"

"That'll be six bits."

Tom paid him. Something seemed off about the man, but that didn't mean anything. He'd been honest about the rock. Tom had already had the gold in it evaluated. Noble had also been right about the mines being nearly played out.

He stepped outside and headed down the road. The scent of freshly baked corn bread drew him toward the café. The breakfast he'd had at the hotel might be enough for the proprietor and his wife, but it barely filled him and it was noon now. He stopped in front of the large window. The sign Elizabeth had placed yesterday was still there. It brought back the memory of her shocked expression and the flush that had come over her cheeks when they'd startled each other.

A dance. Saturday. New school opening.

So that's what she and her friend were up to with the bucket of supplies and cleaning agents. Now he knew a little more. Enough to stay away from the new schoolhouse.

He strode through the door and into the café intent on ordering a big bowl of ham and beans and corn bread. After eating, he'd ride the Coleman Grade and survey the Wells Fargo route all the way to Witch Creek, maybe all the way to the San Vicente Valley if the weather held. He could camp there and head back tomorrow taking a southern route to better read the trails. He'd be one step closer to being prepared for the day of transport, and with any luck he'd be too busy to let thoughts of Elizabeth derail him.

Chapter Eleven

It took half the day, but Elizabeth and Gemma finally had a flatbed wagon hitched and loaded with the crates that they drove out to the school-house north of town. They positioned the wagon as close to the building as possible, but even then the crates were too heavy for the both of them to slide off and carry inside. So, resourceful as always, they decided the only way was to unload them piece by piece. Thank goodness the rain was holding off. As it was, the sky continually spit at them—just enough to be an annoyance.

"I still cannot believe that you rallied some of those women to contribute," Gemma said as she pushed her desk toward the center of the room. "As I remember there are several who are not inclined to be of a generous nature."

"I just hope the people here realize how lucky

they are to have you. If they don't already know, I'm sure it will become apparent in the very first month of your teaching."

Gemma, apparently encouraged by her words, smiled and motioned to the door. "I can smell the rain heavy in the air. Let's get the crates emptied and moved in before it downpours."

Elizabeth climbed atop the flatbed and used a crowbar to pry the top of the crate off. She removed a layer of packing straw and handed it to Gemma before it could blow away in the light wind. "Good for kindling," she said. She pulled out an 1875 *Dictionary of the English Language* and *Walker's Statistical Atlas of the United States Ninth Census 1870* that were both wedged in along each side of the crate. Gemma squealed with delight as she took each oversize book and read the titles and then danced into the schoolhouse with them.

Elizabeth leaned back into the first crate and burrowed through the straw for the next item. Her toes dangled inches above the wagon bed while her hips were balanced uppermost over the wooden edge of the crate as she stretched for the contents buried deep in the protective straw. Pencil boxes, chalk, books and individual slates were pushed aside as she struggled with a world globe, trying not to separate it from its base and still get the thing out of the crate in one piece.

"Elizabeth?"

At the odd inflection in Gemma's voice, Elizabeth let go of the globe and raised herself up. Gemma stared off toward the road leading away from town. There a familiar-looking figure urged his horse off the main path and toward them.

Tom.

The sight of him took her breath away. He hadn't shaved that morning, which made him look that much more rugged than he already was. His dark brown vest hung casually open and loose. A forest green bandanna circled his neck and fluttered in the breeze. What was he doing here?

He reined his horse toward them and slowed to a halt at the end of the wagon. "Miss Starling." He touched the brim of his hat to Gemma. Then he looked purposefully at her. "Elizabeth."

He dismounted and strode toward her. "I'll give you a hand with that."

"But I thought…" She placed her hands on her hips.

He scowled.

How dare he come and growl at them. How

dare he totally confuse her. "What are you doing here?"

"I saw the sign in the restaurant window, remember? Looks like you have a lot to do before Saturday and there's quite a storm brewing."

"You are offering your assistance?" She pulled back, remembering that he was not happy she was here in the first place. "Gemma and I can handle this ourselves. You don't have to do this."

"Do you want my help or not?"

The first large drop of rain plunked on her forehead. She wiped it off and then realized she had straw in her hair from rummaging in the crate and picked that out, too.

Tom bit back an amused smile, but she noticed—oh, she noticed!

Gemma stepped forward and grasped the Major's reins. "Gladly, Mr. Barrington. We'll gladly take your assistance. Thank you for stopping by."

Elizabeth glared at her.

Gemma shrugged and walked the horse to the back of the wagon where she tied him. "We could use a strong arm. There are only two full days left before the celebration. We will need those for baking."

Tom climbed onto the wagon, the motion a bit awkward with his stiff knee, but he managed, and with a stoic face yet.

That injury again. How much pain did he hide? The confused jumble of anger inside Elizabeth evaporated. "You don't have to do this, Tom," she said softly so that Gemma wouldn't hear.

The tense set of his jaw relaxed. "I was halfway down the mountain when the weather turned worse. It's coming and this isn't going to be a light sprinkling when it hits. I wanted to check on you."

His voice, his look…it was almost as if he were reluctant to admit it. She pulled back, flustered and…of course, flattered.

"About yesterday…"

"When you kidnapped me?"

He grimaced. "I might have overreacted some."

She arched a brow.

"All right. I overreacted a lot."

"And now? What about your job?"

With a third of the effort she had expended, he reached down into the crate, pulled out the world globe and handed it to her. "I figure I can spare a little time here."

"Then…thank you," she said, bemused.

He gave her a spare nod and then shoved the crate toward the edge of the wagon. Sliding to the ground, he maneuvered the crate onto his right shoulder. He grunted a bit under the weight—the thing still half-full. "Where do you want this?"

Elizabeth was still absorbing the thought that he'd wanted to check on her. That…he'd thought about her at all since their last meeting.

Gemma hurried past. "I'll show you, Mr. Barrington."

They disappeared into the schoolhouse.

Another raindrop plopped and slid down Elizabeth's cheek. She climbed off the wagon and carried the globe inside, setting it on the teacher's desk at the front of the room. Tom emptied out the first crate of pencil boxes, crayons, paper and individual slates in short order. Then, directed by Gemma, he moved the crate to the corner of the room. When he headed outside for the second crate, Gemma scurried over.

"Such a man!" Gemma whispered, hurrying over to speak while Tom was out of earshot. Her eyes danced with merriment. "He is very handsome, and I find him rather fascinating—

in a surly, mysterious kind of way, of course. I can see why he would be so difficult to forget."

"He's certainly won you over quickly enough." Elizabeth gave a small shake of her head. How could she keep her thoughts off him if Gemma was going to encourage them?

"Maybe he will come to the dance."

"No. I doubt he'll be able to do that," she interjected quickly, shaking her head. She was clearly anxious about such a prospect. He would leave. He would. And she'd be worse off than before. It would be best not to spend too much time with him. "Please, Gemma, don't encourage him."

"Why ever not?" Gemma asked.

She shook her head mutely, unable to voice that she was scared she might succumb to his magnetism.

"I see. Like today when you all but told him that he should leave immediately? It's a wonder he comes around at all considering your attitude."

It simply wouldn't do to dwell on what he'd said or what he did. He was just being…oh, she didn't know what he was being, but to place any more intent on his words and actions simply would not do. Not at all. She couldn't cope with another broken heart! And from the same man, no less! She couldn't let it happen.

"Point taken." The smile she forced was brittle by her count…but it fooled Gemma. And she knew, with the same determined practice she'd given it in the past, it would fool everyone else—herself included.

With that thought, the sky opened up and rain started pelting the roof and windows in earnest. Outside one of the horses whinnied and stomped its foot.

Tom stepped back into the room with the second crate on his shoulder. His vest and shirt and pants were soaked through and sticking to him like a second skin. His felt hat tilted precariously on his head, the water running off the brim and down his chest.

"Been through worse," he said cryptically. And truly he didn't seem to be bothered in the least by it as he looked to Gemma to direct him where to place the crate. She couldn't keep from staring at him the way his cream-colored shirt, pasted to his skin, stretched across broad, strong shoulders. His dark hair curled slightly more around his ears and neck now that it was wet and had big drops clinging to the spiked ends. At the urge to find a cloth and dry him off, she realized she'd been staring too long and needed a distraction.

She grabbed some of the straw from the second crate and stuffed it into the woodstove at the front of the room. Tom, realizing her goal, walked over and pulled matches out of his vest pocket and lit the fire. He waited a moment to make sure the kindling took before sliding his match tin back into his pocket. Then he removed his leather vest and laid it over the teacher's chairback to dry.

Elizabeth headed to her task of sanding the benches once again while he strode across the room and began emptying the second crate. She watched him furtively, very aware of him and every movement he made. He filled the room with his warmth and his presence, making a very comfortable addition…and yet a very disconcerting one. Piles of books were stacked around him by the time he finished. He shoved the empty crate into the corner next to the other, turned them both over and set boards across the top to use as a table. After moving the books across the room, Gemma kneeled on the floor and organized them on the bookshelf.

Tom found Gemma's sanding block, settled astride a bench nearby and began sanding along with Elizabeth. Twice she felt his gaze on her for an extended period. Her face warmed and she knew her cheeks must be flushed a bright pink. Since it was to be a workday and she had only expected to spend it with Gemma, she had chosen her sturdiest dress—a brown one—and layered a pinafore apron over it. She'd even left her braid to dangle to her waist instead of looping it into a knot and pinning it on her head. She was more comfortable this way, but now with the addition of Tom in her midst and feeling tendrils tickling her cheeks and neck, she wished she had taken more time with her appearance.

The scent of wet leaves and needles from the nearby cedars and pines permeated the small schoolhouse as the rain continued drumming on the roof. The warmth of the woodstove coupled with that would have made for a pleasant afternoon had she been able to relax. With Tom so close that was impossible. He kept glancing over at her and try as she might she couldn't concentrate on what she was doing. The sight of him set off flutters deep inside.

"You sure are using every bit of your strength and gumption to sand that part of the bench," he said when he stopped to stand and stretch his back.

She glanced up. His clothes were slowly drying, with patches of a lighter shade over his shoulders and chest. His canvas pants, still wet, clung to every inch of him. Oh, my! She averted her eyes, turning back to her work and furiously hoping her face would cool down immediately. She didn't realize he had come near until he put one large, cool hand over hers and stopped her.

"You might want to slow down a bit. That bench isn't going anywhere and you'll wear yourself out before you wear out that wood. You can take it easier, you know. Thought you were supposed to be visiting…maybe even relaxing."

Beneath his fingers, her skin tingled. Being so close she could feel his breath on her. His nearness was overwhelming.

"This…isn't…just a holiday." She spoke in a soft whisper, staring at his hand covering hers. "I want everything to be perfect for Gemma."

"I see that." He took the hint, glancing up at her friend and then back at her. He lowered his voice. "Look at me, Elizabeth."

"No. There's work to do. Please…just kindly remove your hand."

"Not until you look at me."

"Stop it, Tom." She mouthed the words silently, knowing he was watching her.

He didn't budge.

She swallowed hard and slowly raised her gaze to his. He was so close she could feel the heat emanating off his body and smell the dampness of his vest. So close she could see each individual whisker darkening his strong chin. Butterflies danced in her stomach. "What?" she demanded in a whisper, irritated with herself that she couldn't control her reactions to him any better than she was doing, and peeved with him for making her have those reactions in the first place.

"I figured there was more to your coming here than a simple visit," he said slowly. "A person doesn't just take off like you did without good reason. Especially you."

She might just get lost in the ocean of his eyes if she let herself.

"For your information..." She didn't finish the thought, but let out an exasperated sigh instead. How was she supposed to keep her guard up and keep her distance when he kept coming near? Why couldn't he just stay away?

"What else is going on besides this party?" he prompted.

She must remember that he would leave for another job when this one was finished. As long as he didn't touch her again or come too close, perhaps she could keep a watch over her heart. She took a deep breath.

She pointed back to the other bench he'd just vacated. "If you'll sit over there, I'll tell you."

He finally did as she asked, although she thought she detected a slight quirk to his lips, a slight male arrogance, as he did so. She pressed her lips together. He would think he had won a certain victory in that small challenge, but she had, too. At least he now sat across the aisle on the opposite side of the room.

"Sunday was not an easy day for me. The news you brought about my brother disturbed me immensely, but just before you stepped into my store I had learned that he has taken out a loan on my store and now it is being called in."

He focused his full attention on her.

"I brought documents for Gemma…Miss Starling…to look over. I have hopes that she will be able to find something within the papers to help. She's very good at that sort of thing."

"You don't own the store?"

"Father left me half interest in it." She sighed, thinking of all the work she'd put into the mercantile over the years. "I wasn't worried before because Terrance has never cared for the town or my little store. I thought I was safe enough there while he ran his huge store in the city. I should have suspected something when he started asking me how I felt about selling. He joked about it at first, but a month ago he became much more insistent. I learned about the loan Sunday—right after dinner at the restaurant."

"No wonder you were on edge when I showed up. You had a lot on your plate and then I added to it." Tom huffed out a breath. "If you have a stake in the store, how could he get a loan without your written permission?"

"I don't know."

He returned to sanding. "Where will you live if it sells?"

"I suppose with him. He has a store in San Diego now—on Broadway—with plenty of room in his upstairs apartments. He has asked me to manage the store."

"With him! After what he's done?"

She cringed as his voice boomed across the room. At the bookshelf, Gemma looked up from her sorting and reading. "Do I have another choice?" Elizabeth demanded.

"You should have some say in all this. You've been there for years." He studied her with a thoughtful expression, his blue gaze piercing. "You really care about that old building."

"I do. It's my home. I'll figure things out somehow." She debated within herself whether to say any more and then decided it couldn't hurt for him to know. "Preston had plans to expand the store, and plans for a town park, and another restaurant. Terrance was going to oversee all of it while Preston stayed in the city. I was the glitch in the plan. After I stopped seeing him, he pulled all of his money out of the town. That's when the bank closed."

"And then the army left."

"Yes, but with Gemma's help, I…we…turned things around."

"You certainly did."

At the warm appreciation in his gaze, her cheeks warmed again. It was so like the looks he'd given her years ago. A low-level buzzing started up inside her as if lightning were about to strike. She glanced away. He *would* have to be charming all of a sudden. It only made it harder on her.

He chuckled and the sound of his rich, deep voice brought her back to the present, back to the sound of rain pounding on the roof and the smell of new wood for the walls of the schoolhouse. She stood, wiping her hands on her apron to rid them of the dust caused by the sanding. Then she fingered the brooch at her collar, opening it and focusing on the dial of the watch inside. "It's nearly four o'clock and will soon be dark. Rain or no rain, we better get the wagon and horses back to the livery before Mr. Jolson comes to fetch us." She kissed the face of the watch before closing the brooch.

Tom eyed her with an amused expression.

"It's my mother's," she said by way of explaining her action. She flipped the brooch over to show him the inscription. *Love to my ray of sunshine, Mother.*

He rose from the bench and closed the gap between them. Taking the brooch in his fingers, he read the inscription for himself. A whisper of a smile turned up his mouth. He turned the brooch over and examined the dial.

His fingers were so close to her breast that if she took a deep breath they would brush against her. The thought made her skin tingle and her heart start to ache. The scent of rain on his damp thick hair wafted up to her. She swallowed and pulled away. Why couldn't things be different between them this time?

He lowered his hand. "The only item I have

of my father's is his gun. He probably would be surprised that I still carry it today. He always hoped I'd be a lawyer or a judge. Said the West needed good men because there were so many bad ones ruining it for everyone else."

"What happened to him?"

He blew out a breath. "It's not an easy story. I doubt you'd be interested."

"I wouldn't have asked if I didn't want to know." His reluctance only increased her curiosity.

He took a moment to gather his thoughts. "I don't know if I told you…"

"He was a sheriff. I remember that much."

"Yes…well…I was twelve. Mother and I brought his supper to the jail. We did that a lot whenever he had someone he had to keep an eye on in one of the cells. That way we could spend more time with him. After we ate, we were outside getting ready to leave when a friend of his stumbled out of the saloon waving a gun and shooting every which way. He was drunk. Pa pushed us back into his office so we'd be safe. When he turned his back to see to us, he was shot. The judge ruled it an accident and the drunk went back to drinking."

"Oh! Oh, my!" Elizabeth murmured, her hand covering her mouth.

"I told you it wasn't a happy ending," he said darkly. "After that there was no money for law school or much else for that matter. Mother lost heart afterward."

"I'm sorry, Tom. To lose your father so young...I'm sorry." She couldn't think what else to say. Her heart went out to the boy he'd been.

"Pa always worried about the two of us getting hurt because of his job as sheriff. In the end, he was the one that lost his life."

"You were hurt just the same."

"Yeah. Well," he said in a clipped tone, dismissing her empathy. "Pa always said being married to a lawman was no life for a woman. It was too tough."

She recalled that he'd repeated nearly the same words to her last week—the day she learned of Terrance's duplicity. *"Maybe he did us a favor,"* he'd said. *"There really was no room for a woman in my life."* She understood so much more now. He had seen his family destroyed and he didn't want others to hurt, the way he had been hurt. This was not a vague inclination to Tom. It went deeper than that—soul-deep. He had lived with the consequences most of his life. "Then it is a good thing you decided to be a soldier."

He huffed out a breath, his expression flat. "About the same if you ask me. A hard life for a woman to be hitched to."

She should have given more thought before speaking. She fell silent at that.

Gemma finished organizing her books and now rose from the floor.

Tom glanced over at her. "Looks like your friend is ready to start back to town."

"All set, Gemma?" Elizabeth asked, glad to strike the mood that had come over them both with her questions. She hadn't meant to dredge up such sad memories for him.

"I'd like to do one more thing before we leave," Gemma answered. "Can we move the benches to the sides of the room so they'll be all set for the dance?"

She stood and picked up the end of the bench she had been sitting on, dragging it across the floor. Suddenly it was much lighter and she realized Tom had grabbed the entire thing and in one strong move placed it for Gemma. After that, they worked together, each taking an end and moving each bench, positioning them to line the edges of the room.

"We still cannot manage the slate board," Gemma said when they were done, hands on hips at the front of the room. "Not just the three of us."

"Seems like some of the men coming to this shindig could help get that up in no time," Tom said.

Gemma clasped her hands together. "A fine idea. I'll just get the bolts and screws from the shed and then I'll be ready to leave." She caught her cloak from its peg in the small alcove made for cloaks and lunch boxes and then dashed outside into the rain.

Tom donned his leather vest, slipping his arms through and shrugging into it, and then followed her to the alcove.

Elizabeth grabbed her wine-colored cloak from the peg. He took it from her and held it open as she stepped into it. "Thank you. And thank you for everything today. Gemma and I... we appreciate it." She grabbed tight to the collar at her neck.

Tom lowered his voice. "How long do you intend to stay here, Elizabeth?"

"Until after Gemma's first day of teaching. I wanted to be here to hear all about it. Maybe even help if she'd like."

"School starts Monday?"

She nodded. "The stage has a run to San Diego on Tuesday. I'd planned to go back then."

His eyes were as gray and stormy as the dark clouds scudding across the sky outside. "Wells Fargo has a stage leaving tomorrow."

"I want to stay for the celebration. Gemma is nervous about how it might go. She could use a friend by her side."

He glanced about the room. "Looks like you are ready here."

"Except for the food. It will take a day to prepare that even with Mrs. Birdwell's help."

He tightened his jaw, still not entirely pleased.

"Is that why you came today? You hoped to convince me to head back to La Playa?"

He huffed lightly. "It seemed a longshot."

"It might be easier if you just let me know what your job entails."

"Can't do that. But I like your persistence." The small lines at the corners of his eyes deepened.

It was pointless to press him. He wasn't going to tell her. And she had to admit that she liked that about him, too. He had integrity—and a stubborn streak that made a mule's temperament appear quite agreeable.

"Can you at least tell me how long this job will last?" She only asked so that she would know when he left town and was out of her life for good. A peace would come with that. At least, she hoped it would.

"Like I said—tenacious. Ready for me to get out of your life again?"

Irritated at his response, she considered his smart little grin rather insufferable.

"Can't say for sure how long it will last," he finally said in answer to her question.

"There seems to be a lot you can't say." She was growing perturbed again. "Or won't say."

The amused look on his face faded to serious. "I keep things about my jobs quiet. It's kept me alive, Elizabeth."

She felt immediately contrite. "Oh, I see. Good reason, then."

"You're not worried about me…?"

"No. Absolutely not. You can take care of yourself." Her voice was nearly a whisper. He was now so close that she struggled with thinking coherently.

"Good. You hold on to that thought."

She remembered how he'd said just that when she'd worried about his injury and searched for a place for him to rest. He didn't like being looked after. "I've wondered about something ever since seeing you again."

He waited.

She felt vulnerable asking it but really wanted to know the answer. "Would it have changed anything if you had known that I didn't marry Preston?"

There was a long pause before he said anything. "Yes…and no. I would have left. There's no doubt in my mind about that. I wanted that new assignment. I wanted the extra pay and the challenge. I'd been waiting for the chance to prove myself."

Odd how his words could hurt…even when she understood now, even when it was over and done with years ago. "I shouldn't have asked…" She heard the tremor in her voice and bit the inside of her lip to stop it, looking anywhere but into his eyes.

He took her hands in his. "I did care, Elizabeth. I would have made sure you knew how I felt before leaving. I wasn't the heel Terrance made me out to be."

She glanced up. If a person could really see into a person's soul by their eyes, then she was afforded a look into his. He had been hurt also by her brother's machinations and he had cared—a lot. She could see it now.

But it didn't change his answer. He still would have left her. She took another deep breath and forced the next question out, knowing she was asking for more darts but wanting the truth… needing the truth.

"Would you have asked me to wait?"

Another lengthy pause. She began to suspect she might dread the answer.

He released her hands. "I did. In my letter."

"What?"

"I asked you in the letter that didn't make it into your hands."

Her world crashed in on her then. He had wanted her to wait! She gasped in a short, jerky sob. She covered her mouth with her hand, distressed.

"Oh, Elizabeth…" He gathered her into his arms.

"T-Terrance took so much."

He smoothed the hair back from her forehead. "Yes. He did," he said softly, yet his tone held frustration.

"What else did the letter say?"

"I can't remember much. Just a lot of hopes for us. But, Elizabeth…it wasn't right of me to ask that of you. I realized that once I got to Texas. It wouldn't be fair to tie you down like that without knowing when or if I would ever see you again. It was too wild. Too rough. I just didn't see how it could have worked."

She swallowed hard, absorbing the truth in his words, but nonetheless aching with them.

He gave a mirthless chuckle, which she felt against her cheek.

"I don't think your brother expected me to do so well there. He probably hoped I'd end up with an arrow in my chest."

She shuddered. "Don't say that. Not even in jest." She closed her eyes, remembering the deep ache that would never go away when she had thoughts of Tom back then. Hearing his answer had hurt, but she was glad she had asked him and glad she knew the truth. How in the world was she going to protect her heart now?

He cupped her chin, his fingers and palm warm against her skin.

Her eyes fluttered open to see him searching her face, his own eyes steely blue and compelling.

"I did care for you a great deal back then, Elizabeth. But that was then. This is now." Bending down, he pressed his lips gently against hers.

Stunned, she barely moved. It was the softest of kisses—tender and searching. Her heart began to pound and her breath quickened. This was opening a door she'd shut on her life years ago. She should push him away! She should... but she had no more strength to flutter an eyelash than to move from the very spot she stood. Just the touch of his lips—his soft, moist, gentle, very pleasing lips—and she wanted to stop time so that the moment would never end.

Sensations swirled through her and she blocked out the clamoring warning in her head. She only wanted to sink farther into his kiss. Too soon, he pulled away. It took her a moment to remember her surroundings. The schoolhouse. Gemma. She stepped back, disoriented but with a slender thread of fear growing inside at her reaction. "What was that?"

He swallowed—as affected as she was by the kiss. "That was me saying this time I want things to be different."

Astounded at his words, she watched as he strode out the door and into the rain, untied his horse and mounted up. He just sat there staring at her a good long moment while the rain ran in rivulets down the V in the brim of his hat. He wasn't the least concerned about it. Then he reined his horse toward the road and headed away from the direction Gemma and she would take back to town.

An hour later, Tom rode into the livery under the cover of darkness. Outside the rain continued, making a relentless drumming on the high roof overhead. Immediately, he checked for the flatbed wagon the women had used and found it in the far corner of the large building. Mr. Jolson was just finishing up currying a roan gelding.

"Closing up for the night. Latch the door when you leave."

Tom nodded his assent. He dismounted and led his horse back to the farthest stall. The temperature had dropped with the storm to at least forty degrees. His coat and hat were soaked from the downpour. Shucking them on a nearby railing, he searched the livery for a dry cloth. Finding a few old burlap sacks stashed in the corner, he unsaddled the Major and then used one to wipe him down.

He was sliding headfirst into a mess and doing it willingly. Meaning Elizabeth. He'd been a fool to stop by the schoolhouse. He huffed out a breath, realizing it didn't matter one whit. He had wanted to kiss her ever since the moment he saw her again standing in the mercantile, although he hadn't admitted it to himself. The impulse had been there, starting out low and beneath the surface of his careful plans so that he'd hardly been aware of it. Once he learned she wasn't married, he had told himself it was about getting right with her and making sure she knew the truth about her brother. He had only been lying to himself.

He'd hoped kissing her once would get the urge out of his system. Maybe then he could concentrate on his job. What a fool. That virginal kiss hadn't been nearly enough to satisfy anything. It was meant to stifle his desire but all it had accomplished was to fan a fire that had been banked and controlled for years into flames.

While he worked, he thought about the glimpse Elizabeth had unwittingly revealed about herself. He could tell by the way she froze when he kissed her that she wasn't used to men getting close enough to touch her. She had melted readily under him...which made him recall thoughts of their first kiss when he'd all but taken her there on the beach. His body tightened in response to the memory.

Why her? Why only her in all his days? He'd

gotten along just fine these past four years without her or the thought of her bothering him. Seemed as long as he had the excuse that she'd deceived him by marrying that pompous fool, he could steam ahead full of righteous resentment. Now, knowing the truth, things weren't nearly as clear.

He wadded up the burlap and pitched it in the corner in a wave of frustration, angry at himself for thinking he could withstand her temptation. Trouble was, what tempted him wasn't just her beauty, although that was considerable by his estimation. This was more than a physical urge to expunge. It went deeper. Stronger. It felt like something that would last…maybe a lifetime. And if that were the case, he didn't want to ride away once his work here was done. When he finished this job for Wells Fargo, he wasn't going anywhere until he had a chance to find out how Elizabeth truly felt about him now, today, and more importantly…how he felt about her.

A drip from his wet hair traveled down into his eye. He swiped it away, amused that when he'd been scouting out the stage route earlier in the day he'd escaped the worst of the weather. It was only when he stopped at the schoolhouse that the clouds had released and the rainstorm doused him good. If he were a superstitious sort of man, that might make him leery of anything having to do with Elizabeth. As it was, he'd decided nothing was going to change his course. He'd see this through to the end—whether it ended well or not.

He measured an extra scoop of oats into the feed trough and latched the stall gate behind his horse. After barring the livery door as Mr. Jolson had asked, he strode to his hotel and changed from his wet clothes into a dry shirt and pants. His vest, boots and hat would have to stay wet. They were all he had.

He joined Adolph Green and his wife for supper, which turned out to be a quiet affair. For all the list of rules he'd been accosted with the first night he'd arrived, he was surprised at their lack of curiosity about why he was in town. He had mentioned about half of what he'd told Bart Noble and they'd been satisfied. After thanking Mrs. Green for the supper of stew and greens, he excused himself and headed for the saloon next door.

He picked up a whiskey at the bar, and then chose an empty table against the wall toward the back. He wasn't a heavy drinker, but he enjoyed a glass now and then. Settling in his hard-backed chair, he stretched out his injured left leg to rest on a second chair. Seemed damp weather like this would make it ache. He surveyed the large, open room filled with round tables for playing cards. On the south side of the room stood a billiard table. The piano he'd heard last night from his hotel room was positioned near enough to the table so that he imagined whoever played a tune had to keep one eye on the billiards game so that he didn't get poked in the back of his head with a cue stick.

He hadn't been sitting for ten minutes when a pretty young girl in a pink dress sashayed over to him and asked if he'd buy her a drink. He bought her a sarsaparilla—her choice—and invited her to sit if she liked, but let her know he wasn't interested in anything else. He figured it made him look a little more approachable should things pick up and she might even have something to say about the mines and the gold. Either she could have heard something herself or she might know someone he'd be interested in striking up a conversation with.

An hour later, after giving him the life history of nearly everybody who had walked through the door, she got to her feet. "Better get to work.

I see my boss came in a few minutes ago. If things slow, I'll be back."

Before he could thank her, the saloon doors swung open with a bang, drawing his attention. A young man swaggered in and slapped two coins down hard on the bar. By the scarcity of his facial hair, Tom placed him around the age of eighteen. He was tall and skinny as a rail with big bony hands, and wearing a long canvas coat, along with a dirty wide-brimmed hat that should have been cream colored but looked to be soiled to a questionable shade of sweat-stained brown.

"Haven't seen you in here for a while," the bartender said as he scooped up the money with his arthritic fingers. "What'll it be?"

"Some of that forty-rod whiskey. Make it a double."

The pink saloon gal sidled up to the boy. "You sure you can handle a double, sugar?"

"Shore 'nuff, sweet thing. You jest watch me." He cupped his arm around her shoulders and pulled her close.

Tom listened to the exchange with interest— mainly because the young man looked so much like the one he'd seen coming out of the assayer's place earlier that day. It wasn't the same kid. The other one was filled out more compared to this yahoo and had a good five years on him. Bart Noble had been rough on that young man.

"You hit the jackpot or something, Farnsworth?" the bartender asked as he set up a small glass on the bar. He poured out two fingers of whiskey and shoved the glass toward the boy.

"Naw. This is the last of it."

"Then what you spending it in here for?"

"Spreading it around, that's all. I had a pint down at the RE just now."

"Well, that's downright noble of you. How come you are still here? The last I heard you were leavin' town. What happened?"

"Chet is holdin' off. He likes it around here even though we got took by that chicken of an assayer, Noble. Chet got word on a possible job. Says he'll take care of me till I'm on my feet again if'n he gets it."

"Mighty good of him," the bartender said. "Don't think my brother would give me a drink of water if I was lyin' in the desert dyin' of thirst."

"Yeah. Everybody likes Chet. But they don't know him like I do."

The barkeep quit wiping his glass and waited for Farnsworth to continue. It was obvious the boy was feeling no pain of a physical nature.

Tom expected he was a few cows short of a herd and the liquor he'd imbibed had challenged even that assumption.

"Jenny…she was my girl until she met him. I would have married her once I got a place, once I had my stake. She knew it. She was a'willin' to wait. She was a'willin' to do just about anything for me. Well, in one ratty afternoon Chet ruined all that."

"Hard to believe he'd do something like that. Him bein' your brother and all." The barkeep motioned with a jerk of his head for Pinkie to move away. She extricated herself from the boy's embrace and moved to another table of regular customers.

Farnsworth didn't seem to notice. He hung his head a minute, lost in thought. "He always ruins things," he muttered. "Always stickin' his nose in. So I got no reason to…"

"To what?"

He looked around, his eyes bleary, but suddenly seemed to realize that others were listening. "To do like he says. I got my own ideas. Good ideas. Just 'cause that mine was a bust, don't mean I can't make my own way."

"Sure you can." The barkeep finished wiping

down the glass he held and set it on top of the pyramid of glasses behind the bar.

Farnsworth raised his glass in a private toast and then swigged down the rest of his whiskey. He pushed himself away from the bar and stumbled toward the door.

Tom looked around at the few men left inside. He'd give it another fifteen minutes, then head to the other saloon—the Rawhide Emporium that Farnsworth had mentioned.

After the allotted time, he exited the saloon and headed down the boardwalk. The road was dark except for the two saloons spilling light out onto the street and the glow from the parlor of the hotel. As he approached the RE, two men standing by the side of the building broke away and skulked around the corner, disappearing into the night. Just a little suspicious, but probably nothing.

He moved into the shadow between the bakery and the saloon. Scrunching down he slinked along the outer wall of the saloon toward the back, hoping to get a better look even though it was dark. He could hear the garbled sound of the men talking in low voices and along with that a scratching noise in the dark just ahead of him. He paused. Waited. And then a skunk, visible only by the white stripe down its back, sidled out through the opening ahead of him and veered toward the trees a short distance away.

The men stopped talking and Tom heard the sound of boots scuffing against earth. He inched forward and peered around the back of the saloon. Whoever had been there appeared to be gone now. He detected no movement in the opening between the back door and the stand of trees. He pulled back and leaned against the building, waiting, but no further sounds came to him.

He entered the RE and took a seat toward the back, just like at the first saloon. This place was brighter, cleaner and busier. He kept his ears open and his eyes peeled, but his thoughts kept returning to the two silhouettes of the men he'd followed.

He doubted that they would have even registered with him except that one looked skinny and tall—very much like Farnsworth. And the other, squat and square, looked vaguely familiar. He couldn't place it—or match it—to anyone he'd met here in Clear Springs. Probably nothing…but still…

Chapter Twelve

Call it a sixth sense, but Tom couldn't let go of the feeling that something was happening in town that he wasn't privy to and should be. He'd known the feeling a number of times in the past and he didn't like it. Anything was better than sitting and waiting for something to happen, so to head off the feeling, early the next morning he rode out to the Palisade Mine south of town to speak with the supervisor and double-check things.

Yesterday's heavy rain had left remnants of its passing with the muddy roads in all directions from the main street of town. Although the day was now sunny and crisp, every time a slight breeze blew up, the leaves and branches overhead showered down leftover raindrops. Ahead of him he could hear the groan of the five-ton stamp mill as it rose on its chains and then dropped from a high height to pound the quartz into crumbly bits and extract the ore. The ground and air reverberated with the shock every few minutes.

His ride took a quarter of an hour and he figured during it he pictured Elizabeth and that kiss they had shared a total of fifteen times—once for each minute. Imagining her was a lot more interesting than thinking about the four hundred pounds of ore awaiting transport. As he neared the entrance to the mine, he corralled his thoughts and started thinking seriously about how the move would take place.

The load of ore would leave from this particular mine, although it would include ore from three other mines in the area. Nothing like putting your eggs all in one basket. It was obvious to him that the mine owners had been holding back, squeamish about another robbery, until it would be foolish to wait any longer. He hoped it wasn't obvious to the thieves. That might bring on more men than he counted on or could be ready for. Yet Wells Fargo had a good reputation around these parts. It could be that no one bothered the load and he would have a safe journey all the way down the mountain. If that were the

case he'd be real happy. Considering his premonition, that wasn't going to happen. Likely
there would be at least three men. He figured he
could handle three if they didn't get the jump on
him—maybe even four, but no more than that.

He ducked into the mine office and introduced himself again to the supervisor.

"You'll have a new driver," the mine supervisor informed him. "Ferrill pulled himself out."

"What happened?"

"Fell off his roof yesterday trying to cover
a leak in all that rain. Wrenched his back. Can
hardly walk."

"I'm sorry to hear that." In more ways than
one. Ferrill was a large man. They could have
used his size and strength to great advantage
during the transport. "Any other prospects?"

"Yep. Name's Chet Farnsworth. He's sitting
out by the mine cars waitin' to talk to you. If
he's not to your liking let me know and I'll pull
out another worker from the mines."

Tom glanced through the windowpane. He
recognized the young man as the man leaving
the assayer's office yesterday. Yesterday he had
been full of frustrated anger. "Did you just hire
him on?" he asked the supervisor.

"Yeah. Just yesterday afternoon, but I've

known him awhile. Came by a year ago asking a lot of questions on how to go about mining. Never saw a kid work so hard for a used-up claim."

Tom recalled the conversation he'd overheard with the assayer. "He's younger than most. Does he have any idea how dangerous this could be?"

The man shrugged. "He's getting extra pay."

Dissatisfied with the answer, Tom headed outside to speak to the young man. When he approached and introduced himself, the fellow jumped to his feet and dragged off his dirty felt hat, which caused lots of dark blond hair to fall into his eyes. "Sir, you can count on me. I won't let you down."

"Call me Barrington…or Tom if you want. You are on the young side for this type of job. How old are you?"

"Twenty-two, sir. I'll work as hard as anybody you ever had. I need the job. My brother and I… well, we ain't had much steady work for the past year. I'll do whatever I have to to get the wagon down to San Diego…go any route. Anytime you want. You just name it."

The image of a skinnier, taller beanpole version of Chet came to Tom's mind—the boy he'd seen last night at the saloon. "You got a brother?"

A guarded look came over Chet. "You know him?"

"Saw him for the first time last night at the saloon. We didn't speak. I just listened."

"That's Jimmy, all right. Has a thought and out it comes. A talker. He's my kid brother. That won't be a problem, will it?"

It could be if he talked a streak like his brother. "Not if you can keep your mouth shut." Tom watched, wanting to see how Chet reacted to his slur. If he fired something back all hot-headed and brash, he'd know he was of the same breed as his brother and not to hire him. Tom needed someone with a cool, unflappable attitude. Someone who wouldn't run if things got tough and shots were fired. He couldn't afford to be wrong about the young man.

Chet looked down and pressed his lips together. "Jimmy is…" He gave Tom a slanted look, one that carried despair on its edges. "Like I said…I'll do whatever it takes to get the job. I need it."

Encouraging. He didn't excuse his brother or dwell on him, but made it clear this was about himself…not his brother. Tom respected him for that. He also liked the spark of challenge he saw now in Chet's gaze. "Have you handled a big rig before? Six mules?"

"Yes, sir."

"A gun?"

"Only a rifle."

He had to make sure the boy was aware of the danger. "Could be we'll transport the ore without mishap. Even so this won't be a cakewalk. We'll have to keep alert and watchful the entire trip—sixteen hours straight through. If there is shooting—and I believe there could be— I'll need someone with nerves that can take the pressure. I can't have you crying wolf and deserting halfway down."

Chet raised his chin, his gaze steady on Tom. "Won't happen. I ain't yellow."

"I'll expect you to keep anything you learn to yourself. Your brother isn't part of this deal."

"He won't hear a word from me."

Tom studied him a moment more. Something about Chet reassured him—his resolve, his earnest manner. Something. "All right. You're hired." He reached out his hand.

Chet grabbed it and pumped it hard. "Thank you, mister. You won't be sorry. I won't let you down."

Tom covered what details he could with Chet and then spoke again with the mine supervisor, ironing out a few more things. Then he started back to town. Halfway there he decided to check out the southern route that the wagon would travel once more and reined his horse toward the road.

Elizabeth hoisted the basket of apples onto the table and began peeling and quartering them. Mrs. Birdwell had given her and Gemma complete access to her kitchen for the afternoon in order to prepare food for tomorrow night's celebration at the schoolhouse. Then the woman had donned her bonnet and cloak and left to help a friend who was feeling poorly.

Gemma came into the kitchen and tied an apron on over her lavender gingham dress, watching her all the while. "Do you want to talk about it?"

"No. Why?"

"You are attacking those poor apples like they've done something to anger you. At this rate, although we may have a several pies, you may lose a few fingers in the making of them."

Elizabeth slapped the paring knife down on the table. "You studied those documents all morning! I cannot believe there is nothing in them that will help me keep the store."

"I read through them three times hoping to find something. It just isn't there. I think you should talk to Mr. Furst—the young one. He has known you and your family a long time and now that he is living back in La Playa and reopening the bank he won't want to start off making enemies or hurting his friends. It wouldn't be good for his business. Maybe he will work something out with you."

"All right. I'll do as you suggest," she said as disappointment settled over her. "At least I know which step to take next."

"I'm sorry I couldn't help you more."

"I guess you can't manufacture words or clauses that aren't there. Thank you for looking the papers over, anyway. And you are right… perhaps Sam will be of help, although I suppose it makes a difference whether he truly wants the store or not."

Gemma watched her work a few more minutes before declaring, "I will start on the pie-crusts." She glanced about the small kitchen and started rummaging through the cupboards. "Now where does Molly keep the flour?"

Elizabeth kept paring apples and unobtrusively watched Gemma stumble through sifting and measuring the different ingredients. When she started to add an additional teaspoonful of salt to the mix, Elizabeth finally had to ask, "Have you ever made a piecrust before?"

"You found me out." Gemma sounded miserable and tossed the salt back into its crock.

"Why didn't you say something? Now that I think of it, when you lived in La Playa, I can't remember one time that I saw you do any baking."

"I never have. In Boston we had a cook and I've gotten by since then knowing just a few basics. Nothing as fancy as a fruit pie."

"Well, I want the children at the celebration to appreciate you for your intelligence—not for your salty pies."

Gemma smiled at that.

"Switch positions with me. There are plenty of apples here to keep you busy and that way maybe you will save me from losing a finger."

They exchanged places and Elizabeth finished measuring the ingredients.

Gemma peeled and sliced one apple before she stopped to observe Elizabeth. "You would make such a good mother. Your children would love your pies—and all of your cooking."

Elizabeth pressed her lips together. The only man she could imagine as a father for her children would be Tom. The kiss they had shared had got her thinking along those lines even before Gemma said anything. She had thought of Tom and that kiss half the day now, wondering what he'd meant by it and by what he'd said.

What kind of a father would he make? He would be patient, she suspected. And tough, but fair. And if the things they'd done over their summer together were any indication, he would also be fun. She could imagine him carrying a son on his shoulders while hiking on a trail, or teaching him the fine art of fishing or rowing. It would never happen, of course. Tom was not the settling-down type. "Thank you for saying that. I do love children but I don't think a family is in my future."

"You are not that old. My grandmother married at thirty."

"Spoken from the ripe old age of twenty-three."

"Maybe you should become a teacher. Then you would have more children than you would know what to do with. Like the old woman in the shoe."

Elizabeth cut butter into the flour and worked

it in. "Maybe I shall and give you some competition."

Gemma smiled and then gave Elizabeth a searching look. "You were quiet after Tom left yesterday. What happened? Weren't you happy I coerced him into staying and helping?"

Other friends might share things immediately, but Elizabeth wasn't like that. She'd been alone managing that store for so long that she was comfortable with herself, comfortable holding things in…for a while, anyway.

She had wanted to talk to Gemma about Tom ever since seeing him yesterday but first she had wanted to savor the thought that he'd stopped by of his own accord…and definitely kissed her of his own accord. She smiled to herself thinking of that. He was still attracted to her! She realized, of course, that it couldn't lead anywhere. He might want things to be different this time, but she was a realist. After hearing about how he had lost his father, it was abundantly clear to her that as long as he pursued dangerous jobs, there really would be no room for her in his life. He would still leave when the job he was doing was over to start another one. He would leave, and if she let herself give in to his charms, she would be nursing another broken heart.

"His real reason for stopping by was so that he could *encourage* me to take the stage back to San Diego as soon as possible."

This time it was Gemma who slammed down her knife and fisted her hands on her hips. "That rat! That's not what he was supposed to do."

Amused at her friend's admission of her blatant matchmaking attempt, Elizabeth smiled. "Don't worry. I told him no, that I wanted to be here for the dance and for your first day of school."

"Good. I am depending on you." She went back to peeling and paring the apples.

Elizabeth smiled and watched her for a moment before she admitted, "And then...he kissed me."

Gemma's eyes widened. "He *kissed* you! I knew it! I knew he liked you that way."

Her cheeks warmed, embarrassed. "I shouldn't have told you."

"After all this time? After all your pining years ago? Of course you should tell me. I am invested in this!" Gemma giggled and threw a slice of apple at her nose.

Elizabeth gasped—surprised—and stopped just short before throwing a dash of flour right back at her.

Gemma jumped back, fast on her feet, and twirled once, her arms wide. "Just imagine! That amazingly strong and handsome man kissed you and of course you loved it! I can tell by that ridiculously red glow all over your face."

"Gemma!" But her friend's enthusiasm was contagious. Giving in, Elizabeth reached into the bowl of apple slices and threw one across the table at her. "You are impossible."

She laughed. Then they both laughed.

"I knew I could make you laugh," Gemma chortled, and aimed another apple slice.

Elizabeth's face began to ache and she realized suddenly that it was from grinning so hard. Really, this was too much. She had to set Gemma straight.

"Enough! I give!" she said, picking up the apple pieces. She brushed the flour off her apron. Really.

"How was your Mr. Barrington at kissing? On a scale from one to ten."

Elizabeth rolled her eyes. "All I know is that for me…it was wonderful." She sobered then. "Gemma… The kiss… It can't mean anything."

"Of course it does!" But seeing Elizabeth's expression, Gemma's eyes clouded over. "It must."

"No." Elizabeth shook her head firmly. "That

is not to say he doesn't feel *something* for me. I know he does. He went so far as to say he hopes things will be different for us, but he isn't seeing clearly. He will leave when this job of his is over. He will. That is one thing I must be practical about."

"Maybe he won't," Gemma insisted.

"He did before. I...I don't blame him for it anymore. He said some things and I understand how it is with him."

"No. You said that he had to leave. He was a soldier and he had his orders. That's much different than now."

She shook her head. "We talked about it yesterday...when you had gone outside to the shed. Back then he wanted to go. He had orders, yes... but he was excited about it. He has always loved what he does and the thrill, the danger, of it all. There is no way I can compete with that. No woman can." She swallowed hard. "And I wouldn't want to. I wouldn't want to change him that way. When his job here is done, he'll leave. And I'll go home. Alone. And that's just the way it will be."

Gemma plopped into her chair again, a curious expression on her face as she studied Elizabeth. Uncomfortable under her scrutiny,

Elizabeth turned and found the rolling pin. After separating the dough into two portions, she began rolling out the first mound into a circle. She was aware when Gemma rose...aware when she walked over to her, but she kept rolling out the dough.

Gemma placed her hand on Elizabeth's forearm, stopping her rolling motion. "It's all right to be a little selfish—to be happy," she said quietly. "You are worth it. You know that, don't you?"

She pulled from beneath Gemma's touch and attacked the dough with more force, rolling it to the thinnest crust she'd ever made.

Gemma frowned. "Don't let Terrance win after all this time. He's bullied you into thinking you don't deserve your own slice of happiness."

She didn't understand what Gemma meant. "My brother doesn't have anything to do with this. He's not 'winning' anything. I just happen to care for a man who puts his work ahead of everything else. The same could easily be said of Terrance, except I'd wager to say Tom's work surpasses my brother's in importance."

"I don't think that is what is going on here but I'm glad you can at least admit you care about Tom."

"All right—I admit it! But Tom doesn't want 'tethers.' He said so himself. Caring for someone in his line of work only complicates things."

"I'm not speaking about Tom," Gemma said gently. "It's you. You are afraid…"

Her chest ached with the tightness she held inside. She could not listen to any more. Gemma had no idea what it was like. "I can't let my guard down. Don't you understand? I won't make the same mistake twice."

"But, Elizabeth…"

"No! I won't give my heart—battered as it is—to him a second time. I won't do it." She would shatter if she did. With the back of her hand, she swiped at the sudden moisture in her eyes.

She felt Gemma's gaze on her.

"Let's just get on with this," she said, motioning to the empty pie tins, although her entire body trembled with volatile emotions.

"All right," Gemma said slowly. "For now…" And she stepped up to the table and started sliding the rolled-out pie dough onto the tins.

By four o'clock, Tom had circled around and was nearly back to Clear Springs. He urged the Major into a faster pace, anxious to return before dark. He was still of the opinion that if the robbers struck, it would be while the wagon was on the mountain. Hiding would be easier among the trees and ravines, especially if they intended to head toward Mexico. It's where he would choose to strike if he were intent on taking the gold. If they waited until the load made it to the valley where the change station stood, it would be too easy for a posse to catch up to them. The open fields didn't give them any means of cover.

He entered town from the west, dismounting in the small stand of trees behind the saloon. He held his position and surveyed the area. There was just enough light to make out two sets of footprints, now dried in the mud, from the two men he'd come upon last evening. He saw where they'd been standing, and then noticed they split and went different ways. One headed off down an old Indian trail through the brush. The other set entered the saloon's back door.

So he'd established someone had been out in the rain yesterday talking to someone else. They'd acted a little suspicious but it wasn't enough to go on.

Gathering up the Major's reins, Tom walked him around the corner and over to the livery as dusk turned into night. As he stabled his horse and made sure he had food and water he heard Jolson giving directions to someone. He didn't think anything of it until he heard the man reply in a familiar voice.

His gut tightened. No. It couldn't be…

He peeked over the half wall of the stall. In the doorway, talking with Mr. Jolson, his voice too low to be understood, stood a stout, square man. He turned slightly, enough for Tom to see the outline of his face. He recognized it.

Hodges.

Tom moved swiftly, silently, and grabbed his rifle from its scabbard. When he returned to his vantage point, the two men had disappeared.

He'd be hanged if he let Cranston's murderer slip through his fingers. He raced to the large livery doorway and checked the main road. Down the way, Jolson entered the dry goods store, and looked to be alone. There was no sign of Hodges anywhere.

His first thought was to alert Sheriff Parker.

His second was to find Elizabeth.

Had Hodges seen him? There was no way of knowing. How had the man escaped from jail up north? How long had he been in town without Tom aware? Too many unanswered questions. Too much risk.

Tom strode across the street and checked the sheriff's office. A quick glance through the darkened windows told him Parker wasn't there. The place was closed up tight. He walked around to the back of the jail area, to the small room he'd heard about. He rapped on the door. No answer.

Great.

He wasn't sure where the man hung his hat. He did have a rough idea, however, where Mrs. Birdwell's house stood from talking to the sheriff that first day he arrived. While he was there making certain the women were all safe, he'd make sure to warn Elizabeth and her friend. Hodges was dangerous. They had to be careful.

The fact that Hodges might have been in town awhile unsettled him. The man might have been here watching him. Instead of walking straight to the boardinghouse, he took a roundabout way, paying particular attention to his surroundings. He stayed off the main road and instead used the back way and deer trails until he came to the house pressed against a small hill and hidden among the pines and gnarled oak trees.

A few minutes later he stood at the back door to Mrs. Birdwell's place and knocked on the weathered door.

"Who is there?" Elizabeth's voice came from inside.

"It's me. Tom."

She cracked the door.

One big pretty brown eye stared back at him and two of the softest lips he'd had the pleasure to kiss. Too bad this had to be a different type of discussion. "I need to talk to you."

He could see her hesitation—and her frown—through the crack. "Molly...I mean, Mrs. Birdwell isn't home."

"It's important."

Her eyes blinked and she opened the door enough that he saw she held onto a broom—and wielded it like a shield in front of her. A heavenly sweet scent wafted through the opening. "Dessert?" He drew in a long breath.

"Pies for tomorrow night. They're cooling."

She wore a cream-colored apron over her skirt and blouse. Judging by the amount of flour dusted on her dark green skirt, the apron hadn't done a thorough job.

"It's better that I don't stand outside."

"Gemma isn't here, either."

He moved close, close enough to breathe in the scent of apples that clung to her skin and to see the delicate, individual black lashes that framed each of her pretty eyes. Slow and gentle-like, he wrested the straw broom from her hand, leaning it against the wall. "Let me in, Elizabeth. Like I said, it's important."

She swallowed. "Very well." She moved back to let him enter.

He closed the door behind himself.

The desire to kiss her slammed into him. Knowing that she was alone gave him ideas he needed to keep to himself. It was hard to look at her and not think about the kiss they'd shared yesterday—even harder not to repeat it. Seemed like once he crossed that line and touched her, he could think of little else when she was near. To counter the urge, he reached out and looped a dark brown wave of hair around his finger, then let it fall softly against her cheek. She had braided it loosely in one thick braid that fell down her back to her waist. In that moment she looked the same as she had four years ago— innocent, wide-eyed and beautiful. "You wore your hair this way back when I first met you."

Her cheeks turned a light pink and she avoided his gaze. "I'm really too old to wear it like this, but…"

"I like it this way. You're not too old for it." Though he guessed certain days he worried about the same thing—when the damp weather hit his injured leg and made it ache. He didn't like the fact that he was slowing down because of it.

"You have your gun on now."

Yesterday, upon approaching the schoolhouse, he had stowed it in his saddlebag. "That's what I need to talk to you about. An old acquaintance is in town. His name is Jack Hodges."

"Acquaintance. Not friend?" she asked cautiously.

"Definitely not a friend."

"Should I warn Gemma or Mrs. Birdwell?" She sat down as she questioned him, then suddenly she gasped and shot right back to her feet. "What about the party? Should we call it off? I wouldn't want anybody to get hurt."

He wanted to allay that look of alarm right now. "That's not necessary. He's not here for anyone that lives here in town. I'm just telling you so you will be cautious and keep a wary eye out. He's not a pleasant sort." He moved farther into the kitchen, took her by the shoulders. "Settle down, Elizabeth. Forewarned is forearmed."

"You haven't told me nearly enough to be forearmed. I know nothing of what you are doing here in Clear Springs." She broke from his grasp and paced the floor, completely agitated. "Considering your jobs in the past, people here could be in danger. I want to know."

"I've held off hoping it wouldn't come to this."

"Well, the time has come. I need to know the facts so that I can watch out for myself and Gemma and Mrs. Birdwell. If you feel anything for me—and I believe you do—you'll tell me right now."

Oh, he felt something for her, all right. "Sit down, Elizabeth, and I'll tell you."

It took her a minute to calm down enough to sit, but finally she seated herself on the chair opposite him at the table. He started first with the details of the train robbery in Carson City.

"We surprised Hodges. He didn't expect us to be there when he jumped the train with his gang to collect the gold. We cornered him in the dining car. I got there first and took aim but he had grabbed a passenger on his charge through the train cars—a little boy—and held him in front of him for a shield. I couldn't shoot, not with the boy in the way. I hesitated a second too long. Hodges used that second and shot me in the leg. He was aiming to shoot me again when Cranston rushed in and charged him. I heard a shot, but thought it went wild. We tackled Hodges and handcuffed him before I realized my partner was bleeding. He died a few minutes later."

"Did the boy survive?"

He nodded.

She reached across the table and clasped his hand. Her palm and fingers were warm, her skin milky white next to his own darkened and toughened skin. So different from each other, yet she comforted him in so many ways. Light to dark.

"Tom," she said once he'd finished. "You are being too hard on yourself. If the government didn't charge you with wrongdoing after a thorough investigation, how can you? Or, for that matter, Amanda? I know she is still grieving, but it's not right for her to blame you. Your job is full of risks. She had to accept that when she married Lieutenant Cranston."

He pulled away from her grasp. He couldn't think straight when she touched him and he didn't deserve her compassion. Not in this instance. "Yes, but we were a team. He'd just learned that Amanda was expecting and things weren't going well. We were in Nevada. Being that far away was bad enough. The news that Amanda might be losing the baby was uppermost in Jeff's mind that morning when we boarded the train and came face-to-face with Hodges. Not the sting."

The look in her eyes was a far cry from the condemnation he'd seen in Amanda's eyes or Sam's.

"It sounds to me like Lieutenant Cranston died protecting you." She was quiet for a moment, studying him. "I'm glad you told me. I didn't realize…I think I understand now. It's not just about getting the gold down safely. It's personal. That's why you have to catch Hodges."

"I have to pay him back for Cranston because Cranston isn't here to do it. And with this injured leg I have to know I still have it in me, that I can still do my job and do it well. If I can't… well…guess I'll hang up my holster for good."

"What exactly do you mean by that? You'll quit?"

"No."

Her face drained of color. She understood now. "You mustn't think that way," she warned. "You can't afford to. I couldn't bear it, Tom."

The unspoken fear and longing in her eyes stopped him. Suddenly, he realized, the stakes had become much higher.

"So…you don't think this person—this

Hodges—will be at the school dance tomorrow night?"

"No." He huffed out a breath, slightly amused at her innocence. "Men like Hodges are too hardened for something like a school dance. He might slip into one of the saloons for a drink or two and hide in the shadows, but more than likely he'll lay low and let others scout out the territory and gather information. That's more his style."

He wouldn't tell Elizabeth, but he figured he'd stop in at the saloons tonight and tomorrow just in case he could get Hodges behind bars again. He didn't relish running into the man. It had taken a lot to catch him the first time. But he did it once; he could do it again. Having him in jail would make getting the gold down the mountain a sight more easy. He'd only have to contend with Hodges's gang—not Hodges himself.

He could see the relief spread through her as she relaxed her shoulders and breathed easier. "Thank goodness. Then he won't be anywhere near Gemma or me tomorrow night."

"No."

"I don't suppose that you are coming, are you?" she asked tentatively. "It's just…I'd feel safer if you were there."

The backhanded way that she asked amused him. He would get a chance to hold her again, maybe even dance with her. She sure looked interested in his answer, the way she leaned across the table toward him. He hated to burst the faith she seemed to have in him all of a sudden. He surely didn't deserve any of it. Not yet.

"No. Things are happening that need my attention. Just go and have a good time. Stay close to your friend Gemma." He raised her chin with his fingertips to get a better look at her bright eyes. For the first time in his life, the thought of a new assignment held no appeal. "If it weren't for this job…"

"Believe me," she said, disappointment lacing her words as she avoided his gaze, "I understand entirely."

"I'm not so sure you do." He hadn't meant the words as a challenge. Then again…maybe he had.

"You love what you do—all the danger and excitement. It's important to you and to others." She sighed. "And I…I can't compete with it."

What?

She raised her chin farther.

He had figured out yesterday that she still cared for him, but this sounded as if it were something else. He stood and pulled her up to him, watching the conflicting emotions on her face. Her eyes were big, and luminous. He reached up and smoothed his thumb over her lower lip.

It trembled and she closed her eyes.

Her pulse jumped in her throat. "Stop, Tom."

He hesitated. "I want to kiss you in the worst way. Guess it's obvious I have feelings for you. Feelings that never completely stopped." The air thrummed between them.

She shook her head tightly, avoiding his gaze.

He lowered his hand. "What are you afraid of?"

"I'm not afraid. I'm careful," she protested quickly, emphatically.

"Careful?" he prodded.

"Practical." A stubborn look came into her eyes as she bit her lower lip. "Despite what you said yesterday about things being different this time, when this is over you will leave. You'll say goodbye and go on to your next exciting assignment and I won't see you again." She clenched her hands into fists and then took a deep breath. "If I'm not careful…you will break my heart— again. I won't let that happen. I won't ever let that happen again."

He stood there, stunned. Emotions that he hadn't felt in a long time were swirling around in his gut. He wanted to pull her into his arms and soothe away that part inside her that hurt. He just wasn't sure how to go about it. And was it smart? Would it only make things worse when he had to leave with the gold transport? Probably. But looking at her now, he didn't want to imagine leaving. He didn't want to consider leaving at all.

"I think you should go now," she said dully. "Thank you for the warning. I…we will be careful. Please…you can let yourself out." And with that, she turned and walked away.

As he left the boardinghouse he realized suddenly what was happening. He was giving her little bits of himself, letting her see parts of him he'd always kept hidden, and the same with her. He was learning about her all over again—learning what he gave up all those years ago.

He swallowed hard. He was falling in love. Again.

Elizabeth stood in her room, waiting until she heard Tom's footsteps to the kitchen door and then the closing of the door behind him when he left. She sunk to the bed.

He knew now.

She had laid her heart out for him to see—honestly and completely. Surely her declaration had scared him off. She probably would not see him again.

She hugged herself.

It was for the best. Better now than let things go too far. Better now than when it was too late to pull herself back and save herself.

Then why was she crying?

Chapter Thirteen

~~~~~~

After leaving Elizabeth at the boardinghouse, Tom tried once more to inform the sheriff. Parker was nowhere to be found. He waited in the RE saloon, hoping the man would stop in there eventually. He'd been there thirty minutes, listening to the conversations around him for any talk of the mines or the gold, when the piano player arrived. As Tom nursed his whiskey down to the last drop, he listened to several pitiful renditions of "Oh! Susanna" and "Aura Lee" on the piano.

Each song had a way of making him think of Elizabeth and it just proved too much for him to continue listening to the maudlin renditions of the tunes. All he wanted was to head right back to her and plant a kiss the size of Texas on those sweet lips of hers and tell her everything would be all right. Trouble was, he wasn't sure that was true. He also wasn't sure what she'd do if he showed up on the porch there again…especially as the hour had grown late. The more he realized what her brother had stolen from Elizabeth and from him, the more he hated the man. A reckoning was coming. He'd make sure of it when everything was over here in Clear Springs. On the fourth go-through of each song, he shoved his glass across the scarred tabletop and stood. Nothing against the old piano plunker but that was about all he could take.

The next morning, Tom walked into the law office and the sheriff was waiting for him.

"Where were you last night?" Tom said without preamble. He hadn't slept well, thinking of Elizabeth half the night.

"Well, aren't you in a huckleberry mood this early in the morning? Slow down and take a seat. I haven't had my coffee as yet."

"It can wait." However, it was Tom who waited until Parker had poured them both a cup and sat down across from him at his desk.

"For your information I was up at the Palisade Mine finishing up details. Got word the load is nearly ready and will be transported in the morning. No one will be suspecting we'd move it on a Sunday with the bank closed. There's hope the gold will slide right on down the mountain without incident." His eyes narrowed on Tom. "Now what has got you all fired up?"

"I saw Hodges yesterday."

Parker set down his mug. "Where?"

"The livery. I just caught a glimpse, but it was enough to satisfy any misgivings. It was him, all right."

"Fancy that. This was shoved under my door this morning." He handed Tom a telegram. Tom didn't have to read it to have an idea what it said.

HODGES JAIL ESCAPE STOP SEPT 21 STOP

"Little late, I guess. Got a wanted poster from before somewhere in here…" He shuffled through the papers on his desk and finally withdrew a drawing with the likeness of Hodges. He studied the poster for a moment before he tacked it to the wall with the other wanted posters. "Welcome back to my wall of fame."

"Are the mine owners still set on using the decoy coach on the Wells Fargo route?" Tom asked.

"It's leaving fifteen minutes ahead of the real wagon, which will take the Old Grade."

"With the extra man on horseback?"

Parker nodded. "And the driver. Four in all with the gold."

"Then keep four on the decoy. It has to look real. Hodges will step things up a notch."

"I'll keep that in mind."

Tom walked over and stared at the large area map tacked onto the wall. "That's a lot of men that need to keep quiet and a lot of country we'll need to cover fast. Hopefully Hodges will take the bait."

"The others won't know about the run until tomorrow morning. They are getting paid extra. Each one had the chance to back out without repercussion on his regular job. They know what they are getting into and they are ready."

He wished there was some way he could do this himself. He still didn't like putting them in harm's way, but there was no way around it. He couldn't guard the gold by himself. He didn't expect this to be a one-man heist, not with the amount of ore they were transporting. Looking over the map, Tom poured over the scenarios of how the day could progress—and how it could come apart. "If the thieves follow the decoy and stop it, those men have to be prepared for trouble. Tempers will run high."

"Anything else on your mind?" Parker stood and walked over to the map.

Tom took a deep breath. He still wasn't satisfied with the situation. "This plan might get the gold down to the city, but it won't stop the thieves."

Parker's forehead furrowed. "According to my wire from Mr. Furst, that's your job. To get the gold down safely. Nothing more."

Tom didn't comment for a moment. "I want to send a message to other would-be outlaws. I want others to think twice about messing with this gold route."

"What aren't you telling me?"

The speculation in Parker's gaze made Tom straighten up. Craig Parker was no fool and Tom had come to respect his opinion on the situation that was brewing. He should let him know the truth of the matter. Especially since he might come up on Hodges.

"A run-in like this killed my partner, Jeff Cranston. And left a bullet in me as a souvenir."

Parker returned to his seat behind the desk and took a long, slow gulp of his coffee. "Cranston…as in Amanda Furst Cranston?"

Tom nodded. "One and the same."

Parker's expression, puzzled at first, slowly

cleared. "I've read about you…Barrington. The name didn't register before. Not until you mentioned Cranston."

"We'll keep that part of my past between you and me. If things go bad, no one is to know I had anything to do with the gold transfer. Sam's order."

"No connection. Why is that?"

"Sam's a smart man. He doesn't want any bungled attempts being traced back to his bank. Might cause people to withdraw their money if they have reason to believe the bank can't keep things secure. People tend to be able to excuse one mess-up, but not two."

"He's playing you," Parker said, sounding disgusted. "He's sitting there all safe and warm and criticizing the man in the field who is going through the muck."

Tom didn't want problems between the sheriff and Sam after this. "I took on the job willingly enough. I'm here under my own steam. Matter of fact…I asked for it."

Parker raised his brows. "You've really got a vested interest in this outcome, don't you?"

"One hundred percent."

"This might not be the same gang. The entire situation could play out differently."

"I'm aware of that. But I'll stake my horse that Hodges is in on it. Why else would he come here after escaping? He's the one I want."

Parker raked a hand through his hair. "Look, Barrington. I'm fairly new to all this, this being my first time as a sheriff, but I'm not entirely unaware of the difference between going after a man as a criminal who broke the law or going after him as a personal vendetta. If you catch any of the thieves, I expect you to bring them in for questioning and for trial if at all possible. I won't condone out-and-out murder as a way to get your revenge."

"Even in self-defense? Men like this usually don't go quietly. You at least know that or you wouldn't have lasted even this long as a sheriff."

Parker sighed. "We both know the gray area of self-defense in this situation so I'll just let that remark pass by. Tell me what happened between you and Hodges last night."

"Nothing happened. He didn't see me. He was talking to Gil Jolson."

"Where was your gun?"

"The minute I recognized him I grabbed my rifle from my horse. When I turned back they were both gone."

Parker studied him a moment before he spoke.

"Probably a good thing in your case. If you'd had your gun on, you would have used it. I know how revenge can eat at a person. Messes with their heads."

"That's not happening here." He leaned forward to make his point. "Hodges wasn't exactly standing in the middle of the road. He was in the livery, and then he kept to the shadows. The fact that he was in town at all says a lot. I don't think he realizes that we are on to him. Or he thinks he is intelligent enough to outsmart us."

"So you don't think he's out for you personally?" Parker asked skeptically. "Wasn't his pride hurt when you sent him to jail and broke up his gang?"

"Maybe. But I think he is more interested in the gold than in any personal thing against me. Especially if he doesn't know I'm here. If he successfully gets the gold and then gets across the border to Mexico, he's won." He hoped he was telling Parker the truth. It's what he believed, but he could be wrong. "I'll question Jolson this morning. Maybe he will have more information for us."

"Good idea. You handle it. I've got a few other things to check on today." The sheriff eyed him earnestly. "You ready for this?"

"Ready as I'll ever be," he answered, making a mental check of everything. He stood. "Will someone be at the bank tomorrow night to meet us? Depending on the conditions of the roads after that rain, this could take anywhere from fourteen to eighteen hours."

Parker nodded. "Have you scouted the route again?"

"There's one steep grade the mules might have difficulty with. I think that's where they will try for the gold."

"I know the place." He rubbed his jaw and cracked an uncommon smile. "Would be nice if the thieves were nursing a hangover from Saturday night and decided to sleep instead of messing with us."

"Don't suppose we can count on that." Times like this Tom wished he could get into Hodges's mind and be a step ahead of him in whatever he tried. He still didn't think the decoy would work.

"Anything else I should know?"

Tom walked to the door. "Hodges *has* killed. I don't want anyone else in his crosshairs." *Especially Elizabeth.* He took another look at the large map on the wall, committing it once more to memory, then tipped his hat at Parker. "I'll be around if you can think of anything more. Might take in that dance at the new schoolhouse."

"Guess it's a good thing to act normal, like nothing unusual is happening."

"That's the idea."

"Hmm. May catch a dance or two myself. I heard the new schoolteacher is easy on the eyes."

Tom grinned, thinking of Miss Starling. She actually was kind of cute. Guess he'd been too blinded by Elizabeth to really notice. "She is. Smart, too, from what I've seen. Thanks for the coffee. See you later."

He felt Parker's gaze follow him as he left and walked down the boardwalk.

Elizabeth refilled the bowl of apple cider on the table and stood back, checking napkins, cups, silverware. She had kept busy, dishing out pieces of pie and filling cups with cider for the first half of the celebration. The twelve families that had come tonight, along with Mrs. Birdwell and owners of several of the businesses in town, were more than Gemma had anticipated. To top it off, a man called Mr. Sykes had brought his fiddle to supply the music.

In spite of her professed worries, Gemma appeared collected and radiant as the center of attention. The blocked and quilted dress she wore, a woolen material, was a bit warm for the number of people in the room and all the dancing she'd done. So much so that her hair had curled tighter, and the tiny strands surrounding her face were damp with perspiration. She smiled and waved to Elizabeth, and then started toward her.

"I cannot believe this!" she said, extending her arms, her eyes shining.

"Looks like there is no need to worry about who will support the school. It is obvious you have many here willing to help out."

She shook her head in wonder. "Apparently reading, writing and figuring numbers are important for their children." She raised her head, concentrating on an altercation occurring across the room. "Those Shalbot boys are going to be a challenge. Just look at them teasing poor little Moira."

"Oh, you'll rise to any challenge they can dish out," Elizabeth said. She wasn't worried in the least about Gemma's ability to control the children.

Gemma drew closer, lowering her voice. "Have you seen your Tom?"

Just hearing his name, whispered, as though he belonged with her, made Elizabeth glow on the inside. "Would you stop? I don't expect him, Gemma. I told you that."

Gemma squeezed her hand. "There's time yet."

She had kept the details of Tom's present job with Wells Fargo to herself, realizing that she might jeopardize his work and possibly his life by letting Gemma or Mrs. Birdwell know. He had trusted her with that information and she would safeguard it. She shook her head. "I doubt he'll come. There's too much going on."

The dimples in Gemma's cheeks deepened. "So you have succumbed to the fact that he's a part of your life again?"

Elizabeth had lain awake much of last night after the realization struck her. She knew without a doubt that she loved him. She'd fought it, but this love had always been there, stronger than her will. In the wee hours of the morning, she had finally surrendered and accepted it.

Her cheeks warmed. "No. Not a part, but he is definitely a force in it. I suppose I never completely got over him."

"Maybe that's why other men never interested you. When I lived in La Playa you were blind to the things men did to catch your attention."

"Not blind. Just not interested." She huffed

out a breath as she remembered one particular officer. "There was a soldier who came into the store for the most obscure items just so I would have to order them for him and he could come back. I started to dread his appearance after several months of that. He was rather exasperating."

Gemma grinned. "I'm sure he thought the same of you."

"Tom did practically the same thing...but with him whatever he wanted to order was actually for me—special flowers, a lace shawl and once a collar for Patches that he fancied up with red, white and blue decorations for the Fourth. He made it a game."

"How could anyone else compete with that! I think I'm growing to like him even though he scared the daylight out of me when he kidnapped you."

"I supposed he has always been on the edge of my thoughts." She thought back to all he had said about Cranston, Hodges and the gold. This morning she had informed Elizabeth and Mrs. Birdwell of the risk of an outlaw seen about town without going into detail or connecting it to Tom or the gold. They'd all determined they would stick together until the threat had passed.

Gemma shook her head. "Oh, Elizabeth. It is obvious he cares for you."

"I just hope he stays safe." She didn't think she could bear it if something should happen to him.

"Me, too."

The conversation was getting too personal to continue in such a public place. Seeking to turn things away from herself, Elizabeth said, "It has been a lovely holiday and this is the highlight."

Gemma giggled. "A holiday where you worked harder here than you would have at your mercantile."

"It was a good kind of working."

"And for you…it had some benefits," Gemma said slyly. "Why don't you dance? Enjoy yourself tonight. There are plenty of willing young men and you look so lovely. Molly can handle the punch bowl."

Elizabeth looked down at her dark blue skirt and shirtwaist. It was her Sunday best. "I only wish I had thought to pack my one party dress. It doesn't get much use in La Playa. But Mrs. Birdwell did a very nice job with this dress, didn't she?" She swished her skirt once. Molly had simply fancied it up with the addition of a cream-colored lace collar over the bodice and lace at the sleeves.

"Miss Starling? Might I be introduced to your friend?"

Gemma winked at Elizabeth. "Why, of course, Mr. Noble. This is Elizabeth Morley. A friend from out of town. She has been helping me this week, preparing the schoolhouse for the first day of school. Elizabeth, this is Bart Noble. He is Clear Springs's assayer."

Mr. Noble was perhaps ten years older than she, with a thick red handlebar mustache. His clothes, while not the fanciest, were definitely smarter than the other men attending. "I see you are without a partner tonight, miss. Would you like to dance?"

Just then Mr. Sykes put down his fiddle, amid protests, saying his arm needed a rest and his whistle needed a drink.

"I'm sorry, Mr. Noble. Perhaps later when the music restarts?"

"Of course."

"Do you have children that will attend the school here?"

He seemed amused by her question. "No."

"Then you are here to...?"

"To socialize." His smile didn't reach his eyes.

She wasn't sorry when, after another few minutes of light conversation, he bowed and made his way across the room to a cluster of men.

Gemma fanned herself with her hand as she surveyed the families milling about talking and laughing. "My goodness, it is warm in here! I suppose now is the best time for me to say something to everybody." She gave Elizabeth another conspiratorial wink and then walked to the front of the room. She rang her new triangle school bell, the one she would use to start the school day and call the children in with from playtime. The loud clanging made the entire assembly jump in startled surprise.

"Welcome. I want to thank all who have come out tonight. I've enjoyed meeting you and look forward to teaching your children." She went on to talk about the first day of school and what the children would need. Then she introduced Elizabeth, explaining about the supplies sent from La Playa. "Now, if I could request two strong men to help fix the slate on the wall, my dreams will be fulfilled and we can get back to celebrating."

Immediately five men—three of them near Gemma's age—surged toward her.

Flustered momentarily, she quickly took command and had them positioning the slate to her specifications and then fixing it to the wall with wooden brackets. One young man asked her to dance the next dance and she stood talking to him and his family while they waited for the fiddler to start up again.

Elizabeth watched from the back of the room and a sense of well-being came over her. As more parents stepped forward to introduce their children to Gemma and monopolize her time, Elizabeth's worries were put to rest. Come Tuesday when she left, Gemma would be in good hands here on the mountain.

The three Shalbot boys ran past, their pounding footsteps jiggling the table of food as they raced through the door and out into the small meadow to play. Fresh air swirled into the room and made Elizabeth realize she was quite warm by the amount of bodies pressed into the small space. She propped open the door with a chair.

"I wonder how long Miss Starling will remain a 'Miss'?"

Elizabeth looked up from the chair and smiled. Mr. Jolson stood outside on the bottom step. "How good to see you, Mr. Jolson! Did you bring your wife?"

"No and nonsense. She's watchin' our grandbaby this evening so that the rest of the Jolson clan can be here. Baby was a mite fussy cuttin' a tooth. I told her it wouldn't hurt to bring him, but she disagreed. So you can see who won that discussion."

"Well, I'm so glad you could make it. You've had such a big part in making this building ready for the start of school with all the hauling and carrying you helped with." He had never charged a cent, which had surprised her.

He grinned. "If I'm not mistaken, the mountain air has done a world of good for you, Miss Morley."

"I would have to agree. I have gotten to know some wonderful people here—Mrs. Birdwell and Mrs. Kuhn at the bakery. And you."

"You'll likely see us all in church in the morning, too. Even those three wild hooligans who just rushed out of here usually make the service."

Elizabeth smiled. "Won't Gemma have her hands full with them?"

Mr. Jolson surveyed the room. "It looks like the supplies you brought along went over in a big way."

"I'm so glad I could accompany them. To see Gemma's face… It was perfect." But it wasn't

Gemma that had captured her thoughts so completely. Since giving in to her emotions during the night and accepting the fact that she loved Tom, something had changed. In giving up and letting go of the tight rein on her fears, a peace had come to her—perhaps a tad fatalistic, but a peace nonetheless. Whatever was to come would happen and worrying and fretting as she had been these past few days wouldn't help.

"I believe you've changed some while you've been here, Miss Morley. You aren't sounding like the same woman who arrived all prim and proper on Tuesday. Is this what happens on a holiday?" Mr. Jolson raised a friendly, questioning brow.

He had to be teasing. Had she changed that much? In so short a time? "Perhaps…" With all that had happened here in Clear Springs, La Playa seemed so very far away, and the problems with her brother and her mercantile did, too. Now, as she realized she only had two more days here on the mountain, she determined to use them to the fullest.

Tom would be transporting the gold soon. She hoped it would be after she left Clear Springs and traveled back to La Playa. That way, she would be able to tell him a proper goodbye. If the day to transport the gold happened before that, she was afraid he would suddenly be gone, just like before. She wanted that chance to say goodbye.

Beyond Mr. Jolson, a movement drew her gaze. A man tied his horse to the rope line put up for that purpose. No silhouette could be dearer to her—Tom. A weight suddenly lifted from her. He had come, after all.

"Ah…I see now," Mr. Jolson said, his gaze sliding from Tom's tall figure to her. "Looks like Miss Starling isn't the only reason you're looking all sparkly." His mouth quirked up on one side in a lopsided smile. "No need to explain. I'll just step in and help myself to some pie. While I'm at it I'll say my hello to the new teacher."

"You do that. And make sure to get some apple cider. I ran the press myself."

"Will do, miss."

She was already down the steps and halfway to Tom by the time Mr. Jolson finished his sentence.

The night air was cool and crisp. A heavy dew had already gathered on the tall grass and the carpet of fallen oak leaves at her feet. It muffled the sound of her steps as she slipped down the path. A moon, three-quarters full, shone down with enough light to see.

"You came," she said cautiously. "I didn't think you would." Her pulse jumped just seeing him cleaned up, his hair still wet from a recent wash and comb. He had made the effort to shave, something that sent nervous flutters inside as it made her think of how smooth his strong jaw must feel now. At the urge to test the smoothness with her hand, she quickly took hold of her wrist. He certainly was handsome wearing the black pants and dark gray coat she had grown used to seeing him in. He blended into the night except for the flash of his white smile against his tanned skin. "You look…dashing tonight."

A wicked grin crossed his lips. "Wasn't trying for dashing. Just clean. You're looking quite fetching yourself."

She touched the intricate knot Gemma had made of her hair. She had woven an ivory silk ribbon in and out a number of times. "I didn't bring any party clothes with me. Mrs. Birdwell took pity on me and fancied me up."

The look in his blue eyes softened. "You are beautiful tonight."

Flustered, she forgot to thank him for his compliment.

"Before we go in, I want you to know something."

"All right. What is it?"

"I heard all you said yesterday."

She swallowed. "Yes?"

"And I think I understand."

She nodded, unable to look at him. She'd been so embarrassed after revealing all that. She truly hadn't expected to see him again. She knew men shied away from anything emotional—especially female histrionics. "Let's not speak of it again."

He studied her for a moment. "All right. For now."

"Perhaps we should go in so you can say hello to Miss Starling," she said, hoping to get on a more comfortable footing. "This is her party, after all.

He offered his arm.

The action reminded her pleasantly of the days he was wearing a uniform and would escort her places—to a military function or the pier. Sighing just a little, feeling as though she was "coming home," she slipped her hand through the crook of his elbow and let him escort her up the path toward the schoolhouse.

"Sheriff show up?"

"I've never been introduced to him to know who he is."

Tom gave a spare smile. "Good. Wouldn't want him elbowing in for a dance."

She pulled back and stopped right there on the steps. He sounded so much like the man she used to know with that remark she had to ask, "What are you up to, Tom?"

"Just trying to make one of our last evenings together a memorable one."

The reminder that soon they would be parted again hung in the air between them. The gold transfer must be happening in the next few days. Then he would be out of her life again.

"Do you know when?" she asked.

He nodded. "But I can't say."

At the phrase he'd used before that had irritated her so much, she smiled softly and shook her head. "I'm worried."

"No need to be. I've done this before."

"Knowing that doesn't help."

"I'll be all right."

She would have argued that he couldn't know that. Too many things that he might not count on could alter the situation. However, she didn't want this to be a night of worry and fear. Inside she felt a wave of pride for him swell. "You are a brave man, Mr. Barrington."

"Just doing my part." He tucked her hand around his arm. "We'll just enjoy each other this evening. How's that?"

"I'd like that."

"All right. And now, I believe I hear a fiddle. I'd like a spin around the room with you, Miss Morley."

Enchanted, Elizabeth felt a deep contentment as she entered the building. They stopped at the table laden with dessert and drinks so that Tom could say hello to Gemma. Gemma couldn't keep from beaming at them both. Now that Tom had shown up as she predicted, Elizabeth knew she'd probably hear "I told you so" a number of times before she went to bed later that night.

As Mr. Sykes played the first strains of "Down by the River," Tom led her to the small dance area and took her in his strong arms. She placed her hand on his shoulder and felt the muscle move beneath his vest and shirt as they began to dance. Something had happened between yesterday and now. She'd given it a lot of thought in the hours between. He'd said so much…trusted her with so much…that finally she felt like she understood him. Maybe even trusted him a little.

He squeezed her hand and then a second later turned awkwardly, his boot coming down on her toes. Immediately he drew his foot back, stumbling almost imperceptibly. His jaw tightened. "Guess I'm a bit rusty."

She was pretty sure it was more than that. It had been the leg he favored. "You could blame it on that injury."

He snorted softly. "Wouldn't give Hodges the satisfaction."

Tom pulled her close to avoid bumping into Gemma and that young man who had corralled her for a dance earlier. A few steps, and he released her back to a more socially acceptable distance between them. His eyes twinkled and, looking at him, she wondered where the line was drawn between loving someone a little and loving them completely. She needed to watch for that line because she was in danger of crossing it and she mustn't do that. Ever. She would enjoy this moment with him, guard any part of herself that would hope for more and say goodbye to him when the time came. Just like he said… she would make this night a memorable one.

"Do you remember the dance on the pier when you were a soldier?" she asked.

"The Fourth of July." He spoke in a smooth,

low baritone. "Every soldier there wanted to dance with you. I had to promise them favors to keep them away. A bootlace here, a new bandanna there."

She giggled. "I very much doubt that." And then she sighed, remembering the flash of fireworks. "It was a magical night."

"It was at that." The look in his eyes said he remembered the magic, too, and maybe more as his gaze dropped to her lips. "Elizabeth. You are good for me. Every time I see you I am struck by your grace. You make me realize why I put up with the low scum in my life. I couldn't bear having any one of them come near you or hurt you. But lately—" his mouth quirked up on one side "—a lot lately… I wonder what our lives would have been like if things had worked out differently."

"So do I," she whispered softly as the song came to an end, nearly undone by what he'd said. His words washed over her like a balm. Her entire body glowed and she wondered if it showed in her eyes. He made her feel…precious.

"Will you do something for me?" He released her hand and stepped back. "When you get back to La Playa, don't do anything you don't want to.

Your brother has done enough. You make your own choices and don't be swayed."

"I've thought of that, too. I've given up too much in the hopes we would grow closer and it has never happened. Yes, things will change when I go home."

"Miss Morley? I believe you owe me a dance."

Startled at the deep voice nearby, Elizabeth turned abruptly. The man Gemma had introduced her to earlier stood at her side.

He looked at Tom. "Barrington, right?"

Tom shook his hand. "And you are Mr. Noble."

She didn't want to dance with him, but she had said she would, so she'd best get it over with. "He's right, Tom. Earlier I did say I would dance with him."

Tom's jaw tightened, but he bowed slightly. "Then I suppose you are bound to do it."

The worry seized her that he would slip away while she was with Mr. Noble. Something of it must have shown on her face, because Tom gave her a reassuring look and then stepped back to the edge of the room. The music started up and Elizabeth was glad that it wasn't a waltz or a slow song, but a round dance this time.

Mr. Noble promenaded her around the small

circle and she felt Tom watching her. When she neared his area of the room she glanced at him and noticed his brows were slightly knit, his gaze on Mr. Noble.

"I get the feeling I'm the odd man out here," Mr. Noble said.

Elizabeth hadn't meant to be rude. "I'm sorry. Mr. Barrington is an old friend."

He cocked his head. "I thought he just arrived in town this week. From San Francisco."

The feeling that she might have faltered and said something wrong—information that would contradict what Tom had in place—seized her with a sudden worry. She swallowed and hoped she could amend things. "Yes…from San Francisco. It was my fortune to learn he was visiting here during my short stay."

Mr. Noble smiled serenely at her and continued dancing. When the music stopped he bowed. "I would enjoy another dance. However, I would count it brutish of myself to monopolize your time when your old friend is here. Thank you for the dance, my dear."

"Thank you, Mr. Noble." She curtsied…and then turned around, looking for Tom.

He wasn't in the room.

She dashed outside. His horse still stood with the others. He was here, somewhere.

"Nice dance?" His voice came from the shadows.

She spun around, and could barely make out his outline near the storage shed. "You are a much better dancer." She walked toward him.

"Good." He grasped her hand and pulled her farther into the shadow of the shed and then closer, right up against his chest.

She gasped, her mouth dropping open.

"I hate to share." He claimed her, descending with a swift, passionate melding of his lips to hers that left no doubt that he desired her. Her pulse raced. Every nerve ending in her body was electrified, telegraphing signals of sheer pleasure through her. His tongue, his mouth, demanded her attention, robbing her lungs of breath and legs of strength as he kissed her mouth, then her cheeks, and then her brow. Everywhere his lips touched, her skin tingled.

She responded kiss for kiss, a growing need for him consuming her. It was then an urgency that exploded through them both. He slipped one hand to the back of her neck, drawing her closer than she thought was possible. She started to sink, her knees buckling, and suddenly felt his other hand supporting her at the small of her back. As if sensing her need for air, and perhaps his, too, he pulled back and rained quick desperate kisses down her neck and then he buried his face between her ear and her shoulder.

She let out a shuddering breath. "Oh, my…"

She felt flushed from the roots of her hair to the tips of her toes. Her entire body thrummed with energy. "Oh. My."

He drew back and a shaft of moonlight fell on him. He looked at her with such intense longing in his eyes that she was once more robbed of breath. Her knees again felt weak…but for a much different reason than before. Surrendering wasn't an option. She couldn't give him that part of her heart. She couldn't…

She closed her eyes.

He centered his mouth on hers, drawing her last breath into him, kissing her gently this time. Gently…with his soft lips…leaving no doubt in her mind that to him, at this moment, she was precious and cherished.

When he finally pulled away the stars were blurred. An uneasy feeling, a vague warning inside, gripped her. "You're going tonight…or tomorrow. That's why you are here."

He pressed his lips together. "Ever think I might have come to kiss you good and proper?"

She wouldn't be misled. "I think you fooled them at the dance. But just now…the way you are acting…" She dragged in a shuddering breath and let it out. "I can tell."

"If something should happen, Sam knows…"

She slipped her hand over his mouth, not wanting to hear the rest. If anything should happen to him she would never speak to Sam again for putting him in such a position! "Nothing is going to happen to you."

He took hold of her hands in his and brought them to his chest—cradling them. His blue gaze searched her face, her eyes. "I've been doing some thinking lately—actually a lot of thinking. I've had the feeling since seeing you again that you waited for me. Maybe that's not the case. Maybe there have been other men in your life but they couldn't win your heart. Maybe I'm just one of many. I don't know…" His voice trailed off. He swallowed.

"The fact is, I don't want to chance losing you a second time. After this job…I'd like to come back to La Playa. I'd like to court you proper—" he swallowed "—see where things go from here."

It was so much what she had hoped for and

yet so unexpected. "Are...are you making a promise?"

"I am. If you think there's a chance you could abide it—considering what you said yesterday."

She wanted to believe him, but she couldn't silence the warning deep inside. She was afraid. "I wish you would go back to La Playa now, forget this dangerous assignment and let somebody else handle it."

"I can't, Elizabeth. I have to finish this job. I have to prove I can do it—for myself, for Cranston and for Sam. If I don't I will regret it the rest of my life." He looked away for a moment and then met her eyes once more. "And I won't be any good to you."

She blinked back tears of frustration and yearning all at once. She didn't suppose he'd be the man she loved if he felt different about it. It was that part that made him who he was—the part that spoke to his honor. She straightened her spine. "I understand now. Really, I do. However, remember you just gave your word to me. I expect you to honor it."

A slow smile grew on his handsome face. "That sounds suspiciously like a yes on your part, Miss Morley."

He swept off his Stetson and kissed her again like a man who was trying to make up for four years of missed chances, so long and hard that she finally had to push on him in order to catch a breath. Her lips felt swollen, unused to all the attention.

She held him at arm's length as it registered what he'd said. "One of many? Do you think I allow just anyone to kiss me?"

He grinned. "Just got that, huh? No insult intended."

A sigh escaped. "Be careful, Tom. Please… be careful."

Nodding slowly, his blue eyes serious, he said, "I had best return you to the party. Miss Starling will be wondering where you are." One more kiss, tender and brief, and he walked her to the steps of the schoolhouse.

"Be seeing you," she said, a catch in her voice.

He tipped the brim of his Stetson, turned and headed down the path to his horse.

Her heart overflowed with happiness. He'd promised to return. A voice inside cautioned her to be careful. She would, of course…tomorrow. For tonight, she'd enjoy feeling special… and wanted…and very, very desired.

It was getting late. People were saying their goodbyes and gathering their sleepy children into buggies and wagons as Elizabeth began cleaning things up so that Gemma would have a classroom ready for Monday. It wasn't long before Gil Jolson drove a tired group of partyers back into town.

"Such a success!" Gemma whispered happily to her just before turning into bed.

Keyed up from the party and all that had happened, Elizabeth tried in vain to sleep. She hadn't told Gemma about all Tom had said. Gemma had been too busy saying "I told you so" about Tom showing up in the first place. In the morning Elizabeth would let her know, but she was near to bursting with the need to share it. She tossed and turned and then rose again to pace within her small room. She slept for a while and then was restless again toward morning, so decided to forgo the chamber pot and step outside to the outhouse and a breath of fresh air.

The clouds had blown east and the stars splashed across the sky in a twinkling display of the heavens. She paused to gaze at them, wondering at the same time where Tom was just then. Was he asleep? Or already at his task of seeing the gold down the mountain. She breathed a quick prayer for his safety and then tiptoed through the garden to the outhouse.

It was on her way back to the kitchen door

that a small noise behind her caught her attention—likely a raccoon at this time of early morning. She quickened her steps, anyway, her heart rate increasing with each step.

Then a low chuckle sent shivers through her.

"Oh, no, you don't. You are my insurance, little lady."

A sudden rush of movement and then a hand clamped over her mouth and another around her waist. She struggled, trying to scream.

"Hold her, will ya?" another man grated, stuffing a cloth into her mouth.

She struggled harder, but her long nightgown wrapped frustratingly around her, tangling through her legs and making escape impossible. Although she tried to scream, no sound emerged, blocked completely by the rag.

A bag slipped over her head, blocking out the faint shadows and encasing her in darkness.

Suddenly, she found herself hauled up onto a horse, and an arm with an iron grip around her held her tight against the rock-hard form of a man.

Chapter Fourteen

U p before daybreak, Tom was raring to go and get the job done. When he'd made that promise last night to Elizabeth, everything had finally slipped into place like a saddle that molded perfectly to a horse and to the rider. It was as if he had come full circle back to where he'd started and just maybe…where he belonged. And somehow that included Elizabeth. A change was coming and he felt ready for it. A change was definitely coming…

His thoughts jumped ahead to the task of safely moving the gold. His fingers itched to get started. It seemed daylight was taking its own sweet time coming. He recognized the day for what it would be—his chance to reconcile his past. Nothing would bring Cranston back, but in the eyes of the Fursts…and in his own eyes… he'd have done something to put things right.

He dressed with care, stocking extra bullets in his gun belt and pockets. He headed to the livery, his boots crunching through the frost on the tall grass along the road. The sky had lightened just enough for him to start seeing the silhouettes of the tall pines and oaks beyond the row of buildings on the main road. Crisp, cool air filled his lungs.

He was ready.

He ducked into the livery and saddled the Major quickly and quietly. Sheriff Parker was already there waiting for him and held out a package.

"Roast beef sandwich. Figured you might want something to eat about noon."

"You're right. Too keyed up this morning." He took the sandwich and tucked it into his saddlebag. "Thanks."

"I'll look forward to getting a wire when you reach the halfway station."

"Will do. Thanks for all your help, Sheriff." He shook hands with the man. "Hope to see you again." He led the Major out a small back doorway, mounted and headed out of town for the Palisade Mine.

When he arrived the mine supervisor had just finished loading the last of the rocks into the lockbox on the Wells Fargo stagecoach—the decoy that would take the northern stage route into San Diego. The man was sweating despite the temperature being in the forties. He locked the box and gave the key to the driver. "Keep your eyes open. Good luck to you."

The driver snapped the reins and drove off, guarded on all sides by three other riders.

Tom walked over to the short wagon. The gold ore had already been loaded early that morning by lamplight. He had decided when he met Chet that the young man would drive since he'd already had some experience. He shook hands with him and pointed out the rifle that would be stored at his feet. Then he turned to shake hands with the two other guards, Webster and Donner.

"This won't be a picnic. We may have company—matter of fact, I'm expecting it—so be alert. We'll move out in ten minutes."

An hour later and they were well on their way and settling into the fact that it was going to be a long, nerve-racking ride. He was satisfied so far with his ability to keep thoughts of Elizabeth at bay and concentrate on his surroundings. Three days of sun had dried the road well enough to traverse it without worrying about too many ruts.

He urged the Major down a sandy wash. Yesterday's rain had livened up the creek, turning it from barely a trickle to shin-deep in water and mud. It paralleled the road for two hundred yards or so, cutting deep into the earth and producing steep banks with tree roots partially exposed and snarled like snakes. A man could hide here—and be close enough to jump out at the wagon. Trouble was, the man would have a disadvantage, too—being below the level of their prey.

Tom motioned to Webster, the guard riding on the far side of the wagon, to move in closer. He had straggled behind a bit, looking wary and ill at ease. He looked to be much older than Tom but maybe that was just the amount of gray in his hair and the fact his shoulders were already stooped from working in the mine tunnel for hours on end. He had mentioned it was good to get out into the fresh air for a change. His expertise was dynamite, but he was a decent shot with a handgun.

A Stellar jay cawed and swooped over his head as if to warn him to keep alert. They were heading into a meadow, the last open area until they reached the valley below.

"I sure will be glad to have this day behind me," Chet said from his wagon seat. "My nerves are all a'jumpin' inside. The sheriff said you done this type of work before. Are your nerves a'jumpin', too?"

Tom nodded. He liked Chet. Of the four of them guarding the gold, next to himself, Chet was probably the strongest. It sounded as though he'd had a hard life—and a lot of manual labor—since he'd been fourteen and on his own, looking after his younger brother, the whiny kid he'd seen at the saloon.

"Do you ever get used to it?"

"It gets easier, but no, that feeling in your gut never goes completely away. Which is good. It keeps you sharp."

They approached a lone scrub oak. He checked out the branches for anyone that might be hiding as they passed by.

"You seem awfully sure we are going to get waylaid," Chet said, watching him for a moment. "Sure hope you are wrong."

"Me, too." He motioned with a nod of his head that the likely place was up ahead and not too far. Then put a finger to his lips for Chet to keep quiet now. He had an idea where things might blow up.

Chet fell silent as the road curved toward the river and the vegetation thickened. Oak trees and a few scruffy pines bordered the stream. The sound of water splashing over boulders grew louder.

They rounded the bend.

Jimmy Farnsworth stood in the center of the road, his hands clamped tight around a rifle that he had pointed right at them. "Throw down!" he said in a slight sharp voice.

"Jimmy!" Chet cried out. "What are you doing?"

"Keep moving!" Tom yelled, drawing his gun. The look of uncertainty in Jimmy's eyes told him the boy didn't have the guts to shoot his own brother. 'Course that didn't mean Tom or the other guards might not take a bullet, but he hoped by charging ahead with the wagon, the boy would jump out of the way rather than risk getting run over.

"Don't shoot him!" Chet cried, pulling back on the reins.

But in that moment, Donner leaped from his horse across to the wagon and slammed his rifle butt into Chet's face. Chet yowled, holding his nose as blood spurted everywhere. He staggered backward and up against Donner, who shoved him off the wagon into the tall weeds by the roadside. Donner swung his rifle around to aim at Tom.

Tom squeezed the trigger on his Colt. Donner's body jerked backward and toppled from the wagon. "Watch out for the boy!" Tom yelled at Webster and reined his horse over to the wagon. He jumped on and grabbed the reins, preparing to snap them hard and get the gold out of there.

"Hold it!" a familiar gravelly voice yelled from behind him. "Got you in my sights, Barrington, and you know I won't mind pulling this trigger one bit. Drop your gun."

Tom glanced around for Webster and realized he wasn't on his horse any longer, but lay in a heap on the ground, his arms caught tight to his side by a bola, his rifle two yards away. Tom only had a whisper of a chance. With all the ruckus, the mules had stopped and stood before Jimmy, pulling at their traces in an uncoordinated and ineffective restlessness. Tom eyed the rifle he had stored for Chet that lay hidden at his feet. He could get it, if he was quick. Jimmy and Hodges. Just two now...

A twig snapped to Tom's right. Make that

three…and that slim chance vanished like a wisp of smoke.

"Drop it, Barrington. Or you'll be eating dirt like the rest of them." Bart Noble stood twenty feet away, a pistol in each hand, cocked and aimed right at him.

He dropped his Colt on the ground.

"Jimmy! Get the ropes and tie Barrington. While you are at it, get rid of his gun. Then tie up your brother," Hodges said. "I don't think that other guard will be troubling us for a long while. Noble, you start transferring the gold."

Frowning, Jimmy scrambled over to his horse that was tied to a large oak and withdrew a coil of leather cord from his saddlebag. He walked toward Tom, sliding the piece of cord across his palm. "Sorry, mister. No harm meant." Tom thought to grab the boy, but then what? Hodges and Noble wouldn't hesitate to shoot him. And he wouldn't use Jimmy as a shield the way Hodges had that boy on the train. He didn't think that would stop the other two from killing them both and keeping more gold for themselves.

Jimmy pushed Tom on the shoulder only to find Tom was too big for him to manhandle.

Hodge snorted. "Slim. Yes, you," he said when Jimmy looked at him. "Tie him to the wagon." He flicked his gun, indicating Tom should get down.

"You're not going to get away with this." But he climbed down and fumed while Jimmy lashed his wrists to the wagon wheel.

"Sure I am. I already have." His thick lips curled in an ugly smile while his laugh filled the air.

In the grass on the other side of the wagon, Chet stirred. "What are you doing, Jimmy?" he cried out weakly, holding on to his head.

"Getting our share back, that's all." Jimmy sounded nervous.

"Not this way. This ain't the way to go about it." Chet tried to stand, found he couldn't keep his balance and plunked back down.

"No one is gonna get hurt here," Jimmy said. "But for once you gotta do what I say."

Hodges snorted. "Till you grow some whiskers no one is going to listen to you, kid." He stepped into the clearing, a Colt .45 in his hand, and walked over to Tom. He tugged on the rope, checking the boy's knot. Satisfied, he trained his gun on Chet. "I'll keep an eye on your dear brother. You wouldn't have the guts to put a bullet in him if we needed you to. Get him tied up and make it as good as Barrington's here."

Jimmy nodded and headed for his brother.

Chet looked over at Tom. The young man looked like he was itching to make a play. He was bigger and heavier than Jimmy and that might help but with his face battered and his balance off he was in no condition to do anything. With barely a noticeable movement, Tom shook his head in warning. He wasn't going to have anyone else hurt if he had anything to say about it. They'd figure things out after Hodges took off. He worked his bindings, trying to loosen them.

"You don't know who you're dealing with here, Jimmy," Chet said, frustration coating his voice.

"I know plenty. Just keep quiet and you won't be hurt."

"How can I keep quiet knowing you helped do this? You're an outlaw now. What would Pa think?"

"I can't even remember Pa no more. Just hush."

"Quit your kissin'," Hodges sneered. "We don't have all day." He called over his shoulder to Noble. "How's that going?"

In answer, Noble led his horse and the horse Donner had been riding over to the wagon and tied them to the railing. He grabbed two bags of gold and stuffed it into the saddlebags. Then two more. He kept stuffing the saddlebags with gold until they were full.

"Guess it did bother you, after all," Tom said, addressing him for the first time. "Working for peanuts when it'd be so easy to take someone else's hard-made fortune."

"Barrington, Barrington," Noble said smoothly as he kept working. "You know nothing about me. The mines are nearly played out. There's no more fortune to be made in Clear Springs…and I need to put a little aside to get me by in my old age." He finished his job and walked off to lead the other horses to the wagon.

Five minutes later he was done. He had separated the bags of ore between the six saddlebags and was tying the last one closed. "All loaded up with as much as we can carry. Had to use your horse, Barrington, but we left you the mules." He chuckled. "A man without a horse…well… you know the saying."

Chet suddenly rushed toward Hodges. Before he had gone four steps, Hodges whipped up his gun and fired, the bullet whizzing across the clearing.

The young man jerked, his face contorting with shock and pain as he fell to his knees on the ground. Blood spread over his left shoulder and he fell forward onto his face.

"No! You promised!" Jimmy cried out.

"You'll learn the only promises I keep are the ones I make to myself. Calm yourself before I really get mad. That'll teach you to do it right next time when I tell you to tie somebody up. Now mount up."

Jimmy looked forlornly at his brother but he did as he was told.

"About Miss Morley."

On hearing Elizabeth's name, Tom quit working at the cords at his wrists. A cold fear congealed in his gut. He focused on Hodges, sure he wouldn't like what he was about to hear. "What about her?"

"Now, she'll be safe as long as you don't follow us. Should last one more day where she is. Stay smart for her sake and don't come after us. I think you'll agree it is more important you find her before her water runs out or a wild animal gets her."

She was alive—for now, he realized with relief. But where? Likely she was scared to death the way it sounded and all because of him. He looked from Hodges to Noble as Noble rode up holding the reins of three horses. "This was your idea."

He shrugged. "All I did was dance with the lady…and let Jack here know about her. He took it from there."

Hodges mounted his horse and grabbed the reins of Tom's horse. "Yep. I'd say we make a decent team, Noble. By the way, that decoy wagon was a stupid idea, Barrington. You weren't with it, so I knew the gold wasn't there. There's no way you would guard a bunch of rocks."

Tom gritted his teeth and kept working at the cords binding him. He paid little heed to Hodges. The man was getting downright verbose since everything was going so well for him.

"I'm sure someone will wander by in a day or two. Just hope the mountain lions don't get hungry and find you first, especially now that there's blood all over the place." He chuckled, then set his heels to his horse's flanks and the three of them took off in a jumble of hooves and dust.

Tom struggled with the leather cord, trying to stretch it enough to slip his hands free. Jimmy might be young and foolish, but he could sure tie a strong knot. At least he hadn't thought to tie Tom's hands behind his back. If he had there'd be no chance of getting free. This way, facing the wheel, he might have a chance.

He had figured they would get ambushed— that was a given. No way around it. But he had wanted to be able to chase right after them. Take them out one at a time. That couldn't happen now. He had to get Chet and Webster to a doctor and he had to find Elizabeth. She must be somewhere in Clear Springs or the surrounding area.

Think! he badgered himself. He had to free himself! This was just what he had not wanted to happen—someone getting hurt because of him. He looked across the road at Chet. And then at Webster lying in the grass. Fine mess he'd made.

"Chet! You alive?" He thought he saw the boy's fingers move slightly. "You hang in there. I'll be there in a minute. Hang on now."

He struggled at the cord binding his wrists again. Pulling, stretching… This time, the cord caught on a nail head. If he could just maneuver a bit, get the knot over the nail…

It took him at least twenty more minutes. Finally the thin leather cord stretched enough on the nail head to slip over his hands. His wrists were bloodied and burning, but he was finally free.

He stumbled over to the boy and rolled him

over and pressed his ear against the boy's chest. Chet's heart thumped, solid but rapid. The blood had congealed on his shirt. He had to get the boy to a doctor and get him patched up.

Carefully he pulled and tugged him over his shoulder and then strode to the wagon. He stumbled once, the extra weight too much for his bum leg, but then he was rewarded with a soft "Oomph" when Chet landed in the wagon bed and stirred. He let out a weak growl. "I'm madder than a Tijuana bull at the bull ring. My brother will have some explaining to do when I catch up to him."

Tom breathed a sigh of relief. "Glad you're back with me. You had me worried."

"Takes more than one bullet to get me," Chet said. "You, too, I 'spect. How's Webster?"

Tom strode over and checked Webster for injuries. A goose-egg knot had formed to the back of his head; other than that he just appeared to have the wind knocked out of him good.

"Sorry lot we are," Chet said. He shook his head, disgusted with himself and likely his brother. "They sure got the drop on us."

Tom helped Webster into the wagon and covered the both of them with the tarp that had hidden the gold. There were still a few bags of ore left that the men hadn't been able to carry, but they had the majority of it. He searched the river area for his gun and found it among the grass and stones on the bank. With frustration gnawing at him, Tom climbed up onto the wagon seat, snapped the reins and turned the mules back toward Clear Springs and the doctor's house.

He had to find Elizabeth. Hodges had been right about that. Elizabeth was a heck of a lot more important than any gold. A lot more important than any job. There was no competition at all. He loved her. He loved her and he meant to tell her that, too—the minute he found her. He only hoped he could find her fast. After that he had to get to Hodges before the man crossed the border. Once they made it to Mexico he would have a dickens of a time finding them.

They rode in silence for a while. The grade was uphill, a pull for the mules, so the going was slower than he liked. He should be able to figure out where Hodges had taken Elizabeth. At least the general location. In the middle of all that had happened and all that was said there should have been a clue somewhere. He reviewed all that Hodges had said and replayed the scene over in his mind, thinking back to the people he'd talked to that week—the mine owners, Noble, Miss Starling. Somewhere in there was the answer. Somewhere just beyond his grasp.

The wagon jolted going over a deep rut.

"Think you could miss some of those, mister?" Chet asked, his voice weak. "My arm about fell off with that one."

"I'll give it my best," Tom said, but he didn't slow down. As the ground leveled off he flicked the reins, urging the mules to move faster. He glanced back. Kid sure was pale. Sweat beaded on his upper lip.

"I can't believe Jimmy was in on this. Breaks my heart."

"You should stay quiet," Tom said. "Rest."

"He was mad about everything. Thinks I stole his girl when I didn't. She weren't too particular about her gentlemen friends as long as they could buy her nice things—which I didn't. It's just when Jimmy's money ran out, so did she."

Tom remembered the boy's whining at the saloon.

"Then we lost that money in the mine. Fills with water when it rains hard. Stupid to buy it. Noble skunked us good."

They rode on for a few minutes before Chet spoke again. "Guess Donner ratted us out."

"He paid for it."

"He sure did," Chet said, and finally quit talking.

Chapter Fifteen

Tom pulled the mules and wagon to a stop in front of Doc Palmer's house and bounded up the walkway to bang on the door. By the time a woman opened the door, Sheriff Parker had seen them arrive back in town and was striding down the road from the jail. He took one look in the wagon, dropped the end of it and jumped in. Grabbing Chet under the arms, he dragged him out until Tom could grab his legs. Together they lifted him and made their way into the doctor's house.

The small dining room had been transformed into an exam room. The hutch, instead of holding dishes, was stacked with bandages and unguents and instruments. And instead of a dining table, a table for examinations stood in the center of the room. They deposited Chet right there.

Webster was sitting up on the end of the wagon when Tom walked back outside.

"Tried to make it under my own steam. Still feeling a mite poorly."

Tom put his shoulder under the man's arm and helped him into the house and into a side room where the doctor kept an extra bed. Tom explained what had happened with each man as best he could and then left them in the doctor's care and walked into the parlor to speak with Sheriff Parker.

"The new teacher stopped by," he said immediately. "I've searched for Miss Morley at the school and asked around town for any word on her. People say the only one she danced with last night other than you was Bart Noble. I checked his place, but he hasn't been around."

Tom grimaced. "Noble is with Hodges."

Parker whistled. "Never liked that man so the change of occupation is not too surprising. What more can you tell me. How many were there?"

"Four all together. Donner was on the inside. That's how they knew the day and time. They knew about the decoy, too."

"Palisade supervisor won't like hearing any of that. Might cost him his job. Who was the fourth?"

"Jimmy Farnsworth."

Parker raised his brows slightly and tipped his head toward the exam room. "Tough break."

"Hodges said he left Elizabeth with enough water for a day. Gives me the feeling she's sheltered somehow."

"So he didn't have her with him. I don't know if that is for the better or not. The temperature dropped down to forty last night and it's not much warmer now.

"I'm going after them, but first I intend to find Elizabeth."

The doctor walked into the parlor, wiping his hands with a towel. "He's asking for you, Barrington. He's got a broken clavicle. Bullet is out. He has had laudanum to help with the pain. Should be nodding off soon."

"What about Webster?"

"He's drifting in and out of consciousness. We'll keep an eye on him and alert his family."

"Thank you, Doctor." Tom headed back into the small exam room.

Farnsworth was stretched out on the table. What little color he'd had in his face was gone. His shoulder sported a bulging bandage that included his arm and his neck. Kind of reminded Tom of a trussed-up turkey. Farnsworth crooked his finger. Speaking took effort, whether from the effects of the laudanum or the pain, Tom wasn't sure.

"My brother ain't too smart, but he's all I got in the world. If you find him, please don't kill him."

"I don't want to kill anyone. Not if I can help it. But I've got to find Miss Morley. You got any ideas?"

Farnsworth shook his head.

Tom had a thought. "Where is that claim of yours?"

"South of town, just over the east ridge."

"I know the area," Parker said, standing at the door. "There's a shack on the property."

Tom slipped on his hat.

Chet grabbed his sleeve and pulled him close. "I'm thinking I won't see Jimmy again. They won't let him live. Leastways not for long." His face scrunched up as he tried not to snivel.

Tom didn't know what to say to that. He was pretty sure Chet was right. Jimmy would be a liability and by Hodges's way of thinking better dead than a liability. "You've done a good job being his brother. I have a feeling he was in on the robbery last month, too."

"Yeah—been thinkin' that, too."

"He's got to take the consequences for his actions."

"I know. But it ain't easy."

"I'll do what I can to help Jimmy."

Chet twisted his sleeve. "Promise me?"

Tom hesitated. He was making a lot of promises lately. Most of them he was having trouble keeping. "I'll do my best," he finally said. He looked up and realized Parker was listening to the exchange.

"I'll let you know what we find. You just concentrate on healing now. You did a fine job today. Fine job."

Already the boy was drifting off, the pain medicine doing its job. Tom extracted his sleeve from Chet's weakening grip and straightened. "Let's go," he said to Parker.

Elizabeth watched the muted light from the airshaft overhead grow dim. Soon it would be gone. When that happened, when the last rays seeped from the tunnel, her chance of escape or rescue would cease. She swallowed, her throat dry and burning from the constant screaming and yelling she'd done.

A young coyote watched her from the opposite wall, its gold eyes gleaming. After Elizabeth had been left there a few hours, the beast had limped into the short mine tunnel baring its teeth and growling. The one time it came close and nipped at her, she screamed and kicked it hard with the heel of her slipper. After that, wary and hurt, it crouched down and finally settled, tending and licking its leg where a dark mass of congealed blood distorted the extremity.

An uneasy truce existed for the moment. How long it would last probably depended on how hungry the animal became. In the dark, and tied like she was, she didn't stand a chance. And if others joined the coyote…that would be it.

Surely Gemma had alerted the sheriff? Surely they were looking for her? But the trouble with that was, Gemma, the sheriff and anyone from town would think she was with those three horrible men and probably far away by now. They wouldn't think to look for her close to town.

Cold and thirsty and tired, her entire body ached. She had lost one of her slippers when Hodges grabbed her and threw her up over his shoulder. Her nightgown, although a thick cotton weave, did little to keep her warm once the dampness had set in. Her wrists were bloodied from the tight rope that held her snug to the handlebar of the mine dump car. After hours of standing, she'd finally lowered herself to the ground, only to have her hands above her. In a matter of minutes, her fingers and arms had started tingling and then numbness had set in, so she rose to stand again. Up. Down. Up.

A tin of water balanced precariously on top of the car's corner. Earlier she had leaned over it to sip some of the water when a silvery worm slithered across its surface. Recoiling, she then noticed another worm, then another with hundreds of tiny feathery legs. After that, she determined that being thirsty was the better choice. Ironically, considering her thirst, she could hear a steady drip, drip, drip coming from farther down the tunnel.

She had refused to cry before, refused to give in to the doubt and fear that crouched and waited for her defenses to be down, just like that coyote. For the better part of the day, anger at her captors had fueled her strength, but now with the light waning, she allowed the tears to fall. She was so tired. So very tired. And cold. And thirsty. All she wanted was for one second to feel Tom's big strong arms wrapped around her, protecting her, keeping out the cold and the dark. Over and over in her mind she recalled dancing with him and how he looked only at her and made her feel so precious. What if she never saw him again? What if she never got out of here? What if she never got the chance to tell him that she loved him?

At the sound of her soft sobbing, the coyote's large ears flicked forward. "My, what big ears you have…" she said, aware by the singsong quality of her voice that she was getting loopy.

The coyote raised its head and looked right at her. "My, what a big nose…" She didn't think she could say the rest. Just like in the fairy tale, the beast might pounce when she got to its teeth and that was too frightening to imagine.

Its ears flicked back.

Then it stood and hobbled around to face the entrance to the tunnel.

Had it heard something? Friend or foe? Good or bad? She held her breath and listened. Hard. A silent incoherent prayer began to form on her lips—please, please, please…

"Elizabeth! Elizabeth!"

"Tom!" she screamed, the sound emerging from her dry throat as barely a whisper. "I'm here! I'm here!"

"I'm on my way!"

The coyote circled once, then cowered back against the wall. Elizabeth felt a moment of compassion for it. Here she'd expected its friends to show up first, not hers.

"Elizabeth?"

"I'm here! Oh! I'm here, Tom. Please… hurry!" Tears slipped down her cheeks, but this time they were of joy and overflowing gratitude. Relief rushed through her in a shimmery wave. It would be all right. She would be all right. Tom was coming for her. Her Tom.

"Keep talking. I'm almost there."

She had never loved the sound of his deep voice more than at that moment.

A low, feral growl threatened from the shadows and she realized the beast had moved and now crouched on the other side of the mine car, scared and quivering.

Footsteps scuffing hard-packed dirt came closer. "Be careful! There's a coyote in here with me. It is injured, but it might attack if it feels threatened."

And suddenly he was there, a huge, dark silhouette in the gray bend of the tunnel. He stopped short when he saw her. Then he searched for the coyote.

"It's on the other side of the mine car. I think it's scared more than anything."

"It should be if it thinks to harm you." He

stepped toward her and hugged her tightly. His warmth enveloped her, chasing away the horror of the past thirteen hours. Pulling back, he brushed away the loose hair from her face and then kissed her on her dry cracked lips. "Thank God you are all right."

A silver knife flashed in his hand and the ropes fell away. "Come on. Let's get out of here. You first," he said, keeping an eye on the coyote. Another low growl sounded, but it did not seem as threatening as before.

"I almost feel sorry for it," she said, stumbling toward the entrance, her feet aching with every step on the uneven ground. "Almost. If it hadn't been hurt…or there had been more than one…"

She was trying to walk, but her legs were so tired…so very tired. She stumbled again, and she felt his strong grip on her arm supporting her.

"You're doing fine."

As soon as the tunnel widened enough for the both of them to stand together, he pulled her close again. "You're freezing!" He removed his leather jacket and dropped it over her shoulders. Immediately the warmth from his body began to seep into her skin. She snuggled farther into the coat. Then he scooped her up in his arms and carried her.

"Parker, we're on our way," Tom called out. He moved forward and for a moment the darkness enclosed them completely. He stumbled once and tightened his grip on her. "Almost there."

She marveled that, even with his old injury and the favoring of his leg, he had a surer gait than her. Why, everything about him was big and strong and secure.

"Tom? Did they get the gold?"

He nodded. Silent.

They stumbled out into the dusk and she let out a relieved sigh.

A tall man stepped forward. The first thing she noticed about him beside his blond burly body was the star on his vest.

"This is Craig Parker, the sheriff in Clear Springs."

"Glad to see you are all in one piece, Miss Morley."

She looked about at the unfamiliar terrain. A huge hill rose in front of her studded with pines. "How did you find me? How did you know where to look?"

"You can thank one of your captors for that—

Jimmy," Parker said. "I'll explain on the ride back to town. I know your friend Miss Starling is having a time worrying about you. Molly Birdwell, too."

When she tilted her head to look up at the sheriff, she suddenly felt Tom's hand on her chin. He turned her face to the dying light, studying her. "They hit you?"

Gingerly, she touched her jaw. It was tender, achy. She hadn't noticed it hurting until just now. "They were clumsy and I wasn't a model captive."

A furrow formed between Tom's brows, his expression darkening. "They'll pay," he said, his voice low and threatening.

She'd never seen this side of him with vengeance sparking in his eyes. She didn't want him going after anybody. She wanted him safe. And with her. "I can't think of that now. All I want is a soft chair, a warm blanket and a fire in the hearth at Molly's. And maybe a cup of hot tea. Just take me back, Tom. I need to see Gemma and let her know I am all right."

He nodded. Then he looked at Parker.

"You won't get far in the dark," the sheriff said. "I'll go with you in the morning."

"They could be in Mexico by then."

A sinking sensation hit her stomach. He couldn't mean to chase after those men tonight, could he? "Tom. It's too dangerous. Please… stay with me."

"I can't. I have to go after the gold. I have to finish this job."

"Why did they do this to me? What did it accomplish?"

"Hodges wanted me preoccupied. It worked. I couldn't do a thing until I knew you were safe."

"Can't you wait until morning, then? Go together?" Her eyes burned suddenly. He would leave her and she might never see him again.

He stepped closer, turning her away from the sheriff. "No. It has to be now. Elizabeth, I told you I'd come back. I gave you my word last night."

"I won't be here. I'm going home," she said, weary in every bone in her body. "I've had more than enough of my holiday. Two kidnappings in one week is two too many!"

Sheriff Parker raised his brows. "Two?"

Tom grinned. He caught hold of her messy, loose braid and gave it a gentle tug. "You do that if you want but I'll find you, Elizabeth. I'll always find you. Didn't I today?"

She nodded and sniffed. The things he said

made her feel so cared for and special, but her heart would break beyond repair if something happened to him. She hated feeling this way. So…so fragile. It must be the ordeal she'd just been through. But she couldn't send him off like this…half-weepy. With that thought she squared her shoulders. "Then go, Tom. I know you can catch him. You are smarter than he will ever be. And braver than anybody I've ever met before."

"You know all that, huh?" he said gruffly.

"I've known it for years. And I know you can do this." There was such pride in her voice. Surely he heard it? Surely…

"Then you'll wait for me?" He watched her face.

Her breathing ceased. "What?"

"I asked you to wait for me."

"Why?"

He smiled. "Because you love me."

She pressed her eyes closed. She'd never said the words—not out loud, not to him. But he knew, anyway.

His smile grew into a grin.

"That doesn't mean I'll wait. Not again."

"Well, then," he said, with his lips mere inches away. "Wait because I love you and I'm asking you to."

Caught in his spell, she couldn't escape. No, that wasn't so…she didn't *want* to escape the tender kiss he gave her. Her knees might have wobbled a bit as he pulled away.

"Trust me," he whispered against her lips.

Slowly she shrugged from his jacket and folded it over once, hugging it to her before handing it back to him. "I do. All right, Tom Barrington. I'll wait. You stole my heart four years ago and you have it still. All of it."

Something shifted in his gaze. Tenderness crept in.

"Have a care for it," she pleaded in a whisper.

"I promise." He kissed her once more and slipped on his jacket. Then he swung up on his horse and galloped after the thieves.

The moment Tom disappeared over the ridge, Sheriff Parker removed his coat and passed it to her. "Sorry I didn't think to bring a blanket, miss."

"Thank you, Sheriff. Do you think Tom will be all right?"

"No way of knowing. But he's smart. And he's done this before. I think he has a better than average chance."

"I wish he hadn't gone," she admitted, her voice trembling.

He pressed his lips together. It was obvious he had something to say.

"You don't agree with me."

"No, miss. I don't. This is personal between him and Jack Hodges. Barrington would always be looking over his shoulder—and worried about you, too—if he let Hodges get the upper hand. That's no way to live. He knows that."

"Oh. I hadn't realized he was thinking about all that."

"Like I said, Barrington knows what he's doing."

He helped her up on his horse and seated himself behind her for the short ride back to town.

At Molly's, he walked her to the door. "You get some rest now. I'll catch up to Tom in the morning. From there it will be only a matter of a few days until you see us both."

"Thank you, again. I feel better knowing you are going to be there with him."

The door swung open and Mrs. Birdwell stood there, wiping her hands on her apron. "Land sakes, dear! We've been worried sick. Come in, come in. I'll put the kettle on for tea and you can tell us all about what happened."

"Is she here?" Gemma rushed in from the kitchen and threw her arms around Elizabeth. "I've been beside myself with worry. You're all right? What happened?"

"I'm fine, thanks to Tom and the sheriff here," Elizabeth said in answer.

Gemma turned to the sheriff. "I can't thank you enough, Sheriff. Won't you come in?" She opened the door wider.

Sheriff Parker shook his head. "Some other time. Ladies." He tipped his Stetson and strode back to his horse.

"What a nice man," Gemma murmured, watching him go.

"He's catching up with Tom in the morning. They are going after the men who kidnapped me and…" She hesitated for a moment, wondering whether to tell Gemma about the gold.

Gemma's eyes widened, sensing that there was more to the story. "You must tell me everything."

"I will. But for now I'd surely like a cup of tea and something to eat."

Two hours later, her stomach full of Mrs. Birdwell's chicken and dumpling soup, and her head nodding with drowsiness, Elizabeth announced she simply must go to bed.

"I have school in the morning," Gemma said, rising from her chair and taking the tray from Elizabeth's lap. "Sleep in as late as you like."

Elizabeth followed her to the kitchen and waited while she set the tray down. "I hope your first day is everything you wished for. I'll come toward the end of the afternoon and accompany you back here. I will want to hear all about your day."

They walked down the short hall and Gemma paused just outside Elizabeth's door. "Won't you stay longer? Another day or so in case Tom returns?"

Elizabeth shook her head. "I'm going home. It's time. This had been a wonderful visit."

Gemma raised one brow.

"Well, maybe not all of it…but mostly. I must face whatever it is that Terrance and the bank have in store for me. If it means I must move into the city and manage Terrance's store for a while to have a roof over my head…well, then, I suppose I will."

"What about Tom?"

"He said he will find me," she said simply and in a bit of a daze.

Gemma narrowed her gaze. "And you are… what? Going to wait? I thought…"

She shook her head, her eyes burning even though she was amazed at what she was about to tell her friend. "He told me he loves me."

Gemma rushed to her and clasped her hands in hers. "Oh, Elizabeth, how could he not?" She started to hug her when she noticed her face. "What is it?"

She took a deep breath. "He just has to make it back safe! He just has to. He has to stay alive so that I can tell him I love him, too!"

Chapter Sixteen

Tom left signs along the trail to make it easy for Parker to follow him. By noon of the next day he had to rest. Lack of sleep had worn on him until his sight was blurry and he could barely sit his horse. After a few hours he woke and continued on after Hodges.

Trust me… He'd meant those words to Elizabeth. But what if he couldn't recapture the gold? What if he failed? Could he face Sam? Could he face Elizabeth? The thought, always in the back of his mind, made him realize just how much he stood to lose. Not an option. He couldn't live with himself. Like he'd once said, he'd get the gold or he would die trying. He just hoped that didn't become an omen.

By early evening of the next day, Craig had caught up to him. They squatted behind a large granite boulder, just this side of the Mexican border, and watched the three men celebrating their freedom. The outlaws were far enough into Mexico to be out of range for a rifle's bullet. Jimmy had even started a small fire—not the smartest move. The minute Hodges came back from scouting the area he put it out.

"Looks like they figure they are free," Tom said.

Parker slid down to sit on the ground, his shoulders slumping. "They are by my count. I can't chase them through Mexico. Not with this badge on my chest."

Tom remembered the feeling all too well from when he worked for the government. "You can't," he said, meeting Parker's frustrated gaze. "But I intend to."

"If you are stopped over there, especially if you get the gold back, the authorities will likely confiscate it and jail you…or worse. I don't see it coming back this side of the border."

"Thing is, I don't intend to get caught. I'm not going to lose just because somebody drew a line on a map. Matter of fact, I think that line is a little fuzzy right now."

"That imaginary line carries a lot of weight in a court of law," Parker said gruffly.

Tom turned back to study the men surrounding the small cold campfire. "Looks like something is happening." He could feel the tension mounting.

Their voices had grown louder.

Parker moved up beside him to watch.

Noble and Hodges were upbraiding Jimmy. Tom had always thought Hodges was dangerous. He was smart. Too smart. He liked a challenge of wits. And Noble seemed of the same bent. Between two men like that, Jimmy didn't stand a chance.

Watching them argue, Tom almost felt sorry for the kid. He was no match for the older men—just too young and green to realize what it meant to be outside the law and running with the likes of them. His life was destined to be short.

Suddenly Hodges shouted something and pulled his gun. Jimmy froze. By the whine in his voice he was pleading for something. Then he whirled about, stomped over to the horses and began emptying his saddlebags of the gold, throwing it on the ground like a kid in the throes of a temper fit.

Parker glanced at Tom. "Not lookin' good for the boy."

Tom nodded, his thoughts turning over the

grim prospect of having to tell Chet his brother didn't make it. "I could surprise them."

"This could all be an act, too. To draw you out."

Tom didn't think so. "They don't know I'm here. Or you."

Likely they thought he was still trying to find Elizabeth. Jimmy had made a lot of stupid choices—taking up with Hodges, stealing the gold and kidnapping Elizabeth. He'd have to pay for those choices. The one thing he'd done right by stupidity or design was to leave Elizabeth where Tom could find her. For that, and because he had promised Chet he wouldn't shoot him, Tom felt responsible to at least try to bring him back alive.

He used his gun barrel to point toward the boulders on the far side of the thieves. "I'll circle around. Chase them back toward you."

"All right. Good luck, Barrington."

"You, too, Sheriff."

He slipped silently back and away, crossing over into Mexico as he rounded the small crescent-shaped hill that hid him from the outlaws. At this lower elevation, the trees of Clear Springs had given way to sumac, buckwheat and sagebrush. Overhead, the clouds obscured the moon, making the going slow. A misstep and he might twist his bum leg but good. Then he could kiss the gold and what was left of his reputation goodbye.

He shook off the dismal thoughts just as he came to the small cluster of boulders. One thing at a time. Nothing he could do about the future. All he had was now.

From this vantage point, he was close enough to hear what the men were saying.

"You can't go back, kid," Noble said. "They'll hang you."

"I didn't sign up for none of this. All I wanted was enough gold to make it up to my brother for losin' all our money on that old, worn-out mine. Enough money for a clean start. You didn't say nothin' about kidnappin' or hurtin' a woman. And you shore didn't have to shoot my brother."

"These operations aren't set in stone. You've got to adapt to the situation."

Jimmy frowned. "Well, all I want is the one bag. I'll hide it good. I gotta go back and check on Chet. I gotta know he is all right."

"You're too soft for this line of work, kid," Hodges said, his rough voice way too gentle in Tom's opinion. It sounded like he was sympathetic—which was an impossibility. In fact, it grated on Tom's ears.

"I can't let you do that," Hodges continued. "Not in good conscience. We'll find us a nice little town and lay low for a few months. When they get tired of searching for us you can cross over and see about your brother."

Jimmy looked all done in—a heap of misery slumping on a hard rock. "I just want to go back," he mumbled, his head in his hands.

Noble and Hodges looked at each other in silent communication.

"If you head back now, your brother will likely hate you. It isn't easy being the brother of an outlaw. Folks in town could ride him hard." An ugly smirk moved the handlebar mustache on Noble's face. "Or perhaps he'll die from that wound. Then it won't much matter. Take your pick."

It didn't take Tom a second to figure out Noble's plan. He was goading Jimmy until the boy couldn't take anymore. He'd kill him and satisfy his skewed moral code by rationalizing to himself that it was self-defense. Tom eased his rifle onto the boulder and put Noble in the crosshairs.

Jimmy jumped up and stormed toward Noble.

"You did this! You knew all along this would happen from the moment you told us about that claim that was no good!"

Noble drew and fired. Tom squeezed his trigger a split second later. The man gripped his stomach and then crumpled to the dirt.

Jimmy took three faltering steps backward. He held his chest, blood oozing out between his fingers. "He shot me!" he cried out in a dazed voice. "He shot me!"

Immediately, Hodges dashed behind the boy. He gripped his collar, hauling him in front of him and using him like a shield. "You finally here, Barrington?"

Tom didn't answer.

"Whoo-eeee! Shoulda known you'd come after me instead of going after that woman. She just wasn't worth it, huh? Gold called to you, just like it did me."

Tom narrowed his aim, wishing Hodges would quit swinging the boy this way and that. He didn't want to shoot Jimmy by mistake. The more the boy had talked, the more he had realized that Hodges and Noble had been using him all along. They never planned to split the gold with him.

"That gal of yours is a pretty thing. A bit tall

for my liking—but would fit you just right. You probably could have thought of a thing or two to pass the time with her that's more fun than gold. Eh?"

Tom waited. As long as Hodges kept talking maybe he'd relax his hold on Jimmy. That this was similar to the last time he'd had a run-in with Hodges was not lost on him. He thought briefly of Parker. At least the sheriff wouldn't rush in and draw Hodges's fire the way Cranston had. He was too "by the book" about being on the north side of the border.

"We got an interesting situation here. Step out into the open and let me have a look at you. Hiding ain't your style."

Tom worked his way to a different vantage point. He gripped his gun tighter. Knowing that it was Hodges who had pulled the trigger on his partner made it a lot easier to kill him. He'd give his condolences to the sheriff next time he saw him.

Suddenly he skidded on loose gravel and his feet slid out from under him. Down he went, landing on his elbow. He held on to his gun and struggled to maneuver into a safe position. At the sputtering of rocks, Hodges spun Jimmy around, keeping the boy between them. Jimmy's eyes drooped at half-mast like he was ready to pass out. If Tom was going to be any help at all to the boy, he needed to take care of Hodges now.

"Show yourself, you coward!" Hodges yelled. "Or I'll put another plug in Jimmy!" He turned his barrel and pointed it at the boy's head.

"Wouldn't do that if I were you," Parker called out, emerging from the brush right behind Hodges. "My rifle is trained on your back, Hodges. Put the gun down and no one else has to get hurt. We'll take you in for a trial."

Hodges's laugh was pure evil. Drunk on the raw addictive power he held in his hand with that gun pointed at Jimmy's head, he had no intention of allowing Jimmy to live. Hodges pivoted on the boulder until he could see Parker. "You can't do that, Sheriff. You're in Mexico now."

"You think rotting in jail in Mexico is better than rotting in one in California?"

Tom appreciated Parker's commitment to his office, but trying to talk sense into Hodges was crazy. He didn't know Hodges like Tom did. Parker would end up hesitating. He was too set on taking Hodges in for sentencing by a judge and jury.

"I ain't rotting in no jail nowhere."

He sounded cold and calculating without the slightest amount of desperation or remorse. Tom had to do something *now*. He stepped out into the open fifty yards away with his gun trained on the outlaw. "Drop it, Jack. It's over."

"You!" In a flash, Hodges swung around and aimed his gun at Tom. He squeezed the trigger. Tom fired at the same time that Parker raced at Hodges, dove and knocked the outlaw over. They sprawled on the ground in a heap—Jimmy, Hodges and Parker. Tom had a moment of panic, wondering which man he had actually shot.

Hodges's bullet bit deep into his thigh. For an insane second, Tom realize how ironic it was— nearly the same scenario as Cranston. Only this time, he'd been the one to draw Hodges's fire rather than let Parker get shot.

He took a step and immediately went down, his leg unable to support him. He wanted to swear two ways from Sunday but didn't. Wouldn't help and would only validate his loss of control. He steadied his gun, still aiming at the men, wondering who would come out alive from that pile.

From the top of the heap, Parker was the first to move and push himself to his feet. Immediately, he picked up his rifle and cast a quick glance toward Tom.

"Get him off!" a muffled cry came from beneath Hodges's heavy body.

Parker reached for Hodges and heaved his body off Jimmy. Jimmy struggled and finally emerged.

"Lie still," Tom said, scooting over to check Jimmy's wound. "You'll bleed out if you keep moving."

"I could say the same for you," Parker said.

Tom glanced down at his leg where blood oozed through his canvas pants. He unbuckled his gun belt and cinched it around his thigh, putting pressure on the wound. "Leastways it's the same leg. Burns like fire."

"I'm gonna die, ain't I, mister?" Jimmy blubbered. His freckled face looked a bit waxy.

"Not if I can help it," Tom mumbled. He whipped his bandanna off and pressed it against Jimmy's chest wound.

A hand rested on his shoulder. "Thanks for letting me try," Parker said quietly.

Tom nodded. It had gone down all right. The sheriff and Jimmy were alive for now.

"I'll round up the horses," Parker said.

Chapter Seventeen

Elizabeth stared out the window from the mercantile's second floor at the sun rising over the eastern mountains. She wondered how Gemma was getting on with her classroom of students. Had she maintained control of those three boys who had been so full of energy? And how did Mrs. Birdwell fare? Funny how her time there in Clear Springs had faded to a fuzzy memory. The gold town in the mountains was so different from La Playa and such a far cry from the coast.

She had been back a week with only one wire from Tom—and that shared by Sam. Two days after she'd arrived home Mrs. Flynn had run from the bank to get her, her dress billowing out behind her like a sail. Now the thought made Elizabeth smile but at the time she was sure it would be bad news. Then Sam had quickly followed in her steps and shared the telegram he'd received.

GOLD SAFE IN BANK STOP MEN SAFE STOP HEALING STOP

It was the word *healing* that had put her in a tizzy. She wanted to go to Tom wherever he was convalescing and see for herself that he was truly all right. She wanted to take care of him— cook his favorite meals and…and just *be* there. The need to be at his side sometimes burgeoned up and made her ache inside. Yet she knew instinctively he would not want that. He had handled situations like this before without her help and he would want it that way. He wouldn't want anyone to hover over him. She also had the feeling that he would not be a model patient and his frustration at the slowness of healing might get the better of him at times.

Sam had promised to inform her if he heard anything more, but so far there had been nothing. Not once did he bring up the sale of the mercantile. She wasn't sure whether he was giving her a chance to adjust out of respect for the ordeal she'd been through or he was just waiting to talk business with Terrance instead of her.

Surprisingly, Mrs. Flynn had actually enjoyed

managing the store in Elizabeth's absence. Of course she had reorganized the yarn and material section, and used different "more appropriate" symbols in the ledger. It hadn't fazed Elizabeth a bit. In a few days, it wouldn't matter, anyway. The store would belong to the bank and she would be moving to the city.

Her thoughts eased back to Tom as they always did now when she looked out at the mountains. He said he would come back to her. She had to cling to that promise no matter what. It was more…so much more than she'd had the first time he left her. It gave her hope deep down inside. And that hope gave her strength— strength to wait for him, to hold on.

Before Elizabeth turned away from the window, a one-horse buggy appeared coming down the main road by Rose's Hotel. It drew closer and she recognized her brother at the reins. A sense of foreboding welled up inside. She checked the brooch watch on her shirtwaist. Why was he early? Sam had said the appointment wasn't for another hour.

Descending the stairs, she watched through the front window of her store as he pulled the buggy up to the mercantile. He had a spring in his walk when he climbed down—as if he was

excited to be free of the mercantile and ready
to put this time in his life behind him. Today
they would sign the papers that would release
the store to the bank. All that would be left for
her to do then would be to pack.

She had dressed carefully in her Sunday
best—and it was new. The heavy cotton shirtwaist had tiny shell buttons in a row down the
front and more on the narrow cuffs at her wrists.
Her dark red overskirt had brocade edging and
drew up at the center showing off a cream-colored underskirt with eyelets. Resolutely, she tied
a black silk ribbon over her high-neck collar
and used her mother's silver brooch to clasp it
together. All in all, a most appropriate attire for
the occasion. She wrapped her hair into a knot
low in the back of her head. Done.

Terrance tied the reins around the brake lever
and then climbed down. As he did, he grabbed a
large brown envelope from the seat and tucked
it under his arm. He wore his new suit again…
or was it a new suit of a slightly different shade
than the other but the same cut? It hardly mattered.

"Welcome back," he said crisply, coming up
the steps and into the store. "Was everything in
order when you returned?"

"Mrs. Flynn did a fine job taking care of things."

"You could have at least stopped by my place when you reached the stage depot in San Diego. I would have liked to know you had returned so that we could get on with this paperwork."

She noticed that he hadn't asked about how her trip had gone. He had no idea what had occurred up on the mountain and wasn't even curious. That fact, along with everything else she'd come to realize about her brother, eased her mind about not feeling dutifully remorseful. She followed him into the store. "You are early."

He stopped short and looked down his nose at her. "Now there's a fine greeting."

It was appropriate, she thought, considering the way he'd just greeted her. Why had she not noticed how short he was with her before?

He took his time removing his leather gloves, coat and derby hat and setting them on the counter. Then he walked over to the round table and slapped the envelope down with a loud splat. "I want you to see this before we go over to the bank."

She eyed it suspiciously. "And that is…?"

"Documents from my lawyer."

Slowly she sat down at the table and withdrew

the papers from the envelope. She knew it was pointless to argue. Gemma had looked over her copy of the ownership documents very carefully and found no hope of transferring the ownership solely to Elizabeth.

Footsteps sounded on the boardwalk and then Mrs. Flynn burst through the doorway. "Elizabeth?" Her neighbor was on her way to the ladies' sewing circle at the church.

Elizabeth jumped up and walked swiftly to the counter, grabbing up a hand-size packet of needles and thread she had prepared for the ladies. She handed it off. "If you wouldn't mind, please let me know if you hear any news about Clear Springs. Perhaps someone has learned something new."

"Oh. Of course, dear. After your scare, you must be wondering."

"Yes."

"And perhaps news of your Mr. Barrington?" she asked eagerly.

The woman was so obviously delighted to have a mission that involved gathering information. Elizabeth could barely hold in her smile. Why wasn't she surprised? "Yes. Thank you."

Mrs. Flynn bustled down the steps and onward toward the church.

Terrance eyed her from his seat at the table. "What is this about a scare…and *your* Barrington? How does he figure into anything?"

He didn't sound happy. And he definitely didn't sound concerned for her person. In the past she would have told him everything—about Tom and about the kidnapping and her time in the cave—because he was her brother and she thought he cared about her. But since learning of his lies and manipulations over the years, she decided then and there not to tell him anything.

She studied him, the dark oiled hair combed back from his face. Had she willingly been blind to his faults because she couldn't face the truth—that although she had meant her promise to her mother, it had meant nothing to him?

"What happened, Terrance? Why did you even pretend to care?"

"I don't know what you are talking about." He avoided her gaze and focused on the documents. "I want you to take a look at those papers."

The truth of their situation, their relationship, became clear to her then. Why had she not seen it before? "It's me!" she said slowly. "I'm the one who hasn't been able to see it. I'm the one who has been pretending—with myself." She looked at him. "And it is time to stop."

He cleared his throat. "There is something you should know. Before Father died he changed his will—actually wrote a new one leaving the store completely to me."

It explained so much. "So the will that says I own fifty percent..."

"Is null and void. He wrote that one to appease your mother, but when she died, there was no more point to it." He opened the envelope and spread the papers out before her. "As you can see, I have the proof."

"Father to son."

"As it should be."

She wrapped her shawl around her like a shield and stepped over to the table. She glanced down at the papers, recognizing her father's script. Then slowly, she placed them back into a stack and took them over to the counter. She carefully read through each and every line her father had written. At the bottom, a lawyer had witnessed and dated the papers two months before her father's death. These papers superseded the ones she had always held.

It was true. Everything her brother had said. Terrance owned the store. Well—for about one more hour.

Terrance withdrew a pen from his jacket.

"Obviously, these aren't the sale papers. The bank is drawing those up. But they wanted your signature—Sam actually…wanted your signature—stating that you are aware of the correct ownership." He walked over and placed his pen on the counter in front of her.

"That's because he understands what the store has meant to me." She felt like a part of her was dying. As though, inch by inch, the store was being ripped away from her. Could she actually work for Terrance in San Diego after knowing what she did now? Her hand shook as she picked up the pen. "And to think for a moment I almost considered selling because it sounded like you needed the funds for your political campaign. I wanted to help you. How foolish."

Terrance's brows drew together. He had the grace to look uncomfortable at her words. But then he simply said, "I'm not throwing you out in the streets. I will, however, expect you to attend to household duties and help out in my store. You certainly have enough experience for that."

She took a deep breath and signed her name quickly. "Are there any other options?" she asked crisply, feeling a burning behind her eyes. "Other than accepting your offer to move to the city?"

He seemed surprised at her request, as if he hadn't expected her to decline his first offer. "Ah, well, I suppose I could give you a stipend out of respect for your good stewardship of this store. Three months. That should be enough until you find other employment. However, I don't understand…"

"Tom said not to let you coerce me. He said I should do what would make me happy."

"Barrington again," he said, his voice flat. "Well, I think you'll find that my offer is a good one. Barrington won't be back. Like you said before, he's only interested in his job. The sooner you face that, the sooner you can move on."

She did not like discussing Tom with her brother. "Please, Terrance. Enough about Tom. You don't know what really happened."

He picked up the signed papers and straightened them before putting them back in the envelope and tucking them under his arm. "I've given you a decent offer—to keep house for me and help in my store in return for a roof over your head. I have kept my promise to Father. He asked that I look out for you. I have to the best of my ability, even though I can see you do not appreciate it."

He slipped his pocket watch out and glanced

at it. "Time for me to go. There's really no need for you to come to the bank."

Because her signature no longer mattered. She pressed her lips together. She had no intention of listening to her brother, but she would not walk beside him. Not today.

Terrance hesitated a second, but then with a last look about the store, he stepped outside and walked across the road.

She glanced about the room—the windows, the worn counter—her home for as long as she could remember. Funny…it wasn't even hers now, but it still felt like hers. She stepped outside and crossed the street.

Upon entering the bank she nodded to the one man standing behind the iron bars of the teller window.

Sam's voice came from behind the one closed door—his office—and then she heard Terrance answer. She took a deep breath, walked up to the door and opened it.

Sam immediately stood. Terrance blinked at her from his seat across the desk from Sam, and then he rose, too.

"Mr. Furst, considering that I have lived there all my life and managed the store for the past ten years, I wish to be included as a witness to this exchange."

"You are welcome as far as I am concerned," Sam said. "This situation has troubled me from the start." His gray eyes held nothing but compassion.

He indicated that she should sit and then he and Terrance returned to their seats...rather cautiously. Apparently they worried she might break down into a blubbering puddle of female emotion. She did have her handkerchief tucked in her sleeve if that happened—just in case—however, she truly hoped she could see this event through. For it was an event. The closing of a door in her life.

Sam's words surprised her. In her mind she had envisioned him as the traitor, the interloper. Perhaps that had been due to her brother's shading of the facts. "Thank you. I appreciate your kind words."

Terrance appeared only impatient at the delay, tapping his fingertips on the desk.

Sam reviewed the sale papers with Terrance; however, when the verbiage on the documents caused her to draw her brows once, he made sure to explain in terms she could understand. Terrance emitted a small sigh at that.

Then there was nothing left to do but for her

brother to sign the papers, which he did with a quick flourish.

They stood, all at once.

"Well. That's it, then." She took a deep breath. "Terrance informed me that I have a week to pack."

"That's right," Sam said. "I won't rush you out if you need more time than that. Have you decided to move to the city?"

"Yes. For now. Terrance has offered me a place."

Sam shook hands with Terrance.

She had no more reason to stay. Sam opened his office door for her and quickly moved ahead to open the bank's outer door. She walked out and then stopped on the boardwalk. From here, the mercantile looked no different. The maroon letters, edged in gold on the sign beside the door, still said Morley's Mercantile. Smoke still puffed from the chimney in lazy white bursts as the fire in the stove slowly burned down. Patches still sprawled lazily in the sunlight on the front boardwalk.

Terrance crossed the street ahead of her and climbed into the buggy and circled it around so that he was ready to start back to the city. "I'll return in one week with a flatbed wagon." Then he flicked the reins and headed out of town.

Elizabeth swallowed. One week to say good-bye to this part of her life—to the town and to the families she had come to care about.

Having returned from the church, Mrs. Flynn watched from her porch. Hesitantly at first, and then with a firmness of step more common to her, she walked across the short expanse and looped her arm in Elizabeth's, patting her hand. For once, she remained quiet and Elizabeth was surprised to see tears brimming in the woman's eyes.

Another deep breath. A step. Then another. Unhurried. Each one defined.

They entered the store and Elizabeth wasn't quite sure where to go. Upstairs to the room that was no longer hers? Mrs. Flynn released her arm and hurried over to the stove. "I'll make a pot of tea." Elizabeth took a seat at the table. Patches wandered in and jumped into her lap. She wondered vaguely if the new owners would need help. Maybe she should speak with Sam about that. But no…that would be awkward. Better to make a clean break.

"You know, dear, this could be a very exciting time for you. Change is not always a bad thing. When my dear husband passed away…" She glanced over at Elizabeth. "Well, never mind. We can talk about that another time."

Elizabeth was grateful for Mrs. Flynn's company and grateful that for all her busybody ways the woman seemed to understand how difficult this day was for her. The store, for the first time in two generations, was no longer part of her family.

Mrs. Flynn poured the hot water into the hand-painted teapot and steeped the leaves an extra amount of time for good measure. Then she brought it to the table, poured two cups and sat down with Elizabeth. While they sipped their tea, no one stopped by to make any purchases. It was as if the word had scurried through town—quite probably due to Mrs. Flynn—that the mercantile was now closed.

After an hour had passed, her neighbor stood. "I must get back. I know you have a lot on your mind right now. Just remember, dear—you are a woman of strong character. A shake-up like this…well…it can open up new possibilities. Anything can happen."

Elizabeth was pleasantly surprised. "You just sounded amazingly like Gemma Starling."

Mrs. Flynn looked startled at first and then

held herself a little straighter. "I believe I will take that as a compliment."

Elizabeth smiled. "I believe you should."

When she was gone, Elizabeth climbed the stairs to her room, gathered her crochet hook and yarn and sat at her window, sewing until there was no more daylight.

The week went by with no word of Tom. Every day Elizabeth opened the store as she had for years, sweeping off the boardwalk and wedging the door open for the day. The routine calmed her. She had been doing it since she was old enough to use a broom and her mother had imparted the duty to her.

She lit the stove every morning to take the chill off the room. Then wiped down the counter and table, dusted the shelves if they needed it and straightened the fabric or dishes or whatever needed straightening. It was different now. The love and duty she'd put into the store was seeping into a memory. She felt it leaving her in bits and pieces. The place was no longer hers.

That was her routine for the next five days, along with packing a little bit at a time. However, with each day, she added one new change.

Day two, as soon as the sun had driven the

morning cloud bank out to sea, she brought her rocker down the stairs—rather clumsily—and worked her sewing project while sitting outside on the boardwalk. When it was time for the children to be dismissed from school, she enjoyed watching the Slater children run past her on the road to their home. Lucas even waved.

Day three, she took a walk to the old whaling station out to the very tip of Ballast Point and watched the sailing vessels and fishing boats head out to sea on the current. In the shallows moray eels peeked from between the submerged boulders and watched her.

Day four, she baked a pear dessert and joined the ladies' quilting group at church. Since she was the main topic of news and gossip she gave them an abbreviated version of her holiday with Gemma and the kidnapping. Of course, she left Tom Barrington out of the story except as the man who had saved her in the mine. As it was, that stirred quite a bit of interest.

Day five, her personal things packed and ready, her traveling bag by the door, she waited for Terrance to arrive with the wagon. All that remained for her to do was to gather up Patches into the box she'd readied for the trip.

Chapter Eighteen

❧❧❧

The past few weeks had been a series of things Tom had to do when all he wanted after dropping off the gold was to head straight to La Playa to see Elizabeth. Craig Parker insisted on accompanying him to San Diego, and truthfully, Tom was glad. Parker rigged a travois since there was no way Jimmy could sit a horse, him being so close to death's door. On the journey west, Tom had harbored strong thoughts about joining him on that getup. His injured thigh seemed to be one big cauldron of heat and pain with the wound oozing constantly.

At the bank in San Diego, Mr. Furst, Sr., himself came out of his ivory domain and congratulated Parker and then, a bit more reluctantly, him. After a brief and perhaps rather loud consultation with Amanda, Mr. Furst had him taken to the Furst home and called in his personal physician. For two weeks, Tom had been tended by a crotchety old nurse in the middle of opulence he'd never known. Sam came to visit once and still wanted him to take some kind of reward, but Tom felt it was reward enough having things finally resolved and then healing up in such luxury. He did ask for some of the reward money to be divided between Sheriff Parker, Chet and Webster. By the time they got things squared away between them, he felt like he had made things as right as he could for Amanda and the Furst family. It brought him peace. Finally.

Now, although he wasn't healed up completely, he was good enough to ride again, and hang it all he wanted to see Elizabeth. That's all there was to it. It had been nearly three weeks since he'd said goodbye and rode away—and that was about two weeks longer than he'd counted on. He itched a bit what with the starch in his new shirt and his new trousers rubbing against the tender skin around his wound. That was all forgotten when he got his first glimpse of the town and then the mercantile.

He rode up to the front of the store, taking note of a few changes. A flatbed rig stood outside, the two harnessed draft horses stamping their feet impatiently. On the boardwalk, a rocking chair rocked gently in the breeze, although no one sat in it at the moment. Across the street, that Mrs. Flynn woman waved from her rocker but, interestingly enough, didn't get up. Made him wonder what was going on.

He dismounted and looped the reins around the hitching post, then stepped up to the boardwalk and stopped short.

There in the open doorway stood Elizabeth, prettier than the last time he'd seen her, those big brown eyes of her sparkling with happiness at seeing him. It was strange to see her without her work apron on. She wore a pretty plum-colored skirt and white shirt. Her sleeves were rolled up, which made him wonder what she had been doing, and her hair tumbled in a thick braid down over her shoulder. She looked like an angel and he wanted to grab her right there in front of the world.

"You came," she said, a little breathless.

"You waited."

Her chin trembled a bit at that and then suddenly she was flying toward him as he strode across the boardwalk to her, closing the distance between them in the time it took to blink. Her arms wrapped around him at the same time he took her in his and their bodies slammed together so hard he thought they might fuse into one being. He bent down and kissed her hard and long and ardently, making up for three long weeks of missing her.

He wasn't sure what to say first. There was so much. Then at the corner of his vision there was a movement. He raised his head and watched Terrance straighten himself away from the counter. His stance, his tight jaw, put Tom on alert. Coming from his direction the air was thick with tension, as dense as any fog bank that rolled in nightly over the peninsula this time of year.

Tucked in his arms, Elizabeth must have felt him stiffen. She followed his gaze.

"Look who is back, Terrance!" She turned back to him. "Come on in. We have been packing up things."

Tom followed her inside, removed his hat and dropped it on the counter. "Terrance," he said, nodding once.

Interestingly, Elizabeth scooped up that black hat of his, cradled it a moment and walked deliberately to the door and gently hooked his hat over the peg. Her gaze darted first to him with a soft smile, and then rather defiantly to Terrance.

Tom had no trouble understanding. No trouble at all. She was saying that he belonged here. His chest tightened with an emotion he hadn't felt in a long time.

Then she came back to stand with him and he swept her close.

"Looks like a lot more happened in Clear Springs then I've heard about," Terrance observed in a disgusted tone.

"We got a few things sorted out," Tom said.

Terrance snorted. "Took you four years."

"No thanks to you." Tom narrowed his vision on the man who had stolen that time away.

"I did you a favor. You know you weren't ready for anything more."

"It wasn't your place to play with our lives." He let go of Elizabeth and strode toward Terrance, who, noting the look on his face, backed rapidly down to the end of the counter. He wasn't fast enough. Tom fisted his hand and struck him in the jaw.

Elizabeth let out a surprised squeal.

Terrance stumbled back farther, holding his face. "I know important people, Barrington. You'll be sorry you did that."

"I don't care who you know. And I'm not one bit sorry." He pulled Terrance up by the collar and popped him once more with his fist.

Terrance's knees wobbled and he collapsed to the floor, blood from his mouth dripping on his clothes.

Tom stepped back. He still seethed on the inside and Terrance deserved a whole lot more, but he felt a bit better about things now. "That last one was for Elizabeth because she's too gentle and sweet a woman to do it herself."

Slowly Terrance stumbled to his feet. "I'll have the law after you."

"You'll have trouble with that one." A grin grew on his face. "I happen to know the law here real well."

Elizabeth put her hand on his chest. "That's enough, Tom." She leaned her cheek against him.

His heart expanded inside as he squeezed her close. He could smell the soapy scent in her hair, feel the warmth of her. He wished her brother would take the hint and leave.

"The mercantile is sold, Tom. We were just starting to load things to take them to the store in San Diego."

"I heard. I'm sorry, Elizabeth. I know how much it has meant to you." He took a deep breath, hoping that what he was about to say would help ease her hurt.

He walked slowly across the room, studying each corner of the store. "Do you have to bother with moving things? Whoever bought this place will need help at first—an inventory of sorts. Do you know if they've had experience running a store in the past?"

"I don't know anything about them. Terrance doesn't, either. Sam at the bank handled the sale. I was to have my personal things out by today."

"No, you don't."

"Don't what?"

"Need to move your things."

"Of course I do. I don't want to be in the way."

"Take it from me. The new owner needs you. There's no way he knows anything about stocking a mercantile or the accounting or anything to keep it going."

"You know who the new owner is?" She frowned and looked at her brother. "And we don't? Sam should have come to us first...well... at least Terrance."

"You know, too."

"I do? Is it Mrs. Flynn? She did seem to enjoy running the place while I was in Clear Springs but I cannot imagine her stepping in..."

"No, it's not her." He watched her closely, enjoying this. He wished he could do a better job at keeping his face straight.

"But…" Her eyes opened wide as she stared at him. "*You?* You are the new owner? Tom, you don't know anything about running a store."

"But I know you. And I want you here. Happy."

Terrance snorted and shook his head. He'd crawled into a chair at the table and sat there gingerly dabbing his handkerchief at his cut lip. "It'll be gone in a year. She can't do it."

"She's been doing it for years," Tom said. "She'll do just fine."

"Do you mean that you want me to work for you?" Elizabeth asked, a worried look in her eye. "Tom, what are you saying? This would be much too quiet of an existence for you. There's no excitement here. Just steady work. I don't think you will like it. And… I would hate to see you unhappy."

He hesitated. "You're right about it being too quiet for me."

"Then what?"

"I'm giving you the mercantile free and clear. It's completely in your name…if you'll take it."

At that Terrance shoved himself way from the table and stood. "I've heard all I can take," he said disgustedly. "I'm going for a drink. I'll be

back after that to take you to the city, Elizabeth."
He stormed out, slamming the door behind him.

Tom turned to the woman he loved. "Sure
does slam that door a lot, but it was about time
he left."

Looking incredibly stunned, Elizabeth asked,
"You're giving me the store? But I can't accept
it! It's too much…and I hate to bring this up
but…at such a gift people would talk."

He tucked a wayward strand of her dark hair
behind her ear and smiled as her breath caught.
"We can't have that."

"No. We can't," she said seriously.

"Then I guess the only thing to stop the gossip once and for all is for you to marry me."

Her mouth dropped open.

"I love you, Elizabeth. That's what two people do when they love each other. They don't let
time slip away."

"Oh, Tom, I love you, too. I think I've always loved you as much as I tried to deny it."
She smiled briefly, a helpless yearning on her
face just for him, and then she laced her fingers behind his neck, pulling him to her, kissing him sweetly.

He pulled back slightly. "Is that a yes?"

Conflicting thoughts dashed across her face.
"I couldn't bear it if you were unhappy here."

"Don't worry about that. I plan to have plenty of adventures here with you. And as for work… I meant what I said to your brother. I do know the law here well."

"You do?"

"That will be me…just as soon as our honeymoon is over. It will be quieter than my last job, but I believe it has a lot of benefits on the side."

She arched her brow. "Oh?"

"I plan to come home every night to a woman who'll keep the home fire burning and help start a few new little fires."

"You want children?" A delighted smile broke out on her face.

He had surprised her again. He was beginning to like this. A lot. "I want to give you the world, Miss Elizabeth. I aim to please."

"Oh, you do," she said on a sigh, her eyes shining. "You definitely do please."

"Glad to see I could bring back that sparkle," he murmured, and then he kissed her.

* * * * *

MILLS & BOON®

HISTORICAL

AWAKEN THE ROMANCE OF THE PAST

A sneak peek at next month's titles...

In stores from 28th January 2016:

- **Marriage Made in Rebellion** – Sophia James
- **A Too Convenient Marriage** – Georgie Lee
- **Redemption of the Rake** – Elizabeth Beacon
- **Saving Marina** – Lauri Robinson
- **The Notorious Countess** – Liz Tyner
- **Want Ad Wife** – Katy Madison

Available at WHSmith, Tesco, Asda, Eason, Amazon and Apple

Just can't wait?
Buy our books online a month before they hit the shops!
visit www.millsandboon.co.uk

These books are also available in eBook format!

0116/04

MILLS & BOON®
The Billionaires Collection!

This fabulous 6 book collection features stories from some of our talented writers. Feel the temperature rise with our ultra-sexy and powerful billionaires. Don't miss this great offer – buy the collection today to get two books free!

Order yours at
**www.millsandboon.co.uk
/billionaires**

1215_MB16